W9-AXV-107

He Taught Me To Hope

Darcy and the Young Knight's Quest

P O Dixon

He Taught Me To Hope: Darcy and the Young Knight's Quest

Copyright © 2011 P O Dixon

First Edition ~ October 2011

Front Cover Image Photo © Eagle | Dreamstime.com
Back Cover Image Photo © Andreus | Dreamstime.com

ISBN-13: 978-1466397866
ISBN-10: 1466397861

In dedication to my greatest inspiration—my beautiful daughter.

I offer special thanks to Gayle for sharing the many inspiring images, which I will always associate with the characters in this tale.

Contents

Prologue

And as suddenly as that, she opened her eyes. *Engaged, at last, to the man of her dreams—*

Chapter 1

More than once, he had found himself repeating the oft-asked question, mostly in silence but sometimes aloud. *How on earth do I find myself in such an untenable position?* Try as he might, he could not fathom an explanation that did not baulk at everything he knew to be right and wrong. He could do no more than consider all that had led to that fateful day.

Though some months ago, it seemed to him as if that unpropitious moment in time had occurred just recently. Days had turned into weeks. Yet and still, her prognosis had remained much the same. More than one London physician had been consulted, each of them had been no better equipped to explain her strange malady than the one before. Her mother had declared it all an utter waste of time. There was nothing to be done, for it was quite simple, to her way of thinking. Her daughter was dying of a broken heart.

Poor Miss Anne de Bourgh had lived most of her sheltered life it seemed, for one true purpose—to marry a wealthy gentleman. Though not just any gentleman, for if she had known only one truth, it was that she was destined at birth to marry her cousin, Fitzwilliam Darcy of Pemberley.

The future had not always been so clear to young Anne. As time had passed, she simply had reconciled herself to that prospect. She had allowed her mother's dream to become her dream. Anne had cared for her cousin, and even had looked forward to his annual visits to Rosings Park and her frequent trips to Pemberley over the years. But it was only during their late adolescence when she had begun to appreciate her future state as his intended. He had grown more handsome and charming with each passing year. In social settings, other young women possessing far more beauty and charm than she would ever have, sought and failed to capture his attention, teaching her to appreciate what she had been blessed by Fate to have secured as her own.

By the age of two and twenty, she had begun to think her cousin might not be as reconciled to their destiny as was she. Anne had started to speak of their union as fervently as did her mother, Lady Catherine de Bourgh. So much so, that Darcy's visits had become few and far between and eventually pared to only once a year, at Easter.

Darcy had been a tirelessly vigilant attendee to his poor cousin. His guilt was palpable, as he had not come as soon as he had received his aunt's summons. He had supposed it a scheme, planned by both his cousin and his aunt to lure him to Rosings Park, to bring pressure to bear upon him once again to honour his dearly departed mother's favourite wish. *After all,* considered he, *when of late was Anne ever not sick?*

Alas, the summons of the very physician he had dispatched in his stead persuaded him to come. Dr. Everett had been a loyal and trusted physician to Darcy's family for many years. Darcy could have no reason to think he might take part in any sort of subterfuge or have any cause to do his aunt's bidding.

He did care for his cousin, after all. Just not in a manner which would persuade him to marry her. The inducement of combining the two great estates of Pemberley and Rosings Park was not enough of a consideration for Darcy. However, if there was a chance in the world his presence by Anne's side would aid in her recovery, he felt he needed to be there.

At his aunt's urgings, he sat with his cousin day after day for hours at a time. Darcy's mood soon grew as foul as the air in Anne's sick room. *It is no wonder she does not recover.* He started to bring her fresh-cut flowers each day. Acting against his aunt's counsel, he drew open the dark shades and even opened the windows to allow in the fresh air. Every day, he sat by her bedside and read to her. He often spoke to her—anything he thought might bring about a change.

"Please, Anne; will you not even try to come around? Would that I could do something to see you smile once more.

"I would do anything. Arrange to have you travel abroad with Georgiana and me. Would you not love a tour of the continent?

"I shall visit you here at Rosings Park more often than I have of late. I shall even bring Georgiana. Would you not love to know your younger cousin far better?"

It had torn at his heart to see her wasting away, growing more feeble and colourless before his eyes. He was beside himself with worry. Day after day, with no change at all in Anne's circumstance, Darcy had suffered heavy fatigue, having scarcely slept at all since his arrival. Kind words of comfort and gentle cajoling had given way to desperation and out-right bargaining. *Dare I say the words out loud? She has yet to respond to a single word I have spoken. More than likely, she is entirely unaware of my presence.* In a barely audible, reticent, and uneasy tone, he voiced, "I might even go as far as to marry you."

Darcy was in residence at Netherfield Park with his close friend, Charles Bingley. He thought of it as a reprieve of sorts, one that served two purposes. First, he needed more than ever a change of scenery, or rather time and distance from his *obligations*. Secondly, he had the excuse of being there to offer his friend counsel on the management of his new estate.

For the third morning in a row, Darcy set out on horseback. If he were to be of any help to his friend, it was important that he enjoy a strenuous ride. Ideally, he would be too tired upon his return to think of anything beyond the tasks immediately in front of them. Heavy rains the day before had hastened the descent of the magnificent autumn leaves of amber and burnt orange he had so admired his first time out. They carpeted the paths ahead, rendering them a bit slippery. *So very different from the pristine lanes of Rosings Park,* he pondered. The sharp sting of Darcy's fine leather riding crop urged the stallion on. *It seems I cannot escape that place, no matter where I go.*

My life was not supposed to turn out this way. What have I gotten myself into?

Though the lanes were rather foreign to him, Darcy raced along on his fierce stallion with reckless abandon, utterly oblivious of everything around him. His mind was miles and miles away. Suddenly, a figure darted across the path ahead of him. In light of the breakneck speed of his powerful beast, it was all Darcy could do to avoid what might certainly have been a near fatal collision, by wrenchingly jerking its reins, causing the magnificent beast to rear violently.

As a consequence, there was only one injured party, instead of two or even three, counting Darcy's stallion. Sharp piercing pain flooded his senses, recalling him to the present. Darcy slowly sat upright trying to recover himself fully, whilst nursing what felt like a badly bruised shoulder.

That was not the first time Darcy had taken a bad fall, especially whilst racing about the countryside absent-mindedly. It was the first time, however, he had recovered from a fall whilst finding himself under attack—the blade of a sword aimed squarely at his heart.

If not for the craftsmanship, or rather lack thereof, of his attacker's weapon, Darcy might have been in some danger. As it was, the weathered and splintered blade would have better served as kindling. From his seated position, Darcy looked his attacker straight in his eyes. He did not even flinch, as the aggressor leaned in nearer.

"Identify yourself, stranger!"

"I beg your pardon?" Darcy replied in righteous indignation.

"I demand that you identify yourself!"

"I am in no mood for games," said Darcy. "As you see plainly, I am quite indisposed. Step aside." Darcy braced himself to stand.

"Halt, I say!"

"What is your name? I take it you live amongst the tenants."

"You, STRANGER, are mistaken! I am *Sir Lancelot du lac*. I am merely passing through these lands on my way to Camelot."

"Sir Lancelot, you say." *What an eager imagination this child possesses. I might as well play along, especially if it means quickly sending him on his way.* "Then, surely you forget yourself, young sir. Do you not recognise me? I am *King Arthur!*"

The child swiftly adopted a deferential demeanour. He lowered his sword and knelt beside it. "A thousand pardons your majesty. I did not expect to find you in these parts." The child bowed his head in supplication. "I am yours to command."

"There is no need for all that. Now, if you will pardon me, I must be on my way." Darcy stood and brushed off his clothes. He spotted his horse twenty yards or so up the lane. Deciding not to signal his horse to his side for fear of startling the child, Darcy started gingerly walking in its direction.

"Where are you going, my King? I have waited long for this moment. There is much to discuss if we are to mount a proper defence against the evil *Meleagant*."

"Perhaps you had better run along, child. Your family might soon wonder of your whereabouts."

"I am on an important mission in defence of my family's honour."

"Indeed—why, pray tell, has such a task befallen you? Who is your father?"

"My father is no longer of this world. He was slain by his enemy. Whilst my mother tended to him, I was stolen away by the *Lady of the Lake*. She carried me off to live with her in her Kingdom. Now that I am all grown up," the child straightened himself to his full height, "and have learnt of my heritage, I intend to right the wrongs against my family and restore our legacy."

Darcy stopped in his tracks as he listened to the lad spin his tale. *This child is well-versed in the Arthurian legend. Perhaps he is not the son of a tenant after all, but rather he is from a neigh-*

bouring estate. "Is it true that you have lost your father, young man?"

The little boy said nothing, instead casting his eyes to the ground as a sign of affirmation.

Darcy continued, "You have my deepest sympathy. I, too, have suffered the loss of my father. What of your mother?"

"The Lady of the Lake?" the child responded in kind.

"Is she your mother, young man?"

Here, the lad paused, as if weighing his next response. Finally, he conceded. "She is no longer my mother. I now belong to my true mother."

There is justice in that. Even as I doubt a single word he says, I would hate to think of him as an orphan. "I am glad to hear it. Now, run along." Darcy resumed his long strides. By the time he had closed more than half the distance to his horse, he looked back to see the young child still standing there. Taking Darcy's act as a show of concern, the young boy ran to catch up.

"You own a magnificent stallion. I have never seen one as majestic. May I sit upon it?"

"I am not certain that is a wise idea. Do you not find him intimidating?"

"Do you believe Sir Lancelot might be intimidated by a mere animal?"

"I suppose not." Darcy repressed a chuckle. "How old are you, young man?"

"How old do I look?"

"Just a moment ago, you swore your allegiance to me. Is that any way to respond to your King?"

"A thousand pardons, your highness. It is just that I do not find your question relevant. What age must I be to sit upon your horse?"

Darcy frowned at the young lad's impertinence. "Fair enough," said he, "you may sit upon my horse. However, you must tell me how you plan to carry out that feat, Sir Lancelot."

The young fellow positioned his small hand to his cheek in contemplation. "I suppose I might build a wooden ladder and use it to clamber up on its back. No, no. That might take too long, I fear. And you seem in a hurry." He glanced about his environs. "There is a fence just ahead! Perhaps we might lead the stallion there that I might use it as a mount. Better still, I might climb that tall tree and then jump down on the horse's back," suggested he eagerly, as he pointed to the low hanging limb just ahead. "Or we might elect the obvious choice."

"Obvious? And what might that be, Sir Lancelot?"

The last thing the little fellow wanted to do was to ask to be lifted upon the horse. What brave knight worth his salt would do such a thing? He raised a quizzical brow to his king. A stand-off ensued. Darcy truly was quite taken with the child. He had yet to witness such steadfastness in one so young, or such innate intelligence. After a full minute, Darcy caved in. "Oh, for Heaven's sake, let us get on with this. I shall lift you."

Darcy signalled his horse to approach. Sensing no apprehension whatsoever on the boy's part, he picked him up and placed him upon his stallion's back. The enthusiastic smile on the child's face spoke volumes.

"I shall possess a magnificent horse like this someday."

"So you aspire to own a stallion befitting a king. That is a lofty aspiration, indeed. I wish you great luck in that endeavour."

"I shall require no such luck for it is my right by birth to own such a beast. You shall see."

"If you say so," Darcy patronised the child. "Now, allow me to hand you down."

"Can I not have a ride?"

"No, not today. Perhaps you might have a ride at another time."

"When might that be?"

"The next time I see you. How does that sound?" Darcy responded as he lowered the child to the ground and mounted his horse. He suffered the pain of his bruised shoulder even more having lifted the child. He was eager to return to Netherfield to have it examined and tended.

As Darcy rode away unhurriedly, Sir Lancelot shouted, "Have I your promise?"

Darcy turned about slowly. "Yes, young knight, you have my promise."

❧

Later that night, as was his habit, the young man beseeched, "Mama, tell me the story of the *Lady of the Lake.*"

"Ben, will you never tire of that story? What say you to another?"

"Then, perhaps you might tell me a tale of Camelot. You see, I met King Arthur today. He is my new best friend!"

"Ben, what have I told you about that imagination of yours?" she asked, playfully placing her finger atop the tip of his nose.

"But it is true. I did meet King Arthur! He is very kind."

"If you say so," said she, as she sat on the bed and cradled her young son in her loving embrace. "So you would like to hear another tale of Camelot."

She began to weave an enchanting tale for her son's pleasure, secure in the knowledge that in a matter of minutes, he would contentedly fall asleep. She considered he must have had quite a day. *What an imagination!* Sure enough, he was asleep within ten minutes' time.

She brushed his dark unruly curls from his forehead and imparted a gentle kiss. She then picked up the candle from the table, and headed for her own room, just across the hall.

Pausing at the doorway, she turned to look back at her son. *There is nothing on earth that I would not do for you, my little Sir Lancelot.*

Chapter 2

The fact of the matter was that there truly was nothing in the world she would not do for her son. Her unwavering devotion explained why she had found herself engaged to be married to Mr. Geoffrey Collins.

She often wondered whether she was doing the right thing. Except by reputation, Elizabeth hardly knew the man to whom she was betrothed. She had met him just under a week before she consented to be his wife. *It matters not. I am doing the only thing I can, if I am to give my son the life he needs, as well as be of some service to my family,* Elizabeth tried to convince herself as she placed the candle on her bedside table. She climbed into bed, retrieved her book, and flipped through the pages to where she had left off earlier in the day.

How my life has changed! Elizabeth looked about the bedroom in the place she once again called home, less than a quarter of the size of the apartment she had called her own for the past five years. The bed was less than half the size of the one she slept in just weeks before. But then again, it was her childhood home, the house in which she had spent the entirety of her youth. *My son will spend some of his childhood under this roof as well, at least until my marriage to Mr. Collins.*

Instead of dwelling upon the uncertain prospect of what her future as Mrs. Geoffrey Collins might entail, she endeavoured to focus upon her book.

"What is the use?" Elizabeth voiced in a soft whisper, wishing not to awaken Jane as she quietly slept in her own bed a few feet away. Elizabeth gently closed her book, blew out the candles and drew the covers over her head.

As she had done most nights since her return, before finally drifting off to sleep, she recollected the events that had brought her back to Longbourn just under a month earlier.

Elizabeth thought back to the time when she had once been considered by all who knew her to be the favourite of her father's five daughters. She could no longer lay claim to such a distinction. Indeed, he had never forgiven her for eschewing his counsel and accepting Mr. Randall Carlton's hand in marriage. Although over five years earlier, Elizabeth recalled her father's words as if he had spoken them just the day before.

"Lizzy," he had said, "what are you doing? Are you out of your senses to be accepting this young man?" His anguish had been evident as he paced the floor. "That he cares for you, I have no doubt. Nor am I surprised by his request, as I have admired the friendship the two of you have shared since you were children. But Lizzy, asking for your hand in marriage is what I might have expected of him four to five years hence. My God! He is a young man who is just coming into his own. He has had no opportunity to travel, to see the world, to sow his wild oats as young men his age ought."

"Have you any other objection than your belief that Mr. Carlton is not yet ready to be a faithful husband?"

"Indeed, it is my utmost concern. How can I condone what I know is destined to bring you unhappiness? Your lively talents threaten to leave you in the greatest danger of a miserable alliance should the tender regard he now feels towards you turn into bitterness and resentment for the carefree days of young manhood that were denied him."

"I cannot embrace your sentiments in this respect. I am certain he knows his own mind. He cares for me as I care for him. He has offered me a good home, a good life, and a secure future."

"Or, in other words, you are determined to have him. He is rich, to be sure, and you may have many fine clothes and fine carriages. But will you be happy?"

"I am happy. I am very happy," Elizabeth had declared resolutely.

"I fear you are too young, too innocent to grasp my meaning. He is a young man of nineteen. I implore you; do anything but cause him to grow resentful of you as he comes to know all he has given up."

"You speak as though I am unworthy of him!"

"Do not misunderstand me, my child. You are of an age where it is generally expected a young woman might wish to marry. But it is different for a young man. Young men of his age and station in life are expected to celebrate their youth, not tie themselves down in wedlock. I know all too well the dangers to a young man who rushes into marriage with his heart and not his head. I only ask you to wait."

Any reservations her mother had entertained in seeing her second daughter married before the first, she kept to herself. With four other daughters for whom her primary aim in life was finding rich husbands, she had considered it an act of divine intervention when she learnt her least favourite, and the one she believed she would have the most trouble marrying off, had found a husband on her own. Her choice had not been a poor one. Despite the entail on his family's estate and his being merely a second son, he was the heir-apparent to a substantial fortune on his mother's side.

Not one to bother himself with taking a strong position one way or another, with Mrs. Bennet's overwhelming enthusiasm for the match and Elizabeth's steadfast determination to defy him, in the end Mr. Bennet did not oppose the wedding. With that said, he had done nothing to promote the alliance or to attend to his daughter's future security in the negotiations of a proper marriage settlement.

I doubt I shall ever forget the disappointment I felt on the eve of my nuptials, Elizabeth considered as she lowered the bedcover from her head and sat up and cradled her knees to her chest. *Whilst everyone else at Longbourn celebrated my upcoming wedding, Papa remained secluded in his library.* Elizabeth recalled venturing in to see him, to reassure him her decision had not been made lightly. *He simply stared out the window into the darkness of the night throughout my speech.*

"Will you not even look at me, Papa? It pains me to see how my impending marriage is affecting you. I never intended to distress you. I am exceedingly happy. I wish you would be happy for me."

Upon turning to face her, he had studied her intently, as if seeing his favourite child for the last time. Finally, Mr. Bennet could not have uttered a harsher sentiment according to Elizabeth's way of thinking. "Should you persist in this foolhardy endeavour, you shall be known as a stranger in this home."

To that day, Elizabeth had held fast in her gratitude to her dearest Uncle Gardiner, for it was he who had escorted her down the aisle. Sadly, Elizabeth rarely recalled the joyousness she had felt on the day of her wedding without immediately bringing to mind the circumstances soon after. She had enjoyed only the briefest of wedded bliss with young Randall Carlton. One month to the day after her wedding, she had received the news no young bride would want to hear. There had been an accident.

Not yet eighteen, she had become a young widow, filled with sorrow. She had felt abandoned, robbed, and entirely on her own. Indeed, it was her father-in-law who travelled to Bath to bring her back to Hertfordshire. Deeply saddened himself by the death of his youngest son, his sole comfort had been in the notion that his new daughter might return to his home and live with him. God willing, she and his son might have conceived a child.

The elder Mr. Carlton had experienced his share of grief. His dear wife had suffered the same fate as his beloved son some two years earlier. His first-born son, from his first marriage and the true heir to Camberworth had become a stranger to him; such was the son's vehement disdain over his father having married again so soon upon the heels of his first wife's death. Having reached the age of majority and secure in the knowledge of his inheritance owing to the entail of Camberworth, Carlton's eldest son, Henry, went his own way. He had not seen his father or his younger brother in nearly a decade. He had no wish to see them.

Young Randall had been the apple of his father's eye. When he told his father of his plans to marry Elizabeth, Mr. Carlton had been so filled with hope. A woman gracing the halls of Camberworth would be something. Once again, his house would be a home. He had known Miss Elizabeth Bennet all her life. He held her in considerable esteem. It had mattered not in the least to him that she brought little to the marriage to his son by way of a dowry. Though the bulk of the Carlton's fortune was tied up in property, and an infusion of available capital might have helped, his fortune had been more than sufficient. Any reservations he might have suffered in thinking his son too young for such a step, he had brushed aside. His son had been smitten with Elizabeth ever since the days of their youth. He had no doubt of the extent of his son's love for Elizabeth for it was evidenced on his face whenever he beheld her. The older gentleman would love her, as well, as the daughter he always wanted but never had.

The birth of his grandson just eight months later had been the answer to his fervent prayers. Despite the rift that continued to exist between Elizabeth and her own father, Mr. Carlton had been extremely honoured by her choice of name for his only grand-child. The child had been christened with the first name of Bennet, in honour of her family, and Randall Carlton in honour of his own beloved son's memory.

Through a deep and abiding love for Ben and a shared affection as father and daughter, the elder Mr. Carlton and the young Mrs. Carlton had managed to overcome their grief and move forward as a caring family. Mr. Carlton had watched proudly as Elizabeth assumed the role of mistress in his home. He had delegated the entire management of his household to her. As regarded his grandson, he doted upon him exceedingly. He even engaged a team of nursemaids to assist in his upbringing.

When Ben was approaching the age of four, his grandfather had deemed it necessary to hire a governess to care for him. Elizabeth had attempted to persuade him against the scheme, even as she had suspected her protests would fall on deaf ears. Mr. Carlton exercised no limits when it came to rearing his grandson, a fact Elizabeth had learnt to accept.

Mr. Carlton, despite all his wealth, a loving daughter, and a grandchild who meant the world to him, had come to believe he needed something more. He had buried two wives. He suffered the want of a companion. He was lonely. Anyone who knew him could see it, including the new governess, Miss Garrett. Aged thirty, practically a spinster, she did more to ingratiate herself with the master than she did to exert herself towards Ben's care. Within three months of her arrival, she had established herself as the soon-to-be next mistress of Camberworth.

Elizabeth had cared for her father-in-law. She had been torn over how to navigate the looming disaster as she observed Miss Garret use her feminine wiles to her greatest advantage. Mr. Carlton seemed as happy as she had ever recalled him, believing himself to have found for the third time in his life, the love of a good woman.

Even in his happiness, he had not failed to discern Elizabeth's unease. One day, he had sought her out on one of her favourite lanes to speak with her on the matter.

"Please pardon my saying this, but how do you expect me to be anything other than worried when I sense our world is about to be turned upside down?" Elizabeth had responded to his pressing inquiry on her recent bout of melancholy.

With his arm linked through hers, he had endeavoured to speak reassuringly. "Elizabeth, my dear, I promise you the greatest change to our lives is there will be a new mistress of Camberworth. But you need not fear. My grandson and you shall have a place in my home as long as I live. God willing my wayward son, Henry, shall see fit in allowing Ben and you to stay on in the event of my death. Ben stands to inherit his father's wealth, bequeathed to him by his mother, when he reaches his majority. As long as you reside here, at Camberworth, your own trust fund should meet your needs adequately until Ben comes into his fortune. With that being said, my dear, I intend to stay around for a long, long time."

Alas, Mr. Carlton did not live to see his first wedding anniversary. He had passed away peacefully in his sleep. The widow Carlton had grieved as surely as would be expected of a loving wife. Her outrageous behaviour some nine months or so later had proved her sorrow a lie. Greedy relatives and rather unsavoury friends from London descended upon Camberworth. Most of them had possessed an unwillingness to go on about their way. By then the heir to Camberworth, Henry Carlton, had also returned to assume his rightful position as master. Still unmarried, he was in no hurry to exert his authority over the grieving widow. He rather enjoyed the endless stream of houseguests, in spite of their nefarious ways. Not only was it a place that failed to instil any sense of comfort in Elizabeth, but it had also become an atmosphere in which she did not wish to raise her son.

Thus, Elizabeth and her young son were cast in an untenable position, one that could only be rectified by an appeal to her father to allow her return to her family home almost a year after her father-in-law's passing away.

Echoes of faint coughs drifted across the hallway, effectively breaking Elizabeth from her reverie. She hurried to check on her son. It was taking far longer than she would have liked for him to become accustomed to his reduced circumstances. Many times of late, he had woken during the middle of the night and joined Elizabeth in her room, often with talk of fanciful imaginings and explorations. Mindful of Jane, Elizabeth usually accompanied him back across the hall to listen to his childish musings, and remained with him until he dozed off, once again returning to his dreams of Camelot and the Knights of the Roundtable.

Elizabeth quietly opened the door. She found her son nestled snugly in his bed, resting peacefully. By then, she was fully awake. She decided to curl up on the bed beside him. *What on earth might have caused him to insist that he met King Arthur today? Clearly, he misses his grandfather exceedingly. My greatest wish is that his new stepfather will be half the man Mr. Carlton was.*

Despite the peaceful slumber enjoyed by her son, a half-hour later, Elizabeth remained wide awake. If the past several nights were any sort of example, Elizabeth knew it would be hours before she finally succumbed to sleep, especially if she continued to dwell upon the past. Her philosophy to think only of the past as its remembrance gives one pleasure aside, not so agreeable musings continued to intrude upon her equanimity. *How could my own father have subjected me to such an uncertain fate?* Her mind raced in recollection of the eagerness in which her father had invited her into his library a month or so earlier.

Without even acknowledging their estrangement, he had greeted her with talk of destiny.

"I welcome this chance to speak with you, Lizzy. Since Mr. Carlton's untimely passing, I was certain this moment would come. What with all the outrageous comings and goings at Camberworth of late, I wonder that it took as long as it did before you deemed it an intolerable environment.

"Indeed, it is divine providence that brings you to me today. You see, I have received a letter this morning that has astonished me exceedingly. It is from my cousin, Mr. Collins, who, when I am dead, may turn your mother and your sisters out of this house as soon as he pleases. I certainly bear him no ill will, as he is by all rights entitled. Nothing can clear Mr. Collins from the guilt of inheriting Longbourn. But listen to what he says."

Mr. Bennet then had proceeded to read the entire contents of the letter. Though most of his words escaped Elizabeth's recollection, she would never forget one part.

"*I am very sensible, sir, of the hardship to my fair cousins, and could say much on the subject but that I am cautious of appearing forward and precipitate. But I want to assure you that with your consent to entertain me in your home, I will come prepared to admire them.*"

"This is good news of a sort, but what can it possibly have to do with me?" Elizabeth had asked.

"You are far too intelligent not to understand what this means to our family. Though I have never met the gentleman, I know from shared accounts with other acquaintances he is a widower of three years with two young daughters, twins, aged ten. He wants to come here to select a bride from amongst your sisters. One can hardly expect Mary, Kitty, or heaven forbid, Lydia, to take on such an endeavour. You know your mother well enough to suspect she will not hesitate to recommend Jane.

"Just imagine! Should you consent to an alliance with Mr. Collins, you and your son shall be able to return to live at Longbourn."

Elizabeth coloured. She stared. She spoke not a word.

"Where have you to go? The interest on what little is held in trust for you is hardly enough to allow you to live as comfortably as you might here with your family. Many years will have passed before young Ben comes into his inheritance. What do you intend to do in the meantime? Clearly, Camberworth is no longer a choice.

"No, Lizzy, it must be either Jane or you. You have experienced young love; you have seen other parts of the world. You have even enjoyed a life of wealth and privilege during your stay at Camberworth. Jane has known none of those things. She certainly never will if she marries Mr. Collins. I ask you, Lizzy, is that the life you would wish for your dearest sister?"

Chapter 3

S trains of music rang throughout Longbourn House. It was always the first sounds heard each morning, as Mary faithfully practised on the pianoforte. As poorly executed as was her performance, it was lovely to Elizabeth's ears. It enveloped her with a sense of being at home.

Never ones to be bothered by consequential matters, Lydia and Kitty barely partook of the spread of freshly baked loaves of bread, a cornucopia of seasonal fruit, and meats of the finest cuts that characterised Mrs. Bennet's breakfast table. The two were always engaged in frivolous, girlish banter on one inane topic after another. Mr. and Mrs. Bennet and the eldest daughter, Jane, were also seated around the table. Mr. Bennet had his head buried in his paper. Jane tried her best to appear attentive. Mrs. Bennet could not help smiling with delight at her two younger daughters. Their antics recalled her to the way she and her own sister had behaved in their day.

The two girls carried on about the newcomers at Netherfield Park, and how their father's visit must have increased the chances considerably that the owner might fancy one of them. Most importantly, they rhapsodised over the assembly which was to be held that night, for Mr. Bennet confirmed that Mr. Bingley indeed would attend.

Before long, their chatter intruded upon Mr. Bennet's enjoyment of his paper. He stood and folded it before neatly tucking the paper under his arm and heading for his library. He turned at the doorway to look at the daughters who had so rudely interrupted his morning activity. "You two are the silliest girls in all of England. My greatest hope is the amiable Mr. Bingley will take either of you off my hands. What a blessing it would be if his mysterious guest fancied the other one of you as well."

Far from being embarrassed, his pronouncement only served to bolster the girls' hopes. They stood from the table and danced about the room in jubilation.

"Though I would rather marry an officer, for I greatly favour a gentleman in a red coat, Mr. Bingley is sure to prefer me," said Lydia.

"No, he shall prefer me, for I am the oldest!"

"But I am prettier and more popular than you!" Lydia boasted.

"Which of us do you believe he will choose, Mama?"

"I shall be quite happy should he choose either of you girls!"

Lydia recalled herself to an unanswered question to her eldest sister. "Oh, Jane, I wish to wear your yellow gown. It will surely enhance my chances of capturing Mr. Bingley's fancy."

"No, Jane, allow me to wear it. I should do anything you wish as repayment for your generosity."

Jane's astonishment showed on her face. She tried unsuccessfully to satisfy her young sisters in a manner that did not increase their exuberance. The girls eventually sought their mother's advice to settle their dispute. Mrs. Bennet recalled the surprise awaiting her two young daughters. She prevailed upon them to join her on a trip to Meryton to attend to some last-minute shopping at the dressmaker.

Wholly distracted, the girls danced merrily out of the room behind their mother to don their bonnets and coats. They barely gave any notice at all to their sister Elizabeth as they passed her in the hallway. Elizabeth had just come from the kitchen, where she had seen to it young Ben had a proper breakfast before he began his day of adventure about the estate grounds.

Elizabeth was pleased to find Jane alone in the breakfast room. She took a seat across the table from her dearest sister and proceeded to fill her plate. She was glad to have been spared her younger sisters' company. Elizabeth remarked, "Though I can find very little to agree on with my father of late, I must reaffirm his sentiment as regards my youngest sisters."

Jane said, "Yes, they are very silly. I fear they are bound to make our family ridiculous with their plans for this evening."

"What are they about now?"

"Both Kitty and Lydia are determined they should earn Mr. Bingley's fancy at the assembly tonight."

"Is it a certainty he will be there?"

"Oh, yes! Our father confirmed it just this morning."

"Perhaps you should keep a close watch over them to make certain they do not cause too much damage to the Bennet name."

"I am of a mind to skip the assembly."

"Why should you not go?" Elizabeth asked. "Are you not interested in earning Mr. Bingley's esteem?"

"I have no reason to suspect he will be different from any other man of my acquaintance. I believe even my Mother has given up on matchmaking for me."

"I suppose that to be a good thing, dear Jane. I contend Mama is part of the problem and warrants the greater share of the blame for any disenchanted suitors you may have had. Let her push Lydia and Kitty towards Mr. Bingley and his mystery guest. It can only make you look better by comparison."

Though Jane would never admit it, she had grown quite gun-shy, especially in the aftermath of Mr. Collins's visit to Long-bourn. She might have actually welcomed his attention. Geoffrey Collins was tall, handsome, and though a bit taciturn, he was a kind and respectable gentleman. The fact that he preferred Elizabeth over all the other Bennet daughters, from the moment of his introduction, was clear and somewhat disconcerting for Jane, who was always thought of as the beauty of the family.

Jane certainly harboured no resentment towards Elizabeth. She knew Elizabeth was only doing what she felt she must in consenting to marry Mr. Collins. Elizabeth studied the concern in Jane's face and interpreted it as thinly disguised indecision.

"You should go, Jane," Elizabeth insisted. "I have a good feeling about tonight. It is your night."

"I will consent to go on one condition. You must agree to go as well."

"I genuinely have no desire to attend the assembly. I would rather spend the evening here with Ben. I find his company far more delightful than I would that of those in attendance at a crowded public ballroom. In light of my situation, I am not certain it would be advantageous for me to attend. I am sure my presence would not be well received by the young ladies present and their matchmaking mamas."

"Lizzy, you are engaged, not dead. After all, Mr. Collins is not to return to Longbourn until Christmas. Surely, he does not intend you should sit at home every evening."

"Perhaps you are right. If that is what it takes to get you to agree to go, then I shall go, as well. However, I must warn you. My mother may have ceased her matchmaking attempts, but I certainly shall not. I shall do all I can in seeing that you are admired by Mr. Bingley."

"Dearest Lizzy, the last thing in the world I want is to get my hopes up for this evening."

"Jane, do not be disheartened." Elizabeth thought surely her eldest sister's time was nigh. "Trust me. I really do have a very good feeling about tonight's assembly."

"Then, that is even more reason for you to attend, my dear Lizzy. It seems you have enough confidence for the both of us."

Ben had awakened rather early that morning. He was very eager to see King Arthur. For two days in a row, Ben waited in the same spot as where he had first encountered his new acquaintance. Both days, the pangs of hunger prompted him to abandon his faithful watch.

That day, not only did he eat his breakfast, as his mother had insisted, but he also had stayed behind in the kitchen upon his mother's quitting the room to pack extra provisions. He was intent upon waiting as long as was necessary for King Arthur's return.

Ben raced past his mother on his way out the door.

Elizabeth followed him outside and stood at the top of the porch steps. She called out to him, "Please wait just one minute, young sir. Where are you off to with such a heavy load?"

Ben paused and reluctantly retraced his steps back to his mother's side. "I am off for an adventure with King Arthur, Mama!"

She examined his stuffed satchel. It was weighted heavily with ripe, green apples. She smiled at the thought of how faithfully he kept to his story. "Is that the reason you have so much food?"

"Yes, it is. I have not seen him for a few days, so he must have been on a journey. I suppose he might be famished upon his return."

Elizabeth kissed her son on his temple and tousled his thick dark curls. "Have fun this morning, Sir Lancelot. Remember not to venture off too far away from our castle."

The past couple of days, Darcy had remained secluded at Netherfield Park. It had taken a while longer than he might have hoped for his bruised shoulder to heal enough to allow for a vigorous horseback ride without undue comfort. The one advantage he attributed to his malady was the excuse it had provided him in not having to meet any of the Bingleys' local callers.

He was grateful to enjoy the solace of a solitary jaunt throughout the countryside once more. Mindful of the near collision with the fanciful young lad the last time he was on that path, Darcy approached that same spot with caution.

Ben spotted him from a distance and quickly climbed down from the fence to await his approach. Genuine enthusiasm beamed brightly on Ben's face.

Darcy, who had been in a rather sour mood after having been trapped at Netherfield Park with Bingley's annoying sister Caroline, immediately sensed a lightening in his mood. It was clear the little fellow had been waiting for him. Darcy could only wonder how long that might have been.

He climbed down from his stallion as Ben ran to him.

"Good morning, young man."

"Good morning to you, too, King Arthur! Have you been on a great journey? I have awaited your return for days."

Darcy smiled in recollection of their little game. "I am sorry, young sir. I had no awareness you were awaiting my return."

"There is no need for you to apologise to me, my King."

"I feel I must. I do not like that I might have been a cause for disappointment. How can I make amends?"

"I shall be quite satisfied to enjoy a ride on your magnificent stallion this day. You promised I might have a ride the next time we met. You do remember, do you not?"

"Yes, of course, I did promise you that. Have you ever ridden a horse on your own before?"

"Yes, I rode my own horse this morning!"

"You did! I would love to meet your horse. Where is it?" Darcy asked as he looked about, in search of a pony. He wondered how he could have missed it.

"He is right here!" Ben exclaimed as he ran towards the fence and pointed to his makeshift wooden horse.

Darcy smiled as widely as he had since his arrival in Hertfordshire. "Indeed, it is a fitting horse for a young knight. However, since you will be riding a king's mount, it is better I maintain a tight hold over the reins, in spite of your unquestionable bravery. Are there any objections to this arrangement?"

"I have no objections, my lord. Now, let us not banter about any longer."

Darcy could not help laughing at his impertinent companion. "I am obliged to do whatever you say, sir. Allow me to lend you a hand." Darcy lifted Ben, sat him atop the fierce stallion, and handed over a portion of the reins. Keeping a very firm control of the remaining length, he walked along beside the horse a short distance and then returned to their original spot along the lane.

Once Darcy had lifted Ben down to the ground, the young fellow raced over to the fence to retrieve his satchel. He beseeched King Arthur to partake in sustenance with him. He even suggested their horses might enjoy some of the bounty.

Darcy stood by patiently as young Ben offered his horse one of the apples. He found the young boy's fearlessness to be amazing. Darcy accepted the apple handed to him. He leaned against the fence and took a large bite. Ben faithfully mimicked Darcy's posture as he bit into his own apple.

After a moment or two of hesitation, Ben raised the question that had been foremost in his mind for days. Darcy rested his hands on the fence railing behind him. Still trying his best to imitate Darcy in every pose, Ben looked up to him and asked, "Will you be my new best friend?"

"That is a considerable honour to be invited to be one's best friend—would you not rather bestow such a privilege upon someone closer to your own age?"

"No. The few people I know who are my own age—I find fairly boring."

"Still, one's best friend is a distinction that requires considerable advisement by both parties. What say you we start out as good friends for now? Does that sound satisfactory?"

"Will you come back on the morrow, my King?"

Darcy answered, "I would rather not make any promises." Upon witnessing the dismay in Ben's eyes, Darcy's heart sank. "I shall, however, do my best."

"It is a deal! Shall we shake on it?" Ben offered his hand.

What excitement filled the air! There was not one dour face in the entire room. The atmosphere was boisterous and bursting with enthusiasm and anticipation, especially for the Bennet girls. Elizabeth was obliged to admit to having a far better time than she had expected. Having enjoyed a set or two, she decided that perhaps for one evening, she would forget her troubles and just have fun with her sister Jane and her dear friend Charlotte Lucas.

Charlotte and Jane shared a common, yet unspoken, motive. Both of them secretly harboured the hope that their time to meet a husband finally had come. Their eagerness was evidenced by the fact that both of them had their eyes trained on the door in anticipation of the arrival of the Netherfield party.

It was astounding to them that the newcomers had been in residence for nearly two weeks, and yet remarkably little was known of them. The talk of the town was that there were two single gentlemen and one young lady. Others speculated there were at least three gentlemen and two women. No one was sure, and everyone was eager to find out the truth of the matter.

Elizabeth's initial reluctance to attend the assembly paled in comparison to Darcy's stance. The last thing he wanted to do was to lower himself by mingling with the locals of Hertfordshire, with all of their ill-bred country manners. He was determined he would not attend the Meryton Assembly, despite the adamant insistence by his friend, Charles Bingley. It had been Caroline Bingley's entreaty which ultimately proved persuasive.

"If you do not attend the assembly, then, neither shall I. I shall be quite contented in remaining here with you. I am certain we might find a way to entertain each other." It had been enough said. Darcy was off in a flash to summon his valet.

A hush cascaded throughout the room upon the arrival of their party. It seemed to Darcy that the musicians stopped playing as well, but maybe he imagined it all, as he later surmised. He was decidedly uncomfortable, to say the least. After an awkward pause which lasted an eternity in his mind, a portly gentleman surfaced from amongst the crowd and greeted them. Though Darcy did not have any notion of the gentleman's identity, he seemed to know Darcy's name. Darcy barely acknowledged the gentleman's cordial greeting.

As Darcy, Bingley, and Caroline walked through the mass of gawking strangers who cleared a path in a manner that brought to his mind the parting of the Red Sea, he concealed his growing disdain with a mask of indifference.

It is just as I imagined it would be—a flood of scheming mamas and their unmarried daughters with but one purpose in life, to capture rich husbands. Why on earth did I agree to attend an assembly such as this? Oh, yes! Caroline.

Darcy was half way through the crowd when he nearly stopped dead in his tracks. One young woman off to his right had managed to do what he would have imagined impossible. Not only did she catch his eye, but also in the span of a few seconds, she captured his imagination. Darcy averted his gaze as quickly as did she. Neither of the two managed to look elsewhere for very long.

What amazing eyes! I feel as though I have met her before—but where?

Chapter 4

Elizabeth had thought she had a sense of the world—that which was inherent in knowing of the potency of attraction between a man and a woman. For that perfect moment in time, she had an overwhelming feeling she had gazed into the eyes of the handsome stranger and beheld her future. An incredible prospect the glimpse foretold; she stared into the eyes of her soul mate.

She looked right past the stern countenance he seemed to wear so well and saw a kind and gentle spirit. He was the most beautiful man her eyes had ever beheld.

Oh my, I am staring! She quickly averted her eyes. *He is staring back at me!*

He continued to make his way through the crowd, drawing the attention of the room by his fine, tall person and noble mien. *He looks just as impressive going as he does coming,* she thought with a giggle. She knew without being told that he was not Mr. Bingley. No, all those who had made his introduction had described Mr. Bingley as quite amiable and as one who was determined to please and be pleased. *He must be THE mysterious guest.*

As soon as the Netherfield party completed their procession through the crowd, the musicians began playing a lively tune. All those with partners converged upon the dance floor, and the merriment picked up where it had left off before the arrival of the distinguished guests.

Mrs. Bennet made a point of corralling her youngest daughters. She eagerly approached her husband. "Mr. Bennet, come quickly! We must introduce Mr. Bingley and his friend to our girls!"

"Please have a bit of patience. Allow the gentlemen to catch their breath."

Mrs. Bennet noticed the Netherfield party was breaking up. The tall, handsome gentleman spoke a few words to his friends before walking off

"We must hurry, Mr. Bennet! One of them is getting away!"

"Very well, my dear," said he. He looked about the room for his eldest daughter. Upon spotting her, he signalled Jane to join him at his side.

"What are you doing?" Mrs. Bennet looked at her husband as if he had taken leave of his senses.

"I shall only introduce my family once. The agreeable Mr. Bingley is just as likely to be taken with Jane as any of the other girls."

Within minutes, all the Bennet daughters eagerly stood in a row in front of the newcomers.

"Mr. Bingley, allow me to introduce my family. This is my eldest daughter, Miss Bennet." Jane curtsied gracefully. Mr. Bennet continued, "My wife, Mrs. Bennet, my daughters Miss Mary Bennet, Miss Catherine Bennet, and Miss Lydia Bennet."

The expression on Elizabeth's face spoke volumes. That, in combination with Mr. Bingley's clear expectation of an introduction, caused the eldest gentleman to feel the shame for his lapse.

"I beg your pardon, Mr. Bingley; this is another of my daughters, Mrs. Carlton."

Bingley's happy smile diminished any cause for lingering awkwardness. "It is my pleasure to meet all of you. Allow me to introduce my sister, Miss Caroline Bingley."

Caroline Bingley's countenance bore none of the kindness of her brother. She barely nodded her head without uttering a single word.

"Where is your gentleman friend? What is his name?" Mrs. Bennet asked. "We should all be most delighted to meet him."

"He is Mr. Darcy, of Pemberley and Derbyshire. I shall be delighted to make your introductions during the course of the evening."

After a few moments of conversation, the Bennets were obliged to move along. Several other families seemed to have queued up to meet Mr. Bingley. Not that he noticed. His eyes were decidedly fixed upon the face of an angel.

As it turned out, Elizabeth did not have to work very hard on her sister Jane's behalf. Mr. Bingley requested Jane's hand to dance the first chance he got, and he kept his eyes on her throughout the set.

Lydia and Kitty made quite a spectacle of themselves with that turn of events. They had all stood together when Mr. Bingley had approached their group. The girls had jostled to determine who might be in the best position to garner his attention, even to the point of being embarrassing.

Bingley might not have noticed their antics, but Darcy surely had. From the moment he had noticed the eager mama gather her daughters, all the time with an eye trained on their party; he had known exactly what was afoot. The last thing he had wanted was to be introduced to a scheming mama and her desperate *wives-in-waiting*, so he had made his way to another part of the room. From that safe place, he considered there was only one woman in the room he wished to meet. The prospect that she might be a part of that gathering entourage was unfathomable.

His mind raced with intriguing thoughts of her. *She is extraordinary!* As pleased as he was to have escaped the introductions to the Meryton *determined-to-find-a-husband* welcoming committee, he wanted to curse himself for missing his chance to meet the enchanting beauty who had captured his fancy and who, for some strange reason unbeknownst to him, was amongst that first group who had approached Bingley.

An hour or so later, as Darcy continued to observe the swarm of young ladies surrounding his young friend Bingley, he could only do so with disgust. He was not surprised to see his friend had singled out the lovely young woman with the angelic countenance. It was just as he would have expected of his friend. Darcy thought he had better caution Bingley against spending too much time and attentions in that quarter, lest someone get the wrong idea.

Soon enough, he began scanning the room once again for his own angel. He spotted her on the dance floor. She possessed a measure of grace and poise which set her apart from all of the other young ladies in the room. Darcy wondered at her even being there. *Clearly, she is not of Meryton.* He surmised she must be from one of the prominent families of Hertfordshire. Her manner of walk, her style of dress, and a certain air of accomplishment demanded it. He decided to move closer to her to command a better view.

Elizabeth would have had to be blind not to discern she was the object of his admiration. Whenever she occasioned to look in his direction, she found he always looked back at her. He did not attempt to hide it. The sensations she experienced in being an object of his esteem where pleasantly titillating. Never before had she felt such dizzying emotions under a man's gaze. Yet, the more he stared, the more Elizabeth's courage rose.

She had suffered some disappointment in not having been properly introduced to him earlier in the evening. She saw that as no reason not to endeavour to know him better. Freed from the strictures of maidenly airs, she determined to put herself directly in his path. *If he is bold enough to break with decorum and engage me in conversation, I certainly shall not stand on ceremony.*

Elizabeth approached the refreshment table and stood in the spot right beside him. He had just requested a beverage when he breathed in a hint of the sweetest fragrance of lavender and chamomile. He turned in her direction and was momentarily stunned to find himself face to face with his mind's embodiment of perfection.

"I beg your pardon, my lady." He bestowed a dazzling smile. "Please, accept mine, if you will." He handed her the beverage that had just been given to him by the server. He allowed his fingers to caress hers during what became a teasingly intimate exchange. A thousand words were unspoken between them as they held fast in each other's gaze. Passion fuelled every fibre of her being. He felt the swell of desire. The balmy resonance of his voice was matched by the enchanting allure of her eyes.

Elizabeth's daring fled in the face of such overwhelming magnetism. She demurred. She managed a smile which confirmed his every thought that she was the most amazing creature he had ever beheld. She curtsied and then slowly walked away whilst taking a deep breath to reclaim her composure.

Darcy could only turn and watch her as she made her way back across the room to her group. He could not fathom why she spent as much time as she did with the young woman who had apparently set her sights upon his friend Bingley. He reflected upon his own friendship, and how it put him in close acquaintance with Bingley's particularly annoying sister Caroline, and surmised his goddess obviously must share a close friendship with the young woman attached to the objectionable family. *One can choose his or her friends, but one can hardly choose that friend's family.*

Later that evening, Mr. Bingley, who had danced every set, came from the crowded dance floor for a few minutes to press his friend to join him.

"Come, Darcy," said he, "I must have you dance. I hate to see you standing about by yourself in this stupid manner. You had much better dance."

"Bingley, I shall do no such thing. To dance at such an assembly as this would be unpardonable."

"I would not be so fastidious as you are for a kingdom," cried Bingley.

"Perhaps you ought. I would caution you to think better of your behaviour this evening than you have been doing. You no doubt have cast your eye on another *angel*."

"Indeed, I have. That angel has a name. She is Miss Jane Bennet. I have had the privilege of meeting her entire family this evening. Mrs. Bennet has expressed an interest in making your acquaintance."

"I have no doubt. She is likely trying to foist one of her silly daughters on me, as if such a thing would be conceivable. Your newest angel aside, they are quite nearly the most absurd and uncouth creatures I have ever seen."

Darcy could not have known there would be a lull in music at the time of his speech. Nor could he have known how far his voice might carry. Had he known any of that, or had he looked about to see who was in his close vicinity, he would have espied the change of countenance of the object of his ardent admiration all evening.

Elizabeth was left with the feeling that the voice she found so wonderfully arousing and pleasing a while earlier was, in truth, rather haughty and disdainful. Suddenly, she did not feel much like enjoying the rest of the evening. She was glad she had the foresight to have her own carriage bring her to the assembly. She sought out Jane and bid her good night.

Darcy was infuriated with himself. He could not believe he had failed to secure a proper introduction to his goddess the evening before. He wondered if he ever again would have another chance to meet her. The more he reflected upon the night before, the more he replayed every moment of the evening as he watched her, the more he convinced himself she was not from those parts. He considered she must be a visitor temporarily staying with that ridiculous Bennet family. He would not even allow that she was a distant relative. It was likely she was a very dear friend of Bingley's angel, Miss Bennet. Perhaps, he thought, if he made more of an effort to participate in the local society, he might actually encounter her again.

Elizabeth was just as angry with herself, upon awakening. She felt as though she had spent the entire night dreaming of HIM. Unlike every night before, since her return to Longbourn, the last thing that had crossed her mind before she succumbed to sleep was how it was just as well *Prince Charming* turned out to be a toad. *He might be the most pleasant man in the world, and there would be nothing I can do about it, seeing as how I am engaged to Mr. Collins.*

Darcy arrived to espy Ben teetering atop the fence railing with a long stick to serve as a balancer.

"I caution you against such dangerous feats, young man. What if you should fall and break an arm or a leg?" Darcy asked once he had dismounted and secured his horse to the opposite end of the fence.

Ben continued his perilous journey for another foot or so until he reached a point where he could safely climb down to the ground.

"Do you often engage in such folly, outside the supervision of one of your elders?" Darcy gently scolded.

Ben cast Darcy a befuddled look. "You sound just like my mama!"

"Your mother is very wise, no doubt."

"Yes, she is the smartest person I know," young Ben boasted.

"Tell me something else about your mother."

"What would you most like to know?"

"Anything," he began, "what is she like?"

"Well, my mama says I am just like her. So in turn, she must be just like me!"

"Then I should expect she is kind, she is witty, and she is charming." Darcy immediately brought to mind his enchanting goddess. "Is she pretty?"

"I do not know." The child's face reflected his puzzlement. "Do you think I am pretty?"

Darcy nearly bowled over with laughter! "Men would rather think of themselves as handsome."

"In that case, my mama always tells me I am very handsome. So yes, I would say my mama is very handsome."

Darcy smiled to himself at his young friend's forthrightness. Wondering if the lad trusted him enough to be more forthcoming about his entire family, Darcy asked the next logical question. "Will you tell me more of the rest of your family? What was your father's name?"

"I have told you already all there is to know, my King!" Ben raced over to Darcy's horse, clearly disinterested in the current line of discussion. "King Arthur, I have noticed you do not have a sword. What happened to it?"

Darcy surmised his young friend was not yet ready to open up to him. Rather than press his point, he joined little Sir Lancelot, "A sword! Why, I have never owned a sword. Sword fighting is not my forte. I prefer fencing."

"Fencing? Is it anything like sword fighting?"

"Yes, to a very large extent. Fencing involves the use of a special type of sword as a weapon, as well as the utmost focus and skill."

"Do brave knights fence?"

"I suppose a brave knight can do whatever he chooses. Shall I teach you to fence? Would you like that?"

"Indeed! But what exactly is fencing?"

"I suppose it will be easier to show you than to explain it to you. But first, we shall require foils, the weapon of choice for a beginner such as you."

"Perhaps I shall fence with my sword. I am already an excellent swordsman!"

"What would be the fun in that? If we are going to do this, we must start by doing it the right way. What say you we commence by crafting ourselves two proper foils?"

In no time at all, Darcy and Ben had managed to search the nearby trees to procure branches best suited to their purposes. Ben waited patiently as Darcy carved and smoothed the rough edges. With makeshift weapons in hand, Darcy and Ben stood facing opposite each other.

"*En Garde!*" Darcy advised his opponent upon assuming an offensive posture.

Even though Ben did likewise, his curiosity begged for an explanation. "*En Garde*, my King? What does that mean?"

"I mean to warn you to assume the proper stance in preparation for our match. *En Garde* simply means *on guard* in French!"

"Well, sir, if it is as simple as that, then—on guard!"

The next morning, Elizabeth sat upon the steps reading a missive from her eldest sister. Jane had been invited to dine with Caroline Bingley the day before and apparently had fallen ill. She had been caught in a violent storm whilst on her way to Netherfield Park, foolishly on horseback at the behest of her scheming mother. She had been obliged to spend the night. Judging from the sound of her letter, she suffered a fever, a sore throat, and a harsh cough.

Elizabeth decided to go to her sister's side. Despite the very amiable Mr. Bingley's presence, Elizabeth doubted her sister would receive much comfort from Caroline Bingley. Elizabeth suspected the dinner invitation was merely a poor excuse on Caroline's part to find fault in her eldest sister and thereby discourage her brother's affections.

Elizabeth did not intend to leave Longbourn without first speaking to Ben to tell him of her plans. Elizabeth feared she might have to spend the night at Netherfield Park with Jane. She and her son had never spent a night apart. She set out along the path he was known to take nearly every morning.

She breathed a deep sigh of relief when she finally came upon him. He sat perched upon the fence. He seemed to be waiting for someone.

"There you are," said she. "I have been looking everywhere for you. I did not expect to find you so far out. Do you come here often?

"Yes, Mama, I must come here, for this is the spot where I first came across King Arthur!"

"King Arthur? Where is he then?"

"I expect him very shortly. He has started to teach me how to fence properly. We are to resume our lessons this morning."

Paying little heed to his fanciful tales, Elizabeth knelt to his eye level. "Ben, I need for you to return to Longbourn House with me, at once. Your Aunt Jane has fallen ill whilst visiting the neighbouring estate. I must go to her, and I may very likely spend the night."

Ben uncharacteristically clung to his mother. "Do not leave me alone at Longbourn, Mama! Who shall look after me if you are gone?"

It tore at Elizabeth's heart to witness her young son's anxiety. She sought to reassure him. "Ben, I shall not be very far away. Netherfield Park is but a few miles from Longbourn Village. I will only stay the night if your Aunt Jane truly needs me. Your Aunt Mary will watch over you until I return. She is very kind. Do you not agree?"

"Yes, Mama, she is kind. I like her very much. But she never reads anything of interest to me. She only reads Fordyce's sermons to me. I am not a girl! Will you ask her to read something else to me this evening?"

"I have spoken to her earlier. She agrees to read whatever you should like to hear. How does that sound, my little brave knight?"

"That sounds very agreeable. Thank you, Mama. I shall be happy to be cared for by Aunt Mary whilst you look after Aunt

Jane." Ben reassured his mother with a hug, and the two walked off, hand in hand, towards Longbourn.

Darcy stood at the window of his apartment and watched as the young woman with whom he had spent the past two days alone, at least inside his mind, approached the house. He knew it was she, even from a distance. He ought to have made his way downstairs and perhaps walked outside to greet her. However, despite the thousand times he had kissed her lips in his dreams, they had yet to be introduced formally. He could not have torn himself away from his fortuitous over-looking view, had he even tried. He was mesmerised.

Darcy joined Bingley, Caroline, and their guest in the drawing room some quarter of an hour after her arrival. In spite of his ardent avowal just moments earlier not to seem too eager to make her acquaintance, the emotional intensity and unmasked adulation evidenced on his face captured Elizabeth's attention from the moment he entered the room.

Without giving much thought to the words uttered by his friend Bingley, Darcy stood immediately before her. He then encouraged the offer of her hand by unconsciously reaching for it with his own. He thereupon raised her delicate hand and brushed his lips softly across her pale skin.

Elizabeth. What a fitting name for my goddess divine. Elizabeth—dearest, loveliest Elizabeth! Darcy silently waxed.

Mrs. Elizabeth—Darcy snapped from his trance-like state. *Did he say MRS? My God—SHE IS MARRIED!*

Chapter 5

It had taken all the good breeding that he could muster to summon the strength to maintain his countenance and cool equanimity in the face of such an alarming revelation. *Is this some cruel twist of fate? How can she possibly be married? She has the appearance, the youthful spirit, and the innocent charms of a maiden.* "It is a pleasure to meet you," he uttered.

"Indeed, it is a pleasure to make your acquaintance as well, Mr. Darcy," Elizabeth said. She looked over to Bingley and his sister, "If you will pardon me, I am eager to see my sister."

"Pardon me. Did you say *your* sister?" Darcy looked towards his friend for some sort of explanation.

"Yes, Mrs. Carlton is Miss Bennet's younger sister; she is next to her in age," Bingley explained.

Always a studier of people, Elizabeth easily could discern the thinly disguised dismay that registered upon Mr. Darcy's face with Bingley's pronouncement.

"Of course, you want to see your sister." Caroline was immediately by her side. "I will take you to her, myself." Indeed, Caroline had a compelling motive for taking up the task of escorting Elizabeth from the room as quickly as possible. She had seen the way Darcy had looked at Elizabeth, upon entering the room. Caroline was none too pleased.

Elizabeth entered the room to find her sister sleeping peacefully. On the way up the stairs, Caroline had mentioned that Jane had not enjoyed a particularly restful night. Seeing that Jane was now slumbering soundly, Elizabeth thought it better not to disturb her. Rather, she sat in a comfortable chair beside a window and endeavoured to read the book she had brought along with her from Longbourn. After several attempts at reading failed to garner her complete attention, she gazed out the window and allowed her thoughts to wander to the gentleman she had encountered earlier. She had not quite recovered from her introduction to Mr. Darcy. Lo and behold, the view from her window allowed her an undetected view of him as he walked towards the stables. Clearly distressed, his shoulders slumped as if he had lost his best friend in the world. She felt that perhaps she ought to have corrected his misunderstanding of her marital status. *What was I to say? I am not married; however, I AM engaged to be married.* She reflected on the uselessness of it all. *Knowing how little he cares for my family, it must have been rather a shock for him to learn that I, too, am a Bennet.*

Though Elizabeth sought to read her book, her thoughts inevitably returned to the one thing that most disturbed her composure. *Why am I even thinking of him? He is haughty, proud, and apt to think too harshly of those whom he deems his inferiors!* She briefly considered how his actions at the assembly, as well as his unmasked admiration upon entering the drawing room some moments earlier, undoubtedly suggested he had no knowledge of her being who she was. *His carelessly spoken words at the assembly clearly were not aimed towards me. Nor had he intended them for Jane. I have to wonder who he supposed I might have been.*

Signs that Jane was beginning to stir eased Elizabeth's anxiety considerably. Any thoughts of HIM quickly escaped her mind. Elizabeth put her book aside and approached her sister's bedside. She sat down beside Jane, reached out to rub her forehead, and then rested her hand at her side. Slowly, Jane awakened, grateful to see her sister by her bedside. Lizzy poured a glass of water from the pitcher on the table by the bed and helped Jane sit up enough to enjoy a few sips. She helped Jane settle back into the soft pillows.

"Dearest Jane, how are you feeling? Miss Bingley mentioned you had a fitful night."

"Oh Lizzy, I feel extremely guilty. The Bingleys have been so wonderfully kind. I fear I am taking advantage of them."

"I think you are quite mistaken, dear sister. Mr. Bingley seems pleased to be of service. Even his sister Caroline appears to suffer great concern for your well-being."

Jane hated being a burden to her sister, but she also hated being surrounded by strangers at a time when she felt vulnerable and helpless. She smiled as a testament of what she had experienced as the truth in her sister's words.

"It was very kind of you to come. I know it is an imposition to ask you here, and to take you away from Ben, especially considering the two of you have never spent a night under separate roofs."

"Jane, you must not concern yourself over such matters. I have explained everything to him. Ben understands, and he sends you a heartfelt embrace."

"He is very adorable, but you had better forego that heartwarming gesture, or we might both be beholden to the Bingleys' hospitality."

"Dearest Jane, I think Mr. Bingley likes you very much," Elizabeth cheerfully responded.

"If only that were true," Jane said wistfully. "Mr. Bingley is everything a young man ought to be."

"Indeed, he is. Now, that is quite enough talking and smiling for now. Is there anything I can do for you?"

Jane told her sister how she could better arrange for her comfort, and Elizabeth gladly accommodated her every request.

In the meantime, Darcy's thoughts were a jumble of mixed emotions when he came to the place where young Lancelot usually awaited his arrival. He was a bit disappointed to find that the little fellow was not there. After the double shocks of reality to his fanciful imaginings that morning, a few moments of light-hearted fun picking up where he and *Sir Lancelot* had left off with their make-believe fencing lessons would have been a balm to his battered composure and gone a long way in helping to ease the anguish of his disappointed hopes.

Then again, it was rather late in the day. Darcy reckoned the young lad might have come earlier and simply had grown tired of waiting. Darcy was in no particular hurry to return to Netherfield. He decided to spend the afternoon in that very spot. So much the better should his young friend happen along whilst he idled about. The last thing he wanted was to spend time at Netherfield with HER wandering around the manor.

Darcy had felt the danger of paying her too much attention, first at the assembly and again upon their formal introduction. He meant to make up for his past overzealousness with a show of inattention.

It is just as well that she is married and beyond my reach. Suppose she was not married—she is still a BENNET. How is that possible?

Darcy recalled the disparaging remarks made of the Bennets that Caroline and he had spoken just the night before, as she had imparted details of her conversations with Miss Bennet.

"I have an excessive regard for Jane Bennet—she is really a very sweet girl, and I wish with all my heart she were well settled. But with such a father and mother and such low connections, I am afraid there is no chance of it. Did you know she admitted to me just this evening her uncle is an attorney in Meryton? She has another uncle in trade who lives somewhere near Cheapside. *Cheapside*," she had mocked and then laughed heartily.

Darcy then reflected on his friend's defence of the Bennets. "If they had uncles enough to fill all Cheapside, it would not make them one jot less agreeable."

Finally, he recalled his own words. "But it must very materially lessen their chance of marrying men of any consideration in the world."

Then there were all the things he did not need Caroline to tell him, for he had witnessed first-hand the lack of decorum displayed by the younger sisters, the mother, and even the father, at the Meryton Assembly. Darcy could not help considering that for everything he found abhorrent in the Bennets, he found the opposite traits exemplary in Elizabeth. *She is extraordinary. She has bewitched me. She is all that I can think of. She is all I want to think of. Indeed, she is a goddess divine. Only, she is not MY goddess, nor will she ever be.*

That evening, Darcy was determined to compensate for his blatant display of regard towards Elizabeth by feigning indifference and ignoring the devastating effects on his composure wrought by merely being in the same room as she. The mere thought that he had allowed himself to be so enthralled by another man's wife was abhorrent to his way of thinking and his manner of conducting himself.

Elizabeth had joined them in the drawing room with a report that her sister fared no better than she had around midday. Darcy made no response to her news, but rather continued with the task before him of writing a letter. Caroline expressed her regrets with an assurance to Elizabeth that all that could be done would be done on Jane's behalf. Bingley's countenance reflected his deep concern, and he eagerly assented to the sentiments expressed by his sister.

Elizabeth took her place on the sofa off to Darcy's side and commenced reading her book. His rigid, forbidding posture confirmed her suspicion that he had learnt to think less of her with the mistaken knowledge of her marital status; that, or the undeniable knowledge of her family.

Darcy managed to think of little else but Elizabeth, so much so his thoughts spilled onto the paper before him. *What manner of man must her husband be? Why was there no sign of him at the assembly? How is it that she is here tending to her sister who suffers no more than a trifling cold, when she might be in her own home with her husband? If she were my wife, I could not bear to be parted from her.* Darcy ceased writing long enough to consider his mindless scribbling—*if she were my wife! Get a hold of yourself man!* He quickly reached for a fresh piece of paper and endeavoured to return to the serious business of writing his letter.

Over the course of the next half-hour or so, Caroline tried, as best she could, to garner Darcy's attention away from his letter and towards herself. As all her many schemes had gone unnoticed, she endeavoured to enlist Elizabeth and her brother as allies in her quest.

"Come now, Mrs. Carlton, Charles, and you, too, Mr. Darcy. What say you all that we enjoy a game where one of us is allowed to ask any question we might wish to, and everyone else in the room is obliged to answer truthfully? Would that not be fun?"

"I suppose that is one way to pass an evening," said Elizabeth, whilst laying her book aside. "I think it is a fine way to become better acquainted," Elizabeth remarked in a manner of speaking that compelled Darcy to turn his attention away from his letter to study her intently.

He boldly accepted her challenge. "Indeed, I cannot think of a happier way to pass the time."

"Wonderful," cried Caroline, enthusiastically. "I shall go first. It is not every day that a young lady is at liberty to ask such questions. I am dying to know what a gentleman seeks most in a lady. Likewise, what is it that a lady seeks most in a gentleman?"

Charles was first to respond. "Why the lady must be accomplished; though, I never heard of talk of any woman but that she is accomplished. I should add that she must have the countenance of an angel and the disposition of a saint."

Darcy rolled his eyes at his friend's not so unexpected response. "And to the second half of that question, your answer would be?" Darcy asked impatiently.

"What do I know of what a lady looks for in a gentleman, except that he is kind and amiable, of course?"

"Very good, Charles!" Caroline exclaimed. She then looked towards Elizabeth. "What say you?"

"In truth, I have not given much thought to such things, of late," Elizabeth responded in a less than enthusiastic manner.

"I imagine Mrs. Carlton would have no reason to be concerned with such matters," Darcy spoke to no one in particular, "as the institution of marriage surely renders such considerations as futile."

"I am afraid you may have gotten the wrong impression when we were introduced earlier today, Mr. Darcy. I lost my husband many years ago as a result of an unfortunate accident."

Darcy coloured upon hearing her revelation. *She is not married!* He did not know whether to be relieved or embarrassed by his inadvertent insensitivity. "I beg your forgiveness, madam, for seeming inconsiderate. I had no way of knowing. Please accept my heartfelt condolences on your loss."

"Please accept my condolences, as well," Bingley offered.

"I appreciate your sentiments, indeed," Elizabeth responded to both gentlemen. "As I said, it has been many years since that tragic day, and time does have a way of healing one's pain. I have much to be thankful for in my life."

After such a revelation, no one was much in the mood to continue the frivolous game. The sombre tone in the room soon led them all to return to their earlier activities—Bingley to his silent musings, Darcy to his letter, Elizabeth to her book, and Caroline to her preoccupation with how to garner Darcy's attention once more.

Elizabeth was soon called to her sister's bedside with the news that she had awakened and was asking for her company.

"Dearest Lizzy, having you here means the world to me. How can I ever thank you?"

"Seeing the look on your face is enough. You seem to be recovering."

"Yes, I feel as though I have done nothing but sleep all day. Being here is nothing like being at Longbourn. It is so quiet and peaceful all about."

"If I am any judge of character, I would say Netherfield Park might soon have a new mistress."

"Lizzy, you must not speak that way."

"Why on earth should I not? It is obvious Mr. Bingley is half in love with you already. You should see how he moons about downstairs."

"What of his friend, Mr. Darcy? How does he behave? He stared at you during the entire assembly. Have you gotten to know him? What is he like?"

"I am utterly convinced that, in his mind, the woman who made his acquaintance this morning is hardly a fitting substitute for the woman he so admired during the assembly. Now, I am afraid, he barely looks at me, except to find fault."

"I am sorry to hear that he turned out to be such a disappointment, Elizabeth."

"Why should you feel sorry? My fate is settled. Mr. Darcy might be the most agreeable man in the world and nothing would change the course I have set upon," Elizabeth replied wistfully.

Elizabeth passed a good part of the evening in Jane's room, reading to her and occasionally waiting upon her until Jane was asleep once again. Elizabeth decided if she was to be of any use to her sister in the morning, it was better she venture to the room Caroline had arranged for her, in search of a good night's rest herself. Elizabeth blew out the candles on her sister's bedside table, picked up her book, and walked outside into the hall. She slowly closed the door and without much thought, turned to make her way to her own room, just down the hall. To her surprise, there was Mr. Darcy! His room was just across the hallway from hers. Either he had been waiting for her, or he had heard her leave her sister's room and stepped outside his own bed chamber in anticipation of encountering her.

Despite the lateness of the hour, he was fully dressed, except for his dinner jacket. That was comforting to Elizabeth. If for nothing else, it was exceedingly disconcerting finding herself in the middle of the night, in a dimly-lit hallway, alone with the man who had frequented her dreams for the past nights since she first had laid eyes on him at the assembly. Elizabeth felt her heart race as he slowly drew nearer. He paused directly before her.

"Pardon me, madam," Darcy spoke softly in a manner that took her breath away. "I must speak with you—in private."

Chapter 6

S ome hours later in the quiet still of night, Elizabeth lay awake in her bed. She felt quite satiated having given in to desires, the likes of which had been long forgotten. The intense sensations were far more powerful than anything she had enjoyed thereto- fore, yet reminiscent of those feelings she had thought she might never experience again. The intense emotions that flooded her being pursuant to little more than the touch of his fingers slowly caressing her own, bore testimony to what it must certainly feel like to have those same fingers gently massaging the length of her slender neckline, along the curves of her bosom, and setting upon a lingering, slow-paced, and piercing discovery of her body.

Once again, she recalled the scene that had occurred in the hallway, just outside the door of her apartment. He had stood mere inches from her—close enough that the warmth of his body en- compassed her own. His beautiful eyes subtly swept over her, leaving her to know he was not looking at her to find fault. Her immediate thought had been to rebuff his request for privacy, for what could be more private than the two of them standing alone, in a dim corridor, in the middle of the night with absolutely no one else about, not even a footman. But he overwhelmed her by his presence. She did not say yes; then again, neither did she say no. She stood face to face with her dream-time embodiment of perfection, and met his soul-piercing stare with a daringly inquisitive look of her own.

She could hardly account for the passage of time. In hindsight, it must not have been longer than a few seconds. The next thing she recalled was the gentle touch of his hand on hers.

"I feel as though we have gotten off to a horrible start," he expressed. It occurred to Elizabeth she had been holding her breath. She consciously exhaled.

He continued, "Admittedly, it is entirely my fault. I accept all the blame." He continued to look deeply into her eyes. "May we begin anew?" He then raised her hand to his lips and gently bestowed a kiss without breaking his alluring gaze.

Elizabeth lost her resolve in the wake of his self-assurance and diverted her eyes towards her bedroom door.

"To a new beginning," he said as she slowly began to pull away. Releasing her hand at the last possible instant, he whispered, "Goodnight."

The next morning, Darcy lingered at Netherfield far later than had been his habit. He had hoped for a chance to see Elizabeth and perhaps persuade her to accompany him on an early morning walk. Upon learning she was with her sister, he decided not to delay his morning ride any longer. Somehow, he felt obliged at least to endeavour to ride out to see his young friend. Darcy grew more and more concerned that the young lad had not been more open as regarded the details of his family. He surmised if he remained a patient and attentive listener, in time the young lad might actually give a truthful account of his life. Darcy thought he might even ask Elizabeth if she knew anything of the young boy from around those parts, who called himself *Sir Lancelot*.

Though he did not want to be a cause for disappointment for his young friend, Darcy was not of a mind to stay there long. His thoughts were filled with the pleasing prospect of spending time with Elizabeth, whenever she was not by her sister's side. He planned the greater part of their day. Given her fondness for reading, he considered he might find her in the library. That would present a wonderful opportunity to discover her literary taste. He imagined they might spend hours alone in the library; the likelihood Caroline or Bingley might encroach upon their private time was minimal. After a brisk ride across an expansive, open stretch of the countryside, Darcy decided it was time he returned.

The stark reality of daybreak cast an entirely new light over Elizabeth's sentiments. *Am I out of my mind to be dreaming of this proud and arrogant man with his changeable moods? It is not right that I should be longing for his touch and savouring every fleeting encounter he and I have shared.*

The first thing she did after preparing herself for the day was to return to her sister's room. She was pleased to see Jane out of bed and sitting in the window seat staring out at Netherfield's beautiful gardens.

"Jane, it is a joy to see you looking so much better this morning."

Alas, Jane could not say the same of her sister. Elizabeth did not look well rested at all. "Yes, I feel much better. You, however, do not look very well. Pray tell me you have not succumbed to my ill-health."

"I assure you it is not that which ails me." Elizabeth went on to admit to Jane her heartbreak in having been separated from Ben, even if for the night, and in not being able to tuck him into bed. What she did not confess, but suffered even stronger, was the danger she felt in being so close to a man to whom she found herself irresistibly and, given her circumstance, inexplicably drawn. In light of the devastating effect he tended to have on her composure, she strongly believed if she did not leave Netherfield Park at once, she might do something that certainly was not in her best interest or the best interest of her family.

Darcy returned to the house to find the Bingleys were entertaining morning callers. He entered the room and quickly glanced about in search of Elizabeth. Some of the same people he had thought a vast deal about over the past few days, all sat together on the sofa in admiration of the pleasing ambiance of the room and the elegant furnishings. Elizabeth was conspicuously absent. *She must be with her sister still,* he surmised. As if aware of his friend's disappointment, Bingley quickly relieved Darcy's mind of that mistaken impression. "Darcy, my friend, I am afraid you have missed Mrs. Carlton. She returned to her home whilst you were enjoying your morning ride. But look, her mother and sisters have come to call and to check on Miss Bennet."

The tumult in Darcy's mind was strong. *What do you mean she is gone?* he silently begged. He feigned politeness in spite of his bewilderment as Bingley made the introductions to Mrs. Bennet, Miss Mary Bennet, Miss Kitty, and Miss Lydia.

Darcy reckoned he ought to make the most of it. Though those people were repugnant to him, he realised it would not do to demonstrate his typically haughty and indifferent air, not when he entertained hopes of getting to know Elizabeth better. He supposed he might even be a guest in their home at some point in the near future. The fact that she had left Netherfield Park without saying good-bye vexed him exceedingly. Their late night encounter in the hallway seemed to have set the perfect tone for a new beginning for them. *She must have had a legitimate reason to leave. Perhaps she might even return later this afternoon.*

Every one of his hopes was shattered when the annoying drone of Mrs. Bennet's voice interrupted his reverie.

"Charlotte Lucas, now there is a spinster in the making. However, one might very well say the same of my eldest daughter Jane, I suppose. Although she is a great beauty, and there have been many young men who quite fancied her for a time. I felt sure at least one of them might make her an offer. Alas, nary a one did. Perhaps the tide is about to turn in that regard," she hinted.

Caroline's countenance surely revealed unbridled astonishment. Even Bingley, normally loquacious, knew not what to say. Darcy had his own thoughts of the blatant matchmaking. Mrs. Bennet filled the awkward silence with a soliloquy of another daughter's prospects.

"Lizzy, who is next to Jane in both age and beauty, was blessed with a good marriage, however brief, at the young age of seventeen. Now, she finds herself engaged yet again, to an upstanding gentleman whose name is Mr. Collins. He is the girls' cousin. He stands to inherit Longbourn due to the most unfortunate circumstances of an entail, whatever that means. However, thanks to our Lizzy's engagement, praise the lord, the Bennets shall always have a place at Longbourn."

It was all Darcy could do to keep up his stoic resolve in the face of her shocking disclosure. The more Mrs. Bennet spoke, the more he simmered with concealed rage. *Elizabeth? Engaged? Of all the seemingly insurmountable obstacles I have yet encountered —now this!*

Before Mrs. Bennet could go on to speak of the many other advantages of the match, Lydia, who was eager for a change in the conversation at hand had blurted out, "I think it will be a very agreeable thing if you would have a ball here at Netherfield, Mr. Bingley."

Bingley gushed, "A ball?"

"Oh, yes! It will be a very good way to become acquainted with your neighbours."

Mrs. Bennet agreed wholeheartedly. "Indeed, Mr. Bingley, what a delightful scheme! As it is my Lydia's idea, you must grant her the favour of the first set. My Lydia will be a marvellous partner."

Bingley had other ideas. He acceded to the request for a ball and even suggested to Lydia she should specify the date. He would not agree to the offer of the first dance; rather, he offered up an alternative. "Please accept my apologies in that regard; perhaps my friend Darcy might consent to take the place by your side for the first set. What say you, Darcy?"

Darcy looked at Bingley as if he had taken leave of his senses. Mrs. Bennet did not notice the awkward exchange. She was ecstatic. By then, word of Darcy's wealth had spread throughout the countryside. It was evidenced by the deference and kind regards bestowed on him by Mrs. Bennet from the moment he entered the room. "How delightful! Mr. Darcy, you shall not be disappointed!" exclaimed she. "My Lydia is as graceful a dancer as you have ever seen, if I daresay so myself."

Darcy had suffered all he could tolerate for one morning. Without acknowledging anyone in the room, he immediately took his leave, rendering a room full of stunned spectators by his uncharitable slight.

Mrs. Bennet proclaimed, "I declare he is rude and not nearly so handsome after all!"

Chapter 7

All the Bennet women, including Jane, returned to Longbourn shortly thereafter.

Mr. Bennet greeted his wife at the door. "I HOPE, my dear, that you have ordered a good dinner today, because I have reason to expect an addition to our family party." He went on to impart the news of the pending arrival of a yet another cousin, Mr. William Collins, the younger brother of Elizabeth's betrothed, Mr. Geoffrey Collins. The family's disappointment it was not the latter who was expected was offset by the prospect of the former's being just as tall and handsome as his older brother. Regardless of what he might look like, it was received as excellent news to Mr. and Mrs. Bennet, for it presented the opportunity for another one of their daughters to make an advantageous match with a respectable man. In his letter to Mr. Bennet, William Collins had boasted of his status as the parson in Hunsford and the beneficiary of the largess of his esteemed patroness, Lady Catherine de Bourgh. As had his older brother, he also hinted he would arrive at Longbourn with the purpose of admiring his fair cousins. Alas, to everyone's disappointment, save Miss Mary and the elder Bennets, upon his arrival, their guest had quickly put aside any notion of his suitability as a potential husband, for he had made himself quite ridiculous. Darcy had spent the days leading up to the Netherfield Ball in rather a miserable state. The certain knowledge of Elizabeth's engagement had troubled him far greater than his mistaken impression she was married. He wondered what she was about. He refused to accompany Caroline and Bingley when they called on the Bennets at Longbourn to give their personal invitation for the eagerly anticipated ball. It did not help matters at all that they spoke of Mr. Collins as being a guest upon their return to Netherfield. Darcy could only surmise he was there to court his future bride.

To augment his worries, days had passed since Darcy had last seen his young friend. Two factors had contributed to that misfortune. The weather had rarely allowed for outdoor time. It had rained most days, and on those days when it had not, the lanes were too muddy to allow for an enjoyable ride. The other factor, which Darcy had no way of knowing, was the unfortunate circumstance of young Ben's having taken a cold. He was consequently restricted to bed rest and granted an abundance of tender loving care from his mother who blamed her absence for his illness.

Elizabeth had not decided to go to the ball until the very last minute. It was only the ardent pleas of her eldest sister that brought about her change of heart. The prospect of seeing Mr. Darcy was not one she looked forward to with much aplomb. She had a feeling he might be disappointed with her in light of her tacit agreement to start anew and her subsequent decision to take her leave of Netherfield just hours later, without even saying good-bye. Darcy, on the other hand, had begun to anticipate her presence at the ball. He wanted answers.

Despite the fact that they were amongst the silliest girls he had ever seen, the Bennet daughters made a respectable appearance. Darcy had to admit they all looked quite lovely. Elizabeth was not amongst their party, leaving him to wonder if she would be in attendance that evening. Some moments later, the spectacle of Elizabeth entering the room, accompanied by a short, self-important, and otherwise nondescript gentleman raised his ire.

As Darcy expected, Elizabeth shared the first two dances with that unremarkable man who had arrived with her. He decided to keep a close watch over her that evening, as if he had a say in the matter. Even though her "betrothed" accompanied her that evening, Darcy was not dissuaded. He was determined to speak with her.

When at last Darcy spotted Elizabeth just across the room in conversation with another young woman, who had been introduced to him earlier as Miss Charlotte Lucas, he immediately approached the two of them. Elizabeth was caught unawares for he approached her from behind.

"Pardon me, Mrs. Carlton." The resonance of his voice astounded her. She cast her friend Charlotte a look of utter uncertainty as she wondered if she might have detected the effect the gentleman had on her composure. Elizabeth turned to face him. She returned his bow with a curtsey.

"Mrs. Carlton, may I have the next dance?"

"Yes, you may," said she, without thinking. Darcy bestowed the slightest hint of a smile and then took his leave.

Charlotte regarded Elizabeth with a bit of suspicion. "My dear Lizzy, what was that about?"

"What on earth do you mean?" Elizabeth feigned ignorance. Charlotte would have to be totally devoid of all her senses not to have seen the intensity in their looks, heard the tension in her friend's voice, or felt the subtle undercurrent of their brief exchange.

"Is there anything that you wish to tell me of the nature of your association with Mr. Darcy?"

"There is nothing to tell. Why would you ask such a question? I am engaged to Mr. Collins, am I not?" Elizabeth would not end there. "There is nothing at all between Mr. Darcy and me!"

"Doth the lady protest too much?" Charlotte asked her friend. Elizabeth chose to ignore her friend's gentle cajoling and walked away to recover her composure in privacy.

Darcy kept his eyes trained upon Elizabeth, though he did not follow her when he saw her take her leave of her friend. She was gone but a few minutes, and soon enough had returned to her friend's side. When the dancing recommenced, Darcy approached her to claim her hand. Charlotte could not help cautioning her, in a whisper, that try as she might in concealing it, it was obvious there was more there than not. Elizabeth made no answer and took her place in the set.

If she had but admitted it, she would have confessed to being thrilled with the idea of standing opposite to Mr. Darcy and reading in her neighbours' looks their equal amazement in beholding it. Still, she did not intend to allow him to know just how much he affected her. He had a way of arousing her sensibilities. It was not so much she did not trust him to know how profoundly he stirred her. It was more she did not trust herself.

They went through the dance for some time without speaking a word. His looks spoke volumes. It seemed both were resolved not to break their silence. Though very characteristic of the taciturn Mr. Darcy, the possibility their silence might last through the entirety of the two dances was insupportable to Elizabeth, especially if he intended to do nothing more than to stare at her. She made some slight observation on the dance. He replied, and was again silent. After a pause of some minutes, she addressed him a second time.

"It is your turn to say something, Mr. Darcy. I talked about the dance. You ought to make some kind of remark on the size of the room, or the number of couples."

He assured her whatever she wished him to say would be said.

"Very well; that reply will do for the present. Perhaps by and by I may remark that private balls are much pleasanter than public ones. Now we may be silent."

"Do you talk by rule then, whilst you are dancing?"

"Sometimes, one must speak a little. It would look odd to be entirely silent for half an hour together."

"What I wish to say most, is best if not said in a ballroom. Would you consider allowing me a private audience before supper?"

She almost missed the next step. "No!" replied Elizabeth archly. "What is it you wish to say to me, you cannot say here?"

"Very well, then," Darcy stood close enough to speak intimately. "When were you going to tell me that you are engaged to be married?"

Elizabeth might have been more sensitive to the disappointment he must surely have felt upon learning of her engagement, if not for the presumptuous manner of his speech.

Totally taken aback, she declared, "I did not realise that I owed you an account of my personal life, Mr. Darcy."

"You are making a grave mistake in committing to a union with that gentleman. You cannot love him. I find it hard to believe you have any esteem for him at all. I suspect you have agreed to this farce simply for the sake of securing your family's future."

"I resent you feel as you do and that you feel free to discuss these matters with me. You know nothing of my situation."

"I know all I need to know! You deserve better than to bind yourself to him for the rest of your life."

"HIM? Mr. Collins is a very respectable man! What right have you to judge him?"

Darcy looked about to study Mr. Collins. Something in his manner of standing about the room and his preening and fawning did not sit well with Darcy. He witnessed enough to justify his belief in Mr. Collins's being one of the most preposterous men he had ever seen.

"Respectable? The man is ridiculous. It was painful to watch the two of you dancing earlier this evening. What might the two of you have in common? You are like fire; he is like tepid water!"

It suddenly dawned on Elizabeth—Darcy and she were not speaking of the same person! It did not matter. By then, she was livid at his officiousness. She did not intend to correct Darcy's misapprehensions. *What business is it of his to WHOM I am engaged? Let him think what he will! The material point is that I AM engaged, whether he likes it or not. All the explanations in the world will fail to change that fact!*

"You have said quite enough, Mr. Darcy. I believe I understand your sentiments precisely. You will pardon me, though, if I choose to keep my own counsel on such matters."

"I would by no means suspend any pleasure of yours," he coldly replied. She said no more. They completed the dance and parted in silence.

Charlotte Lucas stood beside Mr. Collins and spoke with him at length to learn more of his situation. At seven and twenty, she was quite determined she would find a husband; there was no reason for her to conclude he would not make as decent a husband for her as he would for anyone else.

"Mr. Collins, no doubt you look forward to the joining of your family and the Bennet family in the near future what with your brother's marriage to my dear friend Mrs. Carlton."

"Oh yes! But I must admit I am equally excited by the prospect of my own marriage to a particular one of my fair cousins, as well."

Charlotte could have little doubt of which Bennet daughter he spoke. It was clear to her that he admired the eldest Bennet daughter exceedingly. That could not be good, according to Charlotte's schemes for herself. She endeavoured to divert his attentions.

"Though it is not truly my place, I feel it incumbent upon me to tell you that the eldest Bennet is likely to be engaged to another very soon."

Mr. Collins cast a wary look. That was not what he had been led to believe, for he had spoken with Mrs. Bennet of his preference for Miss Bennet soon after his arrival.

"Are you quite certain? I have hinted of my intentions to her mother, and she said not a word of any such prospects. No, I believe you are mistaken."

"It is likely Mrs. Bennet did not mention it because nothing is official. However, I speak of Mr. Bingley as the likely intended. If you would but look, then you would see for yourself just how much he admires her."

Darcy and Elizabeth did not have occasion to speak to each other again that evening. She went out of her way to avoid him, and he was none too keen on seeking her out any further. Besides, both of their thoughts tended elsewhere, though, ironically along similar lines. The behaviour of the youngest two Miss Bennets grew more and more boisterous as the evening progressed. The behaviour of Mr. Bennet himself was hardly better as he made Miss Mary's poor exhibition on the pianoforte worse by his admonishment against any further attempts. Poor Mary ran off in tears, a spectacle that caused Darcy to wonder what sort of father would do such a thing to his own child.

All that simply confirmed Darcy's original opinion of the Bennet family and caused him to wonder about Elizabeth's motives. *Surely, she is not mercenary,* he thought. *It is far more likely she is anxious to get away from that family of hers.*

Darcy soon became aware of the general expectation amongst the locals of a pending engagement between his friend Bingley and Miss Jane Bennet. He grew more unfavourably predisposed to that notion the more he observed Jane. He could detect no particular regard on her part towards his friend. He considered just as Elizabeth was willing to bind herself to a man she did not love, so must her eldest sister be, especially as he recalled the hint of desperation Mrs. Bennet had suggested when she had visited at Netherfield.

Within a day of the ball, the Netherfield staff prepared the manor house for an extended absence. The fine furnishings throughout the house were covered with crisp white linens. All the personal belongings were packed and loaded into carriages. The shades were drawn.

None of the occupants of the carriage seemed particularly pleased with the prospect of returning to London that morning. The attitudes of Bingley and Caroline reflected the bitter disappointment of hours of arguing. She had prevailed in persuading him to abandon his hopes for any sort of attachment to Miss Bennet and her dreadful family. Bingley was disappointed in his friend, as well, not that Darcy had spoken a harsh word against Miss Bennet, per se. He simply had not said anything in her favour. He had agreed with Caroline's bleak assessment of the Bennets and what it might mean in social consequence if Bingley aligned himself with such a family.

Bingley recalled the question he had posed to his friend, in an attempt to rally support against Caroline's abusive diatribe. "Do you not agree all of that means nothing, if Miss Bennet truly cares for me?"

"I would agree, Bingley. However, I have seen no evidence of any particular regard on her part. She readily bestows her lovely smiles on you, it is true. How is that any different from any of the many *angels* you have known in the past?"

Darcy was careful to keep his eyes trained out of the window in search of his young friend as the carriage drew nearer to the place where they always had met. Eureka! Darcy eagerly tapped his cane upon the roof of the carriage to signal to the driver to halt.

He climbed down from the carriage and strolled towards his young friend, some twenty or so yards away. Ben was so excited to see him. It seemed as if it had been an eternity since they had last met. Ben had planned many exciting adventures during their time apart. There was so much he wanted to say and do. He ran towards Darcy.

"King Arthur! I have missed you so. Where have you been?" Ben looked in the direction of the luggage-laden carriage. "Where are you going, my King?"

"I am happy to see you this morning, gallant knight. I feared I might not have a chance to say good-bye. You see, it is time I return to my own land, Sir Lancelot. It has been a great pleasure knowing you."

"No, no, no! Do not go!" young Ben cried as he desperately clung to Darcy's long legs. Darcy endeavoured to release the child's tight grip. He lowered himself to his knees to meet Ben's eyes at his level.

"What is this I see? Do brave knights cry?" Darcy removed his crisp, white handkerchief and wiped the lad's tears away.

"I do not feel much like being brave," cried Ben, broken-heartedly. "You are my best friend in the world. You cannot leave me."

"I am afraid that I must. Please try to understand."

What was there to understand to a young lad who had suffered such painful losses during the short span of his lifetime? A father he never knew, a doting grandfather who loved him dearly, and now a friend who meant more to him than even he could ever know—all of them gone. Ben fought mightily to stop his tears from falling. "Shall we ever meet again?"

Darcy endeavoured to keep up a brave front in the face of what he knew must be acutely painful for the long-suffering child. "Brighten up, my young friend. I am a firm believer that good-bye is not the end. The best things in life have a way of working them-selves out. Our friendship is strong. It might even have the potential for greatness. If it is meant to be, then, indeed, our paths will cross yet again."

Chapter 8

Mr Geoffrey Collins was eager with anticipation for many months had passed since he first had met his fair cousin. In under a week, he would see her again. As he sat in a chair staring out the window of his modest house in town, he reflected upon all that had occurred, and how it seemed to him as though life were conspiring against him. As much as he considered it a great displeasure to spend any significant time in the presence of his Hertfordshire relations, he had planned to do just that over Christmas, such was his longing to see Elizabeth once more. Of course, it meant he and his daughters would be obliged to stay in a Meryton inn; what with Mrs. Bennet's brother and his family from town enjoying a standing invitation to visit Longbourn at Christmas, there simply was not enough room at the manor for the huge influx of house-guests. Alas, both of his young daughters were afflicted with colds. In letters exchanged with his intended, the mutual decision was reached that it would not be wise to travel.

He knew the girls would be as taken with Elizabeth as was he. He had observed with some measure of appreciation, just how much she doted on her young son. He had no doubt she would embrace his daughters as though they were her own children. She was just that kind of woman. Though his girls benefited appreciably from a strong female presence in their lives in the form of an attentive and somewhat stern governess, who had been with them for many years and who was considered a part of the family, what they needed most was a mother's tender love and care.

Elizabeth was the object of his ardent esteem from the moment of their introduction. Though the father had intended it as an arranged marriage, Mr. Collins had no intention of taking anything for granted. Geoffrey Collins was everything his younger brother was not. He had a most agreeable countenance, and he comported himself with considerable dignity. More than anything else, he was clever. In his astuteness, he realised merely to have her consent was nothing. What he desired most was her passion, something he knew would never come about without first winning her heart. He decided he must court her properly, but the prospect of doing so at Longbourn was unfathomable. That week he had spent there, under the same roof as the silliest creatures in all of England, had been a torment. And that mother! He had given the matter quite a bit of thought during his stay and was firmly decided—the first thing he would do upon his inheriting Longbourn Village, would be to build a dowager house, should it ever come to that.

Just three weeks earlier he had written to his younger brother, William Collins, to put his plans in motion. He had taken care of all the pleasantries upfront in congratulating him on his nuptials to the former Miss Charlotte Lucas and in apologising profusely for his not being there in person, in spite of his ardent desire to see his own intended. He explained how there was much to do in preparing his country home in Lincolnshire for his own pending nuptials.

Geoffrey Collins correctly suspected his younger brother could not be counted as a favourite of his future Bennet in-laws, what with his having failed in his intention of visiting Longbourn to choose a bride from amongst his cousins, much in the same fashion as he had successfully done. He had learnt that the announcement of his brother's engagement had been poorly received, indeed. The chilly reception was such that the younger Mr. Collins quickly had removed himself from Longbourn and taken up residence at Lucas Lodge, ostensibly to commence his courtship of his fair lady and bask in the hopes and dreams of his newfound felicity.

When he had learnt from his brother that Charlotte was a dear friend of Elizabeth's, he was pleased beyond measure. It was perfect. Collins asked his younger brother to extend an invitation for Elizabeth and her young son to visit them in Hunsford for the spring. He and his daughters would join them. There, he would have an opportunity to court Elizabeth and become better acquainted with her son, away from the prying eyes of Longbourn. Elizabeth would have a chance to become better acquainted with his lovely daughters, as well.

The disheartening situation had gone on for months. Elizabeth fretted over her young son's dismay more each day. Overnight, it seemed, he had gone from waking up bright and early each day eager to finish breakfast and set off on his favourite path, only to return a short time later with one account or another of his adventures with King Arthur, to his seeming total disinterest in waking up at all. By Elizabeth's reckoning, Ben seemed as melancholy as was her sister Jane, who had been rather discouraged upon learning that Mr. Bingley did not intend to return to Hertfordshire during the foreseeable future. He had elected instead to remain in town for the winter, if his sister Caroline's account could be taken as truth. Elizabeth knew her sister was nursing a broken heart. She knew not what to think of her own son's malaise.

Looking out the window, she espied young Ben sitting on the front steps of the manor house tossing bread crumbs to the white geese wandering freely about. It was as clear an indication as any of the height of her son's boredom. Conspiring to do anything that would encourage her son out of his lackadaisical behaviour of late, she donned her coat and went outside to join him.

"Ben, what say you to the two of us venturing out this morning for an adventure with King Arthur?"

"There would be no point in that. He is gone."

"Has he not gone on journeys before? Perhaps, he has returned."

"No, I am rather certain that is not the case. He is never to return."

"Why would you say such a thing?"

"They always leave. They never come back."

"They?" Elizabeth asked her young son in puzzlement. "To whom do you refer, Ben?"

"They! All of them! My father never returned. My grandpapa went away, and he has never returned. Now, King Arthur has gone away. HE will never return."

The tumult in Elizabeth's mind was now painfully great. Had she been remiss in allowing her young son to engage in flights of fancy for as long as she had—even in encouraging it as she had just done? She knelt before her son and took his hand in her own. "Ben, there is a significant difference between your father and your grandfather and your King Arthur. Unlike your King Arthur, your father was a living, breathing human being, as was your dear grandfather. Though your father never had a chance to know you, I assure you he would have loved you very much. You know how much your grandfather loved you. Neither of them departed this earth purposely.

"Your King Arthur, however, is merely a result of your young imagination. Please understand me when I say he does not exist. He simply is not real. Tell me you know the difference."

"No Mama! You are mistaken. King Arthur, too, is a living and breathing human being. He is kind, and honourable and just! He told me he was to return to his own land." Even the eyes of a child could not misread the pain and incredulity shining on her face. He asserted, "You do not believe me."

"Ben, I love you more than anything else in the world," Elizabeth started. The last thing she wanted was to encourage him in his fantastic account. She refused to do so again.

Before she could speak further, Ben responded, "I know you love me, Mama. I want to know that you believe me." The lack of belief upon her countenance did not abate, causing the young lad to withdraw his hand forcefully and run off as fast as his little legs would carry him. Elizabeth decided not to follow him, thinking it was best to allow him some time alone. She also needed time to reflect.

One of the things she had missed about Longbourn during her stay at Camberworth was its proximity to Oakham Mount. Elizabeth always did her best thinking there. In mere months, she surmised, she would be far, far away from the one place of her greatest solace. As much as she was anxious over the prospect of embarking upon her new life with Mr. Collins, she knew there must be significant advantages in doing just that, if not for herself, then surely for her young son. Ben desperately needed companionship; the type a mother, a house full of aunts, a hysterical grandmother, and an inconsiderate grandfather did not provide. He needed the guidance of a strong man and the enduring ties of siblings. In his many letters over the past months, Mr. Collins had spoken enthusiastically of his desire to make them all a family. Elizabeth prayed he did so out of sincerity, that he would indeed be an excellent father for Ben. *I shall find out soon enough. The advent of our trip to Hunsford could not possibly have come at a better time. Indeed, it is just the sort of diversion my son needs.*

Darcy and she walked along the beautiful, windy coastline, arm-in-arm. It had been far too long since he had last seen her. He had missed her terribly. Their frequent letters had been a poor exchange for their time spent apart, prompting him to think to spend Christmas with his young sister at her temporary establishment in

Ramsgate. He also was influenced by his knowledge that his aunt Lady Catherine and his cousin Anne had made plans to spend Christmastime in town. They were two of the last people he wished to see. He had shared his travel plans with no one, other than his sister.

"Georgiana my dear, have you given any more thought to my offer to have you come live with me?"

"Dear brother, as much as I would enjoy that, we have had this conversation before, have we not?"

"You are far too sacrificing for your own good. It will be no hardship at all if Mrs. Annesley and you would come live with me. I would benefit greatly from your company."

"And what might your betrothed say to that? You know Cousin Anne has never had much patience for me. Now that I am older, I find I have no great desire for her company either."

"Please do not tell me you, too, subscribe to the notion that I will ever marry Anne."

"Why would I not? I, along with the rest of the family, believe it is inevitable. What have you done to cause any of us to think otherwise?" *Other than flee to Hertfordshire with your friend, Mr. Bingley, and tuck yourself away for these past weeks,* she silently voiced.

"I confess to being at a complete loss as regards what to do next. Any mention of my true intent only threatens to return our cousin to her deathbed." Darcy looked out over the water, its turbulence reflecting his inner turmoil.

"It is a very convenient malady our poor cousin suffers, if you ask me," Georgiana alleged, half-jokingly.

Darcy returned his attention to his sister, as if the thought never had entered his mind. "Indeed—I do not wish to see her suffer a relapse."

"Trust me, Brother; should you continue to stay away from Rosings Park much longer, I assure you, a relapse is imminent."

Colonel Richard Fitzwilliam had just stopped by the Darcy town house to visit his cousin and find out his plans for Easter. It was their annual tradition to visit their aunt in Rosings Park, and yet Darcy had shown no indication he planned to go that year.

"Why fight it any longer? Everyone in the family knows it is only a matter of time until you and Anne marry."

"The question I might ask of everyone in the family, is why is there all of this concern over my intentions towards Anne."

"That is what our family is for. Have you not read the *Fitzwilliam Family Creed?*" Richard asked Darcy, in a poor attempt to lighten his foul mood. It made no difference. Richard continued, "Look here, the sooner you endeavour to relieve Anne and Lady Catherine of their misapprehension that you have any intention of ever marrying Anne—that you were only speaking hypothetically—the better it will go with you."

"It is not as though I have not attempted to do just that. I have argued with Lady Catherine until I was blue in the face on this very topic. You know, I can only be so firm with Anne."

"I know that—as does Anne. I say she has you exactly where she wants you in that regard."

"Between Georgiana and you, that makes two."

Darcy set off for a stroll in Hyde Park after his cousin's departure. A breath of fresh air was just what he needed to clear his head and decide what he must do. *Should I travel to Kent for Easter or not? Indeed, it is not a decision easily made. If I do not go, Anne is bound to suffer considerable disappointment. On the other hand, should I go, she will also be hurt. I have no intention of spending two weeks at Rosings Park, pretending to go along with this farce. I will not marry Anne! She may as well hear it from me, once and for all.*

Darcy walked along entirely caught up in his own thoughts until the rumbustious sounds of children at play just up ahead of his path caught his attention. Immediately, his thoughts tended towards his young friend from Hertfordshire. Darcy admitted to having grown quite fond of the precocious young boy. He often thought when the time came for him to indeed settle down to raise a family, he wanted a son just like his young friend, *Sir Lancelot*. Despite the brevity of their acquaintance, Darcy had learnt to miss his young friend considerably.

Young Sir Lancelot was not the only one of his Hertfordshire acquaintances he found himself thinking of with some frequency, and even missing to a greater extent than he could have imagined with his hasty departure from Netherfield Park. Not a day went by that he did not think of HER. *Elizabeth.* Never before had any woman held him so enthralled. Day after day, Darcy found himself repeating a dishearteningly familiar refrain. *I shall conquer this.*

What other choice might I have? How he wished things had been different—her circumstances to have been otherwise. He had mixed feelings over there having been so much left unspoken between them. Everything he had ever known of the fairer sex confirmed his belief in her having been not entirely unaffected by him. Far from it. As much as he had felt the intensity of the passion between them, he was sure she could not have helped sensing it too. Alas, nothing would ever become of their mutual yearning. She belonged to another. Still he wondered. *How long had she been married? What circumstances might have led to marriage at what had to have been a remarkably young age? Were any children born of the union?* The more he relived every moment of his fleeting encounters with Elizabeth, the more he thought of his young friend.

The two of them are so much alike in their mannerisms, in their speech, in their countenance.

"In their countenance!" he voiced aloud. Darcy, who happened to be sitting at his desk, rested his face in both hands. He started massaging his forehead in serious contemplation.

What if?

Chapter 9

Elizabeth placed a loving hand on her son's shoulder to awaken him. Within minutes, they were set to arrive at the parsonage in Hunsford. Elizabeth's anxiety was no match for the considerable trepidation Ben suffered in anticipation of the visit. He was to meet his future sisters—nay, *stepsisters* as he eagerly pointed out time and again to his mother. Secondly, he was to get reacquainted with his future stepfather.

Ben had not been nearly so impressed with Mr. Geoffrey Collins as had been his relatives, when he had made his acquaintance some months earlier at Longbourn. To Ben's way of thinking, the gentleman had absolutely no sense of adventure. Try as he might in engaging the newcomer with talk of the Arthurian legend and adventures of the Knights of the Round Table, all his entreaties had met with deaf ears.

When Ben inquired of him, "Perchance you know of *Meleagant?*"

Mr. Collins replied, "Pray tell me, son, who is *Meleagant?*"

"Oh, it is of no consequence," Ben responded coyly. *Who is Meleagant, indeed? Why YOU sir,* Ben thought to himself. No wonder Ben had precious little use for the gentleman from then on. He had endeavoured to maintain a comfortable distance for the remainder of Mr. Collins's stay at Longbourn. The arrival of their carriage at the parsonage coincided with the emergence of the bright afternoon sun. At last, the steady rain had ceased, and the dark clouds that hovered over them during the entire journey from town had parted. Elizabeth took that as a sign everything would work out for the best. An eager receiving line had assembled in front of the gate of the parsonage to greet them. There was Mr. and Mrs. William Collins, the former endeavouring to exhibit a modicum of decorum that befit his overly inflated sense of himself, and the latter, whose genuine smile was gleeful. Alongside of them stood Mr. Geoffrey Collins, who towered above everyone with his tall person and handsome mien. Gillian and Emily, two charming young girls, stood at his side.

Geoffrey Collins eagerly positioned himself to hand down his intended as soon as the carriage came to a halt. He was very reluctant to release her hand after having bestowed upon it a light kiss. Her response was not at all unreceptive. It was a favourable beginning. He was pleased.

Darcy sat in his study nursing a large glass of brandy while he stared into the fire and awaited his cousin's arrival. It turned out the decision to spend Easter at Rosings Park had been made for him. Just that morning, he had received an urgent plea from Kent. Anne's health had failed. The prognosis was not good. He was obliged to attend her.

He recalled an earlier missive from his aunt talking of the parson and his bride from Hertfordshire. *She makes no mention of a son. Perhaps I was mistaken in thinking there might be a connection between Elizabeth and young Sir Lancelot.* Not that it mattered. Darcy had determined against returning to Hertfordshire to clear up the mystery of the young child's maternity. He did not want to know the truth of the matter, for he felt surely no benefit would be derived from such knowledge. She was promised to another.

Hours later, Darcy found himself on the road to Kent with his cousin Colonel Fitzwilliam. It seemed to Darcy his cousin was suffering quite a bit of enjoyment by the sound of his own voice.

Immediately upon entering the carriage, Richard proclaimed, "Let us hope we reach Kent in record time, my friend. It is a shame to think our dear cousin Anne might pass away whilst we are on the way and not have you by her bedside as she breathes her last breath on this earth." The snide smirk that graced his countenance could scarcely be contained.

"I fail to see the humour in your speech," Darcy responded gravely. "This is hardly a laughable affair."

"Of course it is! How convenient is it that Anne has suffered this unfortunate relapse at this time. When last you and I spoke on the matter, you were resolved you would not travel to Kent this spring. Yet, here we are in a carriage en route with all haste to Rosings Park."

"If you would bother to recall correctly, I had not decided one way or the other. Besides, Anne suffers a wholly unrelated affliction this time. Our aunt says Anne's health has suffered a slow and steady decline since Christmas, when they travelled to town to visit me."

"In other words, you are entirely to blame for Anne's grave illness. Thank you for explaining it to me so fully," Richard derided, giving Darcy a sense of the utter foolishness of it all. Darcy said nothing. He decided it was prudent to avoid providing his clever cousin any added fodder for mirth at his own expense.

How he wished his cousin would tire of hearing his own voice, especially as he began to expound on the many ways Darcy might rouse his cousin from her sick-bed. *Heaven forbid!*

After a spell, Darcy was relieved his talkative cousin had been lulled to sleep by the combination of his own reticence towards being drawn into meaningless debate and the steady pour of rain and silent streams of raindrops on the windowpanes of the carriage. It gave Darcy a chance to think.

What might it be like to see HER again—knowing she is married to that ridiculous man, desiring her as much as ever, longing to be near her?

Darcy thought back to the last time he had laid eyes upon her. He recalled his astonishment in being *attacked* by the preposterous man and in being caught entirely off guard by the gentleman's audacity to introduce himself during the Netherfield ball. He recollected his using the words "apology," "Hunsford," and "Lady Catherine de Bourgh" whilst eyeing him with unrestrained wonder. When at last Mr. Collins had allowed him time to speak, Darcy recalled replying with an air of distant civility. The mortification Darcy had espied on Elizabeth's face, after moving as far away from the odious man as quickly and as abruptly as conceivably possible, was priceless. *What is she thinking?*

It is done! Elizabeth has married that foolish man. She has made her bed, and now she must lie in it. Immediately upon thinking such thoughts, he wished he had not allowed his mind to venture there. He groaned aloud with the mere prospect of it all.

Mr. and Mr. Collins brought up the rear as all the Hunsford party enjoyed a leisurely stroll on the day after Elizabeth and Ben's arrival. Evidence of spring abounded with a colourful array of blossoming trees, faint scents of freshly budding flowers, and the delightful sightings of nature's smallest creatures. It afforded the perfect opportunity to escape the somewhat restrictive confines of the parsonage.

The elder gentleman's mind was anywhere but on the conversation with his brother. *What on earth is he talking about now? I love my younger brother, honestly I do. However, I will be unable to account for my actions should he persist in these sycophantic ramblings on the subject of his esteemed patroness, Lady Catherine de Bourgh.*

He endeavoured to turn his attentions towards his lovely betrothed, who strolled just ahead of him, arm in arm with his new sister-in-law. How exceedingly envious he was of Charlotte at that moment. *Elizabeth and I have shared the same living quarters for nearly twenty-four hours, and yet I have had not one moment alone with her. I wish to know everything about her. There is only so much one can glean from letters. Patience. Perhaps this evening, once the children have gone to bed, and my brother and his wife have done likewise, I shall have some time alone with her.*

As to the children, I am gladdened, indeed, by the warmth and kindness she has bestowed on Gillian and Emily. They like her very much. I suspect she returns their regard. I shall endeavour to bestow an equal measure of attention towards young Bon. Upon deeper reflection, Mr. Collins surmised, *He is quite an impertinent young child and profoundly in want of a firm hand and strict discipline such that his mother is unable to provide. All in due time,* Collins considered. *All in due time.*

Elizabeth was far more attuned to the conversation with her dear friend Charlotte, than was the aforementioned gentleman with his own walking companion. She had missed Charlotte dearly. Indeed, she had found Hertfordshire rather lonely since Jane had returned to town with their Uncle and Aunt Gardiner after Christmas. Elizabeth was delighted with the prospect of spending time with sensible female companionship. She spoke to Charlotte of the heartbreak Jane had suffered what with Mr. Bingley's precipitous departure from Netherfield Park. He had not even bothered to say good-bye, and in so doing he had left the neighbourhood with the general impression her dear sister had been badly used.

Charlotte could not help thinking, *far better it is Jane who is crossed in love than I.* Indeed, she considered how providential it was that she interceded as she did in turning Mr. William Collins's head away from his fair cousin. Otherwise, Jane might surely have been the new mistress of the parsonage by then, while she would have been at Lucas Lodge and a burden to her family. At seven and twenty, she rightfully had perceived it as being her last chance. Even her own family had given up all hope she should ever marry. She had known not whether to be pleased or annoyed by her brothers' exuberance over the announcement of her engagement. Charlotte also recalled how fervently her friend Elizabeth had tried to dissuade her from accepting Mr. Collins's hand in marriage. *Elizabeth of all people,* she recalled. *Not everyone could be as fortunate as could she. While it was true Mr. Bennet had coerced her into accepting the elder Mr. Collins, one had but to look at him!* Charlotte could recall only one other man of her recent acquaintance who might even compare to her new brother—*Mr. Fitzwilliam Darcy of Pemberley and Derbyshire. As I recall, he seemed enamoured of my dear friend, as well. Indeed, not everyone can be as fortunate as can Elizabeth.*

Gillian and Emily unhurriedly walked a few paces ahead of Elizabeth and Charlotte. It had been a long time since they had taken a leisurely stroll merely for the sake of diversion, not since the death of their mother three years earlier. From what they could recall of their beloved mama, she had been an avid walker and had enjoyed being out and about in the open air. Their governess, being an older woman, did not relish time spent out of doors, and so the girls largely were confined to indoor pursuits, both in town and in the country. How different their lives would be with their new mother, they both sensed.

They could not help looking at young Ben Carlton with a sense of awe and wonder at his eager imagination. Their feelings were the mixture of a sense of uncertainty and curiosity about the young boy, more than four years their junior. What amount of terror might he unleash on their otherwise quiet and reserved household? They recalled hearing their dear father speak to their governess about the wild and unruly behaviour of the younger Bennet daughters and how he was glad his daughters had yet to travel with him to Longbourn and thus be exposed to the unseemly young women. Questions persisted in the girls' impressionable young minds. *Is Ben anything like his mother's younger sisters?*

Ben exhibited a certain amount of disinterest in the twins. Their initial introduction, just the day before, had sparked his curiosity causing him to conclude the two looked just alike, but did not engage him so much as to bother to devise any means of telling them apart. What difference did it signify to him? They were girls. Poor Ben had his fill of girls.

It was a good thing he had remembered to bring his magnificent steed along on the journey to Hunsford, he considered. It offered him the ideal pretext to gallop ahead of his party without giving offence. Ben decided to cut an uncharted path through the forest for a bit of adventure. What he saw brought him to an abrupt standstill. The opening of the trees just up ahead afforded the glimpse of towering bulbous-capped domes, sky reaching grand pillars, dazzling expanses of windows, glazing that shone like gold, and magnificent castled walls reflecting the sun's fiery tints as far as his eyes could see. The reflection lakes that etched paths through gardens with spectacular bedding brought to the young fellow's mind flowing river streams. Ben had dreamt of this special place for as long as he could remember.

He released the reins of his fierce makeshift stallion and speedily raced back to his mother's side. He grabbed a hold of her hand and urged her to follow him. "Come quickly, Mama!"

Elizabeth hurriedly broke away from the rest of the party to indulge her son's latest flight of fantasy. "Ben, what is it? What have you discovered?"

"Look Mama, just up ahead! It is Camelot!"

Chapter 10

Although Darcy had been in residence at Rosings Park for a short while, he suffered the passing hours as though they were days. Scarcely imparting a proper greeting to his aunt, Lady Catherine de Bourgh, Darcy made his way to Anne's apartment within minutes of his arrival. Sure enough, she was bed-ridden. However, she did not look nearly as poorly as the urgent plea from his aunt had suggested. Not that she looked exceedingly well. She looked much the same as she had before his hasty departure at the end of last summer.

The room was dark and dreary, with the heavy shades drawn tightly closed. Anne's nurse sat off in the corner, sound asleep in her chair. Darcy's sudden appearance startled her, and she immediately set upon moving busily about the room. To his gentle calling of his cousin's name, and the not so quiet stirrings of her nurse, Anne responded not one bit.

Richard had imparted the unsolicited but much offered advice that rather than speak to Anne as merely a cousin upon finding himself alone with her, Darcy should regard her with the affectionate words and gentle touch of a lover. Darcy had considered his cousin's words with greater attention than he would allow. To his way of thinking, what Richard suggested was carrying things a bit far, regardless of how innocuous it seemed on the surface. He was desperate after all, just not THAT desperate. Darcy considered it would be a cold day in Hades before he brushed his lips against those of his Cousin Anne, as Richard had recommended.

Rather he sat down on her bed, after making a point of dismissing her nurse, and took her scrawny, fragile hand in his and caressed it tenderly. He raised it to his lips. Then, he leaned towards her and placed a lingering kiss on her forehead. *I would rather my lips were kissing a dead fish!*

The arousing effect on her maidenly sensibilities was pleasing. Anne opened her eyes almost immediately. "Fitzwilliam! You have returned."

"Yes, I am here," said he, having by then released her hand, and placed his hand on her chin. "It seems I have timed my visit to coincide with your recovery."

"I admit to feeling much better than I have been of late. Now that you have returned to my side, I can only imagine I will soon see a swift and complete recovery."

Darcy ceased his actions and stood by her bed. "I should like that very much, Cousin, for there is a matter between us that warrants great discussion, as soon as you are up to it."

"Oh, I agree, Fitzwilliam," said she with a complaisant smile, "there is much to discuss."

The look on her face led Darcy to know they could not possibly have the same discussion in mind. "Very well then, I shall leave you now so you might get some rest."

"Pray do not leave my side again so soon," she pleaded desperately.

"I am afraid I must. You need your rest. I will return after dinner."

Dinner with his aunt and his cousin Richard was little better than spending time at Anne's bedside, Darcy considered. Whereas Anne's hints were subtle and somewhat indirect, Lady Catherine's words were outright demanding.

After speaking a few words with her staff in regards to the timing of the dinner courses, the grand matron directed her full attention to her nephew. "Darcy, how did you find my daughter?"

"I found her in far better state than your urgent letter suggested I might, your ladyship."

Richard chided, "Why am I not at all surprised to hear that?" The question earned him quite a menacing look from the great lady.

"Silence, Nephew!" Lady Catherine demanded. "When I want to hear your opinion, I shall request it. Besides, why should she not be on her way to recovery with the news of her intended's pending arrival, when it was his own neglect that rendered her thus in the first place?"

"Lady Catherine," Darcy beseeched, "you know as well as does Cousin Anne that I never intended my ill-considered words were to be taken literally. I will not marry her."

"You speak nonsense, nephew! You WILL marry my daughter. It was the favourite wish of your dear mother. Whilst in your cradles, she and I planned this union. Whether you intended to speak the words or not, is of no consequence." Lady Catherine sought Richard's backing. "Is this engagement not frequently spoken of amongst all our family? Is it not widely expected?" To her desperate appeal, Richard spoke not a word, pretending instead not to have heard anything she uttered, in spite of the fact that he had been looking at her directly.

"Well, Nephew, do not just sit there," she demanded. "Say something!"

On and on, went Lady Catherine, speaking words of a similar vein the following morning at breakfast. Darcy had taken about all he could stand. He decided to take a break from the madness of Rosings Park for a breath of fresh air; away from his cousin's sickbed, away from his aunt's pressuring him, and away from his cousin making light of the situation with every chance he could find. He considered his opinionated Cousin Richard certainly was little help in making matters any easier for him.

Fortunately, Anne was *recovering.* Darcy began to consider he might leave fairly soon thereafter, and in so doing, let her know, in no uncertain terms, that she could pretend all she wanted, he would not marry her. Furthermore, for her to persist in her deceitful deathbed schemes, she risked alienating any affection he had previously entertained for her as a cousin. *Enough is enough!* Darcy was quite distracted as he paced about the immaculately groomed gardens.

Denied a chance to visit *Camelot* immediately upon his discovery of the enchanting place because, as told to him by Mr. Collins, it would not be fitting as they had not received a proper invitation, young Ben decided to stand watch over the place from a comfortable distance. As his curiosity, as well as his eager imagination, endeavoured to get the better of him with each passing moment, so too, Ben found himself drawing nearer and nearer to the grand castle. Ben's thoughts were of the evil *Meleagant,* and how he had refused to believe him that this was indeed Camelot! *I will show him,* young Ben considered. He was bound and determined to gather the proof he needed, even if it meant returning every day until his mission was successful.

Ben's tenacity soon paid off! Finally, on the third day of his pilgrimage to Camelot, he espied his king! All nonsensical admonishments addressing formal invitations and the like before setting foot on the grounds of Rosings escaped Ben's head!

He raced towards Darcy, praising and shouting, "King Arthur! King Arthur! I have found you!"

Before Darcy knew it, the young lad had been directly upon him. He jumped into Darcy's arms, and Darcy lifted him to the sky. Darcy bestowed a hearty, pleasant smile before placing the child gently back upon his feet and lowering himself to his eye level.

"Sir Lancelot! What on earth are you doing here and so far away from Hertfordshire?"

Ben threw his arms around Darcy's neck with enough energy to land them both on the ground. Both fellows laughed aloud. Darcy attempted to reclaim some measure of dignity, but Ben had other ideas as he quickly climbed onto Darcy's lap. Darcy allowed the young lad a moment or two to compose himself. It was obvious to him just how much the child had missed him since they had parted company in Hertfordshire. He saw no need to press him for details on the circumstances of his being there.

Ben finally spoke, "King Arthur, I have missed you terribly. Say you will never leave me again."

Darcy knew he could make no such commitment to his young friend. Rather he said, "What say you we take things one day at a time? Pray tell me, what on earth are you doing here in Kent?"

"Where is Kent? This is *Camelot,* is it not? I am here to see you!"

Darcy looked about the magnificent grounds and imagined just how enchanting it must seem through the eyes of a child. He smiled in appreciation of Ben's characterisation, especially as he recalled his own early recollections of the picturesque estate. "Camelot, indeed! What say you to a tour of the grounds? Would you like that?"

"I should like that very much!" Ben shouted enthusiastically upon standing and racing ahead.

Darcy shouted, "Wait for me, young man!"

Ben turned around and raced back to Darcy; whereupon, he quickly grasped and enfolded his tiny hand in Darcy's mightier one. Darcy and Ben walked along the many paths, hand in hand, and Darcy pointed out ordinary sights of interest with embellished descriptions of towers, curtain walls, moats, drawbridges, jousting fields, and the like, and thoroughly entertained the young lad in so doing.

Upon arriving at the stables, Ben was delighted to see teams of impressive stallions all fit for battle. He would not be satisfied until Darcy introduced him to them all. At length, Darcy asked the question of Ben once more, on how he came to be so far from Hertfordshire.

"I am here with my mama! You must return with me and meet her, for she does not believe you are a real person. She believes you are an imaginary friend!"

"Of course," Darcy spoke to no one in particular. *So, Elizabeth IS his mother!* "Where is your mother now?"

"She is at the parsonage with Mr. Collins! Come with me. I will introduce you to my mama!"

"I am afraid that is ill-advised. One cannot simply barge in on another without a proper invitation. Besides, I fear your mother might not wish to see me."

"Of course she will wish to see you! Why would my mama not wish to see you? Moreover, you have a proper invitation already. You will be MY guest. Oh, please come back to the parsonage with me!

Geoffrey Collins had awakened early that morning with his mind pleasantly engaged in the same thoughts which had carried him off to sleep the night before. For the second night in a row, Elizabeth had acceded to his request to spend time alone with him downstairs in the drawing room after everyone else in the household had retired for the evening. As it had been the night previous to last night, it had been again a private and intimate setting. He had enjoyed it immensely as she had seemed to become less and less uncomfortable under his steady gaze. That she had allowed him to walk with her to her bedroom door pleased him exceedingly, as did the warm smile that had graced her countenance after he had bestowed a lingering kiss to the back of her hand.

He could only think of a single thing about his betrothed that had failed to please him. In the light of the day, he had to admit to a sense of unease as regarded her rearing of young Ben. He had not been impressed with the child's behaviour on the day of their outing. He recalled how Elizabeth had eagerly pretended to go along with Ben's insistence on Rosings Park's actually being Camelot. *Where does he get such fanciful ideas, and why does she not do more to discourage it?* He had little doubt had he not interceded as sternly as he did, the child would have raced off towards the grand home, encroached on its aristocratic inhabitants, and thereby embarrassed and brought shame upon them all.

He also considered Elizabeth's thinly disguised dismay in witnessing her son having been spoken to as authoritatively as he had done. *She was wise enough not to speak on it,* he considered. *It is something she soon will become accustomed to, no doubt. A child must know his place. I will be no sterner towards the child than my own father was towards me. He shall be a better man for it.*

The Hunsford party sat around in the drawing room enjoying a leisurely afternoon. Mr. William Collins opined on their immense misfortune in not having yet received an invitation to dine at Rosings Park.

To his older brother's inquiry on the venerable Lady Catherine de Bourgh's family, the younger Mr. Collins began a soliloquy. "She has only one daughter, the sole heiress of Rosings—a most charming young lady, indeed. Lady Catherine herself says that in point of true beauty, Miss De Bourgh is far superior to the handsomest of her sex because there is that in her features which marks a young woman of distinguished birth.

"She is, unfortunately, of a sickly constitution, which has prevented her making progress in many accomplishments, of which she could not otherwise have failed, as I am informed by the lady who superintended her education and who resides with them still.

"Indeed, Miss Anne de Bourgh is quite indisposed even as we speak. I am sure that explains why we have yet to be invited for dinner. However, I have taken it on myself in calling on the family to commiserate with Lady Catherine. This is what I have learnt. It seems Mr. Darcy of Pemberley and Derbyshire, the nephew of my esteemed patroness as well as her soon to be son-in-law has been summoned to attend her daughter."

In the midst of her husband's ramblings, Charlotte considered what a peculiar engagement it must be as she recalled how Mr. Darcy had yet to visit his intended in all the time since she had lived in Hunsford, and especially as she reflected upon how he had regarded her friend whilst they were in Hertfordshire. Collins's last statement drew in Elizabeth, who rarely listened to anything her ridiculous cousin had to say. She considered the audacity of Mr. Darcy not to let her in on that particular fact, especially as he was so happy to inject his strong opinion in her own personal affairs. *It has been weeks since I last thought of Mr. Darcy and the devastating effect he has on my composure.* Her body reacted in recollection of their *encounters* as well, to such an extent she wished she were not in a room full of people.

In the midst of her thrilling reverie, the door of the drawing room flew open. Ben rushed in, leading a somewhat reluctant Mr Darcy by the hand.

"Mama! Mama! Look who is with me!"

"Mr. Darcy! What are you doing here?" Elizabeth questioned before she even realised what she was saying, seeing as how she was a guest in Mr. and Mrs. Collins's home herself. Still, the sight of HIM in the company of her young son was indeed a source of considerable astonishment mixed with intrigue.

Ben adamantly stated, "No, Mama! This is King Arthur. You see, I told you he is real. He is a real human being. He is my best friend in the world, and I found him at Camelot."

An uncomfortable silence filled the room. Geoffrey Collins noted with some deep measure of concern the singular manner in which Elizabeth greeted the gentleman. He noted with serious disquiet the "manner" in which the gentleman regarded HER!

He unapologetically broke the awkward silence. "Ben, you have had quite enough excitement for one afternoon. It is time for you to go upstairs to your room whilst the adults entertain the new guest."

Ben insisted, "King Arthur is MY guest! He is here by my invitation. Why should I not remain to entertain my own guest?"

Darcy did not fail to notice the strong undercurrent of tension in the room. *Who is this gentleman to speak to Elizabeth's son as he does?* Darcy bent to Ben's level to meet him eye to eye. "Perhaps you should do as the gentleman suggests," and anticipating Ben's protest he spoke in a manner only Ben and Elizabeth might hear. "Do not fear. I shall see you before I return to Camelot."

Ben eagerly embraced Darcy about the neck. This time Darcy was prepared for Ben's show of affection. "Do I have your promise?"

Darcy looked up tentatively at Elizabeth. "I promise to do my best. Now, run along."

Chapter 11

Geoffrey Collins commanded the full attention of everyone in the room with his confrontational approach towards Darcy and his ensuing verbal attack. "I insist you do not encourage the young child in his fanciful beliefs. You do so to the child's own detriment."

Darcy regarded the gentleman as one might expect he would towards such an insolent stranger, "I beg your pardon. Who are you to address me so?"

Mr. William Collins nearly tripped over himself as he scrambled to Darcy's side and bowed as low as he possibly could, attempting to make up for his brother's lack of regard for the privilege of receiving Mr. Darcy *himself* at his humble abode.

"Mr. Darcy, I respectfully beg for your forgiveness. My brother could have no way of knowing who you are. Allow me to make amends. Brother, this is THE Mr. Darcy of Pemberley and Derbyshire of whom I spoke just moments ago. Mr. Darcy, it is indeed a great honour to receive you in my home. Might you allow me to introduce my older brother to you?" Darcy favoured the ridiculous man with slightly more reverence than he would have had he been outside the man's home and nodded his approval.

"Thank you, sir. This is my older brother, Mr. Geoffrey Collins."
Geoffrey Collins spoke to Darcy in a manner that clearly conveyed his disdain for his brother's sycophancy. "Mr. Darcy," he said as he nodded his head. "I see there are no introductions needed as regards my *betrothed*."

Darcy looked at Elizabeth intently. He was not at all impressed she had allowed him to believe she was engaged to the younger man when they had danced at the Netherfield Ball.

Elizabeth spoke up rather hastily. "Mr. Darcy and I met in Hertfordshire last autumn."

"Is that so?" Collins asked. Speaking directly to Darcy, he questioned, "And when did you and the child become so familiar?"

"I might appreciate your concerns in this matter; however, as you are not as connected with the child's mother as your manner implies, I suffer no obligation to address your concerns with any particular regard."

"Elizabeth, perhaps you should explain to the gentleman why he is mistaken," Collins spoke in a manner intended to direct rather than to persuade.

Elizabeth did not feel any real need to explain anything. It was not as though she did not have her own litany of questions that demanded answers. She wanted answers; that was a certainty —only not in front of a room full of spectators. "Mr. Darcy, may I prevail on you to join me outside for a walk about the garden?"

Before Darcy could speak, Geoffrey Collins responded. "That seems a fine idea. Shall you and I both have a walk in the garden with Mr. Darcy?"

"No! I beg of you. Your presence is not necessary. I am quite capable of speaking with Mr. Darcy in privacy."

Darcy bowed slightly to Mrs. Collins, and then followed Elizabeth into the hallway. He would not be persuaded to abandon his attempt to help her don her wrap and, in so doing, took every advantage of their nearness to reignite the undeclared yet potent magnetism they shared.

They spoke not a word as they departed the house. Darcy could only imagine the series of questions Elizabeth might have, but he felt they were nowhere near as consequential as those he had for her. He espied a rather secluded area off to the side of the house, away from the direction of the garden. He closed the respectable distance they had established upon first setting off along the observable path, took her by the arm, and guided her there.

"How could you have led me to believe you were engaged to be married to my aunt's ridiculous parson, Mr. Collins? Not that his brother is a great prize, mind you—but how could you?" Darcy insisted. The passion in his voice was matched by the ardour reflected on his countenance and the intoxicating heat that radiated from their nearness.

Rather than shrink from the intensity of his assault, Elizabeth stoked the smouldering fire, stepping closer and lifting her head as high as she could and responded to him in kind, directly face to face. "Pardon me, Mr. Darcy, I am the one who intends to ask questions here!"

"Not until you tell me why you deliberately misled me." How he wanted to take her in his arms. He was sorely tempted to do just that.

"I did no such thing! I chose to allow you to think what you might! Am I under any obligation to you, Mr. Darcy?"

Though Mr. Collins did not have an advantageous view of the spot Darcy had chosen for his conversation with Elizabeth, young Ben certainly did as he sat perched in the window seat of his room. Before they knew it, Darcy and Elizabeth's confrontational twosome had become an uncertain threesome.

Ben grabbed a hold of Darcy's leg and pleaded, "You are not leaving, are you, my King? You promised you would not leave without saying good-bye."

Completely setting aside the raging desire he had for Elizabeth and wanting nothing more than to comfort his young friend, Darcy reached down and picked Ben up. "No, Sir Lancelot! I am not leaving just yet. I am only speaking with your mother in private."

Ben looked back and forth between his mother and his king curiously. "Why are you speaking with my mama in private? Do you already know my mama, King Arthur? Have the two of you met before today?"

"Yes, young sir. Your mother and I know each other *quite* well."

"I would not go THAT far," Elizabeth said, as she reached to hand her son down from Darcy's arms. "However, it does seem as if a formal introduction between the two of you is warranted. Moreover, it is I who should make said introductions. Ben, this is Mr. Darcy. Mr. Darcy, this is my son, Bennet Carlton."

"Oh Mama! Where is the fun in that?"

Darcy playfully repeated, "Yes, where is the fun in that?"

"Pardon me, gentlemen. If it is merely fantasy you two seek, then perhaps I should introduce myself as *Guinevere*."

Darcy combined the titillating thoughts that raced through his mind with a less than innocent sweeping of his alluring eyes over her enchanting body. He took Elizabeth's hand in his and uttered tantalisingly, "I *love* the sound of that." He brushed his lips tenderly against the back of her hand and then looked deeply into her eyes, "Especially, as I consider the *implications*." He spoke in a manner that rendered Elizabeth speechless and trembling inside. They stared intently into each other's eyes as if completely lost in themselves.

Young Ben considered the looks that passed between them in bewilderment. Though the *implications* his friend spoke of were rather unclear to him, it was enough to cause him some concern. He reached up to release his mother's hand from Darcy's gentle grasp. Pretty certain he was not yet ready to share his friend with anyone, he declared, "Allow me to think about it."

Darcy relinquished his gaze from Elizabeth's amazing eyes and regarded Ben with a bit of curiosity. He knelt to his level to speak with him man to man. "Pray tell, what is there to think about, young sir?"

Mindful of his mother's sensibilities, Ben walked away from her side a few steps and beckoned Darcy to join him. With his back to his mother, the young lad spoke in a hushed tone. "She is a girl."

Young Ben did not speak so low Elizabeth could not hear him. She tried mightily to suppress her smile, even as she and Darcy looked good-humouredly at each other.

Darcy directed his attention to Ben. "Well, yes, there is that. However, is there any harm in her being a *girl*?"

"Indeed there is! Girls cannot do anything. They cannot sword fight; they cannot wrestle. Girls cannot climb, and I know for a fact my mama does not ride horseback."

Darcy paused as if in deep consideration of Ben's argument. "That is indeed a long list of failings. Perhaps you and I might teach her to do all those things."

"But she does not even LIKE horses!"

"What say you to giving her a chance? I say we start out bright and early tomorrow morning for a day of games. I suggest you bring her around to the spot I pointed out to you earlier today. We shall test her mettle to determine whether she is worthy."

Elizabeth felt compelled to join the two gentlemen who seemed intent upon making plans for her day, as though she had nary a word to say in the matter. She walked over to them, wrapped her arms about Ben's shoulders, and leaned down to bestow a light kiss upon his forehead. "Where is this place the two of you speak of in guarded tones, as though it were a great secret?"

"Pardon me, my lady," Darcy remarked, "it is just that Sir Lancelot and I believe we have discovered the location of Excalibur! We have plans to return there for a bit of adventure. I am doing my best to persuade him to bring you along for our next exploration."

"And what say you, young sir? Are you quite persuaded?" Elizabeth asked her son, teasingly tickling him until they both found themselves upon the ground. Ben acquiesced as a desperate measure of surrender. Neither seemed intent upon giving up their newly found and rather unconventional, but comfortable, seating arrangement, prompting Darcy to join them and sit side by side with Elizabeth as she cradled her son in her lap.

Elizabeth spoke to the two of them, embracing the younger one tenderly in her arms and embracing the elder with the warmth of her smile. "It would seem the two of you have quite a bit of explaining to do, as regards your close camaraderie. Seeing the two of you together, I can comprehend you going on charmingly, when you had once made a beginning. What I wish to know is how it all came to be. Pray tell, starting with you, Mr. Darcy."

"Where do I begin? Let me see. Once upon a time, a valiant warrior set about on his mighty stallion—" Darcy waxed poetically.

Ben eagerly interrupted, as he sprang from his mother's lap and climbed into Darcy's, "Oh! Allow me to tell the story, my King! Please!"

"Calm down, young man. If you insist upon having your share, then I suggest we do it together."

"I insist," declared he with a smile as wide as could be. "Once upon a time, in a land far, far away, a brave young knight travelled along a long and winding road in search of a place to rest his exhausted and weary soul, when all of a sudden—" he began. And so it proceeded as Ben and Darcy went about telling Elizabeth the story of the history of their friendship, taking turns where they would, and mixing in Arthurian legend where they could, and thoroughly entertaining her in so doing, with little regard for the passage of time.

For the first time in what had been an exceedingly long time, Elizabeth found herself especially relaxed, whilst enjoying a bout of frivolousness. She was more than pleased to see just how delighted her son was in Mr. Darcy's company as she came to know, indeed, it had been his departure from Hertfordshire that had wreaked such havoc on her son's spirits over the past few months.

She eventually decided it was time they returned to the house, but first she needed to spend a few moments alone with Mr. Darcy. "Ben," she began, "I think it is long past time for you to go back to the house. Return to your room, and I shall visit you there shortly."

"Mama, must I return just yet? I do not like parting with my best friend in the world after so short a time together."

Darcy intervened, "You must always do as your mother advises, young man, without questions. Besides, we shall have plenty of time together in the morning." Darcy stood to see Ben off and then directed his full attention to Elizabeth and offered her a hand to assist her to her feet.

Elizabeth felt an uncontrollable quivering pulsation as they locked hands. She was convinced he was not unaware of the effect he had over her sensibilities. Darcy rubbed his thumbs tenderly along the soft skin of her wrists as he gently caressed her hands a bit longer than was necessary. Elizabeth was mindful of the need to interrupt their intimacy, as he surely was not inclined to do so. She was speechless in the face of the one man in the world who managed with the slightest touch to shatter her defences and beget a sense of yearning she was simply unable to put into words.

"I wish we did not have to part just yet," Darcy spoke tenderly. "My thoughts of you have been my constant companions as I struggled to come to grips with your situation. You cannot possibly know what a torment it has been to have to think of you as married to that ridiculous parson, and imagining him as your husband, chasing you about your room each evening, catching up with you, and then having his way with you night after night." For an instant, he raised his hands to cover his face in affected disgust. "Oh! The *horror* of it all! How could you so cruelly allow me to go on as I did?" Before Elizabeth could protest, Darcy silenced her with a gentle touch of his fingertip on her lips. Her heart raced. He bestowed a magnificent smile to signify he was merely speaking in jest. "I know you did not owe me any sort of explanation. I realise now your silence on the matter was a reward for my officiousness."

Elizabeth smiled in acknowledgement of the truth of his words. "There is something to be said of a man who owns his mistakes so willingly."

Darcy extended his arm to Elizabeth, she warmly accepted his offering, and they began to make their way along the path in return to the parsonage.

"Indeed. And, to make up for my past interference, I shall not utter a single disparaging word as regards my opinion of the *NEW* Mr. Collins—how he is all wrong for you, how he would be an extremely contemptible father for Ben, and how I plan to do all that is within my power to see that a wedding between you two never comes to pass."

"A man who willingly admits his past mistake, then endeavours to make up for it by keeping his opinion to himself," she began playfully. "Be still, my heart." At that particular moment, Elizabeth had two choices as she saw it. One would be to point out the glaring inconsistency in his expressed sentiments, and the other would be to continue basking in the easy companionship they had established over the last hour or so. She gladly chose the latter, thinking surely he was speaking in jest, and even if he were not, knowing she would have plenty of time to set him straight over the coming days.

Before either of them would have wished, they stood directly in front of the door of the parsonage, with their next step over the threshold to be met with the reality that was Elizabeth's life. Darcy reluctantly relinquished his hold over her arm, opened the door, and allowed her to pass through the entryway.

Geoffrey Collins had worked himself into quite a state during the entire span of his betrothed's absence. He had stood at the window and observed the two of them as they made their way along the path to the garden. He was beside himself with fury when he observed Darcy steer Elizabeth in the opposite direction, along an obscure path beyond his direct line of vision. Charlotte witnessed all this and desperately wished not to see the proud man react to the unfolding turn of events in a manner they might all come to regret. Her carefully chosen words halted him in his steps after he decided he did not trust the haughty gentleman, *of Pemberley and Derbyshire*, who apparently was no stranger to his intended, to be alone with her.

"I do not envy Mr. Darcy one bit," Charlotte began, in a manner suggesting she merely was thinking aloud. "Elizabeth is quite a force to be reckoned with when she feels she has been crossed." She directed her next words to her perplexed brother-in-law. "Did you see the looks she bestowed on poor Mr. Darcy? No, indeed, I do not envy him one bit by the time Elizabeth is done giving him one of her set-downs."

Charlotte's not so subtle words of caution seemed to do the trick as Geoffrey Collins halted his steps towards the door, returned to his station at the window, and resumed his futile vigil. By and by, he observed an approaching carriage and remarked on it to his brother.

The younger man nearly pushed the elder aside such was his eagerness to see who might be visiting his home. He was so thrilled to see it was one of Lady Catherine's carriages. He hurried outside to greet its occupants. While he did not stay out-of-doors terribly long, the message he conveyed to his dear wife upon his return was heralded as though it was the revelation of a lifetime.

Geoffrey Collins rushed to Elizabeth's side the moment she entered the drawing room and placed himself directly between Mr. Darcy and her. "Elizabeth, my dear, I trust you have told Mr. Darcy all he needs to know as regards any future association with young Ben and how he is not to encourage him in his fictional accounts."

"Actually, I did no such thing. Mr. Darcy does not need to be told how to act together with my son."

Collins was taken aback completely by Elizabeth's words. He thought surely they were in perfect agreement on this subject. "Perhaps you and I can discuss this matter further," he directed his glare towards Darcy and spoke the following words mostly for his benefit, "when the two of us are *alone* later this evening."

Darcy was not especially impressed. He discerned enough of Elizabeth's stark change in demeanour since entering the room to know not to be overly concerned as regarded the power that gentleman held over her.

Elizabeth replied, "Perhaps. Now, if you will excuse me, I must go upstairs to look in on Ben."

"I must bid everyone a good day as well," Darcy began. "Mr. and Mrs. Collins, thank you for having me in your home." Towards the elder Mr. Collins, he simply nodded, though barely perceptibly, in acknowledgement of his presence. "Madam," he spoke kindly to Elizabeth after bowing to her, "until we meet again."

Try as she might in containing her cheerful smile in ardent anticipation of the intriguing possibilities for the day ahead, she was simply unable to do so with any convincing measure of success. Geoffrey Collins was not at all pleased by her display.

Mr. William Collins interrupted the good-byes with glad tidings. "Indeed, we shall meet again very soon, Mr. Darcy. Her ladyship dispatched a messenger whilst you and my fair cousin were out. We have received an invitation to dine at Rosings Park this evening!"

Chapter 12

Who amongst us cares that you are a most active magistrate in your parish? Must we hear every account, of the minutest concerns of which are brought to you by Mr. Collins? Do we truly need to know how you sally forth into the village whenever any of the cottagers are disposed to be quarrelsome, discontented, or too poor; arriving in splendour to settle their differences, silence their complaints, and scold them into harmony and plenty with your august presence? What concern is it of any of ours, other than that ridiculous vicar, that is?

Such were the thoughts that drifted through Darcy's mind almost as soon as his aunt ventured to speak in long-winded, one-sided dialogue accompanied with a steady nodding of the greasy head of the younger Mr. Collins.

Would it be terribly rude of me simply to stand from the table and take my leave? Would that I could persuade Elizabeth to join me?

One can always wish, he considered, having pondered the implications of such a scandalous notion. Darcy looked about the members of the dinner party as they sat around the table heavily laden with platters of meats, vegetable dishes, assorted fruit, and superb wines. *It is a blessing Lady Catherine harbours the anti-quated rule about husbands sitting next to their wives. Otherwise, that ridiculous parson might be seated next to me. Instead, to have Elizabeth seated beside me is better than anything I could have wished for at the start of the evening It is most pleasant to have her by my side.*

It is worth it just to be able to reach over and touch her or perchance brush my hand against hers as we fetch for something at the table. How I wish for some time alone with her this evening! How on earth will I bring that about? Darcy then considered from the moment of her arrival, Geoffrey Collins had not ventured from her side by more than a few inches. *The gentleman seems as possessive of Elizabeth as his brother seems solicitous of my aunt.*

One can hardly blame him, Darcy reckoned. *If she were mine, I would not trust another man to be with her either. Patience man, Elizabeth will see Collins for the man he is not in due time.*

Lady Catherine had been extremely curious about the young widow visiting the parsonage. Indeed, she regretted Anne's health had not allowed them to receive the Hunsford party at Rosings Park sooner. It turned out Lady Catherine and her late husband, Sir Lewis de Bourgh, had been long-time acquaintances of Elizabeth's late in-laws, Mr. and Mrs. John Carlton. Lady Catherine had been fond enough of the late Mrs. Sara Carlton that she had considered her a dear friend.

Darcy honed in on his aunt's discourse as she expounded her history with the Carlton family. She elaborated in detail on that which Elizabeth already knew, as well as some things she did not, and enlightened her nephew Darcy in the process, as well. Upon speaking of the string of tragedies that had befallen the Carlton family, the death of her dear friend, the death of the young Mr. Randall Carlton, and lastly, the passing of the patriarch himself, she expressed her condolences in the sincerest of terms.

I had no notion of any of this, Darcy considered. *Here sits this amazing woman who means so much to me, yet she is scarcely more than a stranger. I hardly know a thing about her at all. Perhaps, had I not spent so much time during our brief inter-*

ludes in Hertfordshire jumping to conclusions, I might have learnt all of this from Elizabeth herself. It is a grave injustice to be parted from one's husband so soon after the marriage—a mere month! It is an even greater injustice that young Ben never experienced first-hand a father's love, that his father never knew his son. How proud he would be. Indeed, if he had loved Elizabeth yet half as much as Lady Catherine suggests, then surely he would be swollen with pride over his son.

Having exhausted the subject of all she knew of Elizabeth's past, Lady Catherine's curiosity could not be contained as regarded her present, as well as her future.

"Where is your son now? Did he travel here with you? Surely, you did not leave him in Hertfordshire. A young child should be with its mother," Lady Catherine began. She lovingly looked towards her daughter, who sat to her left. "I have never parted with my dear Anne, even to this day."

"Yes ma'am, your ladyship, my son is at the parsonage."

"Excellent. Do remind me, if you will, what is your son's name?"

"My son's name is Bennet Carlton, your ladyship," Elizabeth said as she sat her silverware aside, thinking this might be a lengthy inquisition, if her ladyship's preceding discourse served as an example.

"Yes, of course. Now I recall clearly. Bennet is his given name, in honour of your family. Although," she pontificated, "I am not quite persuaded your family deserves such honour after practically having disowned you when you went against your father's wishes in marrying at seventeen."

Elizabeth was not at all pleased to have all her life's history the topic for discussion. She did not know whether to be honoured or deeply offended that Lady Catherine was so inclined to discuss aspects of her past she had not disclosed herself.

Lady Catherine's speech was mixed with praise and condescension. "I commend you on your decision to remove yourself from the way of life afforded by the Camberworth fortune for the sake of providing a good environment for the child. It is admirable that you would sacrifice your own comfort in the interest of what is best for your young impressionable son."

You think highly enough of Elizabeth now and cannot help but bear witness to her many admirable qualities. The question is will you continue to regard her so once it is made known she is the one woman who holds my heart? Darcy silently reflected. In the hours that had passed since he had left her side at the parsonage, he had spent much time thinking of how much he wanted her, but no time at all considering exactly how he would help bring that about. Instead, his mind was flooded with hopeful thoughts. *She is not married. She is not truly lost to me! I am in love!*

Lady Catherine went on to speak disparagingly of the fact that the Longbourn estate was entailed to the male line. Even how happy she was Rosings Park was not similarly encumbered.

"I must also commend you on your alliance with Mr. Collins, to whom your family's estate is entailed. By your act, your family will be protected from what would have been certain destitution when your father passes." There was not one person seated at the table, other than her ladyship, who did not suffer embarrassment by those words. She made it sound to all as if Elizabeth merely was mercenary!

"Though I can imagine the Longbourn estate is nothing compared to Camberworth, I would think it is a decent enough place for your son to be reared."

"My son enjoys his new home very much, your ladyship," Elizabeth politely replied.

"You must bring him around for I dearly wish to meet the sole heir of my dear friend Sara Carlton."

"I thank you for the warm invitation. I shall be happy to honour your request to meet my son."

"Excellent! I shall send my carriage around to bring you here tomorrow."

"Again, I thank you, your ladyship. However, tomorrow is a bit sooner than I had anticipated."

Geoffrey Collins intervened, "Tomorrow is as fine a time as any. We shall bring the child together."

"I beg your pardon, but again I will have to defer until a later time," Elizabeth adamantly affirmed.

"Begging your pardon, my dear cousin, why are you so opposed to bringing the child around tomorrow, especially as her ladyship has taken away any inconvenience with the offer of her carriage?" Geoffrey Collins asked. A little irritation was evident in his tone.

"My son and I have made other plans for tomorrow. I am not in the habit of disappointing his hopes," Elizabeth expressed in a measured response.

"I am most eager to meet your son. I insist it be tomorrow! I, too, am not in the business of having my hopes disappointed. He is but a child. I fear, as an only child, you may have spoilt him. This is yet another of the many advantages to your alliance with Mr. Collins the prospect of extending your family and providing young Bennet with siblings.

"A healthy young woman such as you will likely bear a number of children," Lady Catherine declared. She regarded Elizabeth's youthful appearance in wonderment and thought to ask, "Pray what is your age?"

Elizabeth smilingly submitted, "Your ladyship can hardly expect me to own it."

"I detect a bit of dignified impertinence in your tone that I pray your young son does not possess. I insist on being satisfied! Tell me at once! If my memory serves me correctly, you are in your early twenties."

"I am not yet four and twenty, your ladyship," Elizabeth was compelled to disclose.

"There, that was not so difficult. You young people today have much to learn when it comes to showing the proper deference to your elders. Indeed, I shall be quite interested in meeting your child."

Having assured Lady Catherine in the most earnest manner her wishes would be acceded to over those of the child, Geoffrey Collins thoughts tended towards the gentleman seated at the side of his betrothed. Were he a man of a suspicious constitution, he would have sworn there was some unspoken exchange between Elizabeth and her dinner companion. He had to admit to suffering increasing annoyance. That was three times in a single day she had undermined his authority in front of others. It was one thing to do so amongst close family, but to be so blatantly disrespectful in a room full of strangers was insupportable. Truth be told, in Collins's estimation, there was only one person amongst their party who needed most to be made aware of Elizabeth's unwavering loyalty to the man to whom she was betrothed—Mr. Fitzwilliam Darcy!

That rich, arrogant, sanctimonious prick has some gall. Here he is, engaged to an heiress, the sole heir of all of this property and ostentatious wealth, and yet it seems he cannot take his eyes from MY Elizabeth, and he makes no pretence to hide it.

What is he about? Does he suppose he can marry that cold fish of a cousin of his and take Elizabeth as his mistress? I would not be surprised, knowing of his kind as I do. Such degeneracy is characteristic of his ilk. Well, that is his great misfortune! She is MY betrothed. My intentions are strictly honourable whilst his are dubious at best. I will be damned if my plans will be disrupted on account of that bastard!

Geoffrey Collins decided a change in conversation was desperately in order. "Your ladyship, if you will allow, I would like to offer my congratulations, as well, on the engagement of Mr. Darcy to your lovely daughter." He raised his glass and offered a toast. All who would do so lifted their glasses, as well. Some members of the party simply could not.

Collins went on to speak of the extraordinary prospects that lay ahead with the combining of the two prominent estates of Pemberley and Rosings Park in a manner that could bring no one more delight than Lady Catherine herself and no more vexation to anyone other than Darcy.

Mr. Collins raised the question of when the engagement would be announced publicly, the irony being even his own engagement had not been announced (a matter he intended to correct immediately upon his return to his home).

Darcy was at a complete loss for words. All eyes were upon him, although only two of his silent inquisitors mattered most. Anne, whom he cared for deeply as a cousin and one whom he was not apt to subject to derision, and Elizabeth, whom he admitted to himself he was in love with and whose good opinion meant everything to him. Anne looked at him pleadingly. He returned her look with one of assurance that he did not intend to engage in such a delicate discourse during that evening's dinner party.

Lady Catherine seized the moment finally to have her nephew on public record of his true intentions, strongly suspecting, if not praying, he would not dishonour the family in any way. She asked, "Well, Darcy, Mr. Collins has posed the question to which we are all rather eager to know the answer. When do you intend to announce your engagement to my daughter before the world?"

It seemed to Darcy as if providence was on his side. At that very moment, the butler approached him with a note on a silver salver. With all eyes firmly trained upon him, Darcy picked up the note for his own perusal and within seconds excused himself from the table.

"Where are you off to during the middle of dinner?" Lady Catherine demanded.

"Pardon me, everyone. This is an urgent express—one to which I must attend post-haste. I shall endeavour to return to the party before the end of the evening. Once outside the dining room, Darcy pocketed the card, which turned out to be blank, and said a silent prayer for his cousin's foresight in coming to his rescue.

After dinner, when the gentlemen had joined the ladies in the drawing room and tea was being served, Lady Catherine once again directed her attentions towards Elizabeth.

"Please play something for me, young lady."

"No, your ladyship! I beg of you. You see, I own to playing rather poorly."

"Nonsense! Rarely do I have the opportunity to be entertained. Why, music is my delight! If I had ever learnt, I should have been a great proficient. And so would Anne, if her health had allowed her to apply herself. I am confident she would have performed delightfully."

"I am afraid you might find my proficiency more distracting than entertaining," Elizabeth demurred, hoping against hope such a prelude would discourage her hostess.

"Any degree of accomplishment is better than none. Why! I wager your skills would be quite admirable should you take the time to practise. I have told Mrs. Collins this several times, that she will never play really well unless she practises more, and though she has no instrument, she is very welcome, as I have often told her, to come to Rosings every day, and play on the pianoforte in Mrs. Jenkinson's room. She would be in nobody's way, you know, in that part of the house."

"I am certain my friend, Mrs. Collins, appreciates your magnanimous gesture; however—I," Elizabeth began, but was interrupted before she could continue her sentence.

"Once again, I detect that unguarded impertinence in your speech that is most unbecoming. I insist on being satisfied!"

Geoffrey Collins agreed, "Yes, my dear cousin, I, too, shall be delighted to hear you perform on the pianoforte this evening. It has been far too long since I enjoyed that pleasure."

Elizabeth acquiesced and made way to the grand instrument. She felt if nothing else, she would spend the rest of the evening stationed there, away from Lady Catherine's increasingly annoying regard and her intended's watchful eyes.

Darcy joined the party when tea was over and the card-tables were placed. Lady Catherine was so taken with the elder Mr. Collins's commendations of her daughter's engagement in words that could not had been better expressed than if she had uttered them herself, she supposed they must be kindred souls. This earned him the right to sit across from her as they sat down to whist.

Finally, Darcy saw a chance to speak with Elizabeth alone, and he seized on it. He approached the pianoforte and placed himself so as to command a full view of her beautiful countenance. He stood a few moments in silent, ardent admiration before venturing to speak. He spoke tenderly, "It is not true, you know."

Elizabeth ceased her playing, "Pardon me, but to what are you referring, Mr. Darcy?"

"It is not true that I am engaged to my cousin Anne," Darcy spoke softly.

"Actually, I know nothing of the sort. It is not as though you said anything at dinner to refute your aunt's claims. Why are you speaking to me now?"

"I could not bear to have you return to the parsonage this evening, thinking I was engaged to marry my cousin. I am not."

"Mr. Darcy, it is not as though you owe me any sort of explanation, other than perhaps to explain why you take an eager interest in persuading me against my own engagement. Besides, this is not the first time I have been made aware of your commitment."

"That is all the more reason I feel the need to explain things to you. Do you still plan to accompany Ben for our adventure tomorrow?"

"I am aware of nothing that would force me to alter my plans and disappoint my son, Mr. Darcy."

"To listen to Collins's words one might think your opinion might have been swayed," Darcy expressed, passively taunting her over an earlier moment that no doubt caused her some dismay.

Elizabeth certainly did not like the sound of that. She was far from amused. The look she bestowed on Darcy was more telling than words could ever be. Elizabeth struck a loud chord in a momentary exhibition of her frustration.

Darcy waited a moment or two before speaking again. "Perhaps we shall have a chance to speak of this in the morning."

"Perhaps," Elizabeth ventured to say. She started to say more but thought the better of it once Colonel Fitzwilliam joined the two of them. It did not go unnoticed by him how disturbed Mr. Geoffrey Collins had grown over the sight of Darcy and Elizabeth engaged in hushed whispers.

"How did you find my friend in Hertfordshire?"

The welcome addition of Colonel Fitzwilliam was a cause of considerable relief for Elizabeth, and she endeavoured as best she could to bestow as much of her attention as possible towards him. When Lady Catherine had played as long as she chose, the tables were broken up, the carriage was offered to Mrs. Collins, gratefully accepted, and immediately ordered. The party then gathered round the fire to hear Lady Catherine determine what weather they were to have on the morrow. From these instructions, they were summoned by the arrival of the coach, and with many speeches of thankfulness on the younger Mr. Collins's side, they departed. As soon as they had driven from the door, Elizabeth was surprised to find Mr. Geoffrey Collins sitting as close to her as she could ever recall, with his hand resting securely on her own.

Chapter 13

It seemed the brilliant sun, the crisp blue sky, and the fluffy white clouds conspired to make it the perfect day for the *royal outing*. Ben was impatient to come across the spot he and Darcy had dubbed the possible location of *Excalibur*, excitedly pulling his mother along by the hand, every step of the way. Upon their arrival, neither could be disappointed at the enchanting view that stretched before them.

Darcy, along with a small team of Lady Catherine's servants, had staged the grounds with a makeshift jousting field, a fencing area, and even an archery range. Not even in his wildest imagination did Ben expect all that.

Darcy had awaited their arrival eagerly. He enthusiastically greeted them both with a brilliant smile.

"Good morning, Guinevere," he bowed before directing his attention to Ben. "Good morning, Sir Lancelot. Are the two of you prepared for a morning of excitement?"

Ben could scarcely contain his exuberance. He raced off to explore the grounds. Darcy did not mind. Assured of Ben's safety, with so many servants about to see to it, he took Elizabeth's hand in his own. He kissed it lingeringly as if it were the most precious kiss he ever had imparted.

Elizabeth's heart raced. On the one hand, she knew she would have to establish ground rules with him. To do otherwise would not be fair to either of them. On the other hand, her thoughts cried out, *I hunger for his touch.* Elizabeth tempted fate as long as she dared. Endeavouring to break their contact, she spoke impishly, "Are you to start at this once again, Mr. Darcy?"

"I cannot help it," Darcy said, lowering her hand but still not quite ready to let go of it completely. "I have thought of little other than this very moment since I last saw you. I have missed you. Thank you for coming."

Elizabeth pulled her hand free of his gentle grasp. "From the look of this place, I would say you had quite a few things on your mind. You have outdone yourself, Mr. Darcy. This is unbelievable. I am most grateful to you."

"This is no trouble at all," Darcy said, as he moved to stand by her side and appreciate the same view as she enjoyed. "Besides, I would do anything in the world to bring a smile to Ben's face. Should I succeed in pleasing you as well, it is all the reward I shall ever need."

Elizabeth avowed, "Then, I am very pleased, Mr. Darcy."

The powerful emotions that passed between them were left unvoiced with Ben's enthusiastic return. "What shall we do first, my King?" Ben pleaded, practically teeming over with excitement.

"Let us see, young sir. There is archery, fencing, horseback riding, and I even have a surprise for you."

"A surprise! How wonderful! I love surprises. What is it?"

"I encourage you and your mother to have a seat," Darcy said, directing them to the strategically placed chairs off to their left. Once everyone was seated, Darcy signalled to a nearby servant, who signalled another servant, and soon two horsemen took their places on the jousting field. Ben's imagination overflowed with anticipation as the two riders moved to face one another in combat. He had read about, but never actually witnessed, a true jousting tournament! Such that it was—it was actually quite amusing, as neither horseman knew precisely what the art entailed, having received the briefest of instructions from Darcy just that morning. It was enough for Ben, if one would guess by the look on his face. He was thoroughly entertained.

Next, it was time to move to the archery range. Having secured Elizabeth's permission to engage in such sport, Darcy and Ben walked ahead. Darcy accepted the bow and arrow offered to him by his valet.

"Mind you, Sir Lancelot," Darcy said as he raised the bow and positioned the arrow, "archery is a sport requiring the utmost discipline for it can be quite dangerous." He lowered the bow and arrow. "You must remember always to keep your arrows pointed in a safe direction," Darcy demonstrated as he spoke, "keep it either aimed at the target or pointed to the ground."

Darcy then aimed the arrow at the farthest target and landed a perfect hit.

"Let me try! Let me try!" Ben shouted with unbridled enthusiasm.

"Have patience, young man. There is far more to this sport than simply aiming and shooting," Darcy cautioned. He summoned his valet over to join them once again. "My man will teach you the finer points before you are allowed to start. Pay attention, and remember, Sir Lancelot, patience and discipline."

"What shall you do, whilst I am being tutored?" Ben called out as he watched his friend step away.

Darcy cast a glance towards Elizabeth, who had chosen to keep up a safe distance. "I should like to persuade Guinevere to give it a try."

Some moments later, *Guinevere* wondered at just how easily persuaded she had been. The warm morning sun, combined with the anticipated intensity of his excursions, prompted Darcy to remove his jacket and loosen his cravat just a bit. He then removed his cuff links, placing them on the seat of the chair, over the back of which he had casually placed his jacket, and he rolled up his sleeves. He had managed it all without tearing his eyes from Elizabeth's for even a second. It was not as though Elizabeth had not borne witness to such acts on other occasions. Never before had the experience rendered her weak in the knees. There the two of them stood. It was astounding to her that she found herself such, ensconced in his warm embrace, his right hand resting securely on her upper arm and his other hand gently resting on hers.

Darcy was in no hurry at all. He was ever mindful of the words of caution spoken just moments earlier on the need for patience and discipline. Those words served as his mantra as he held Elizabeth closely. Discipline proved the key as he commanded his body not to betray his innermost thoughts. Patience was also a virtue for Darcy had exercised the utmost patience, standing there breathing in the sweet scent of her hair, the faint hint of perfume, and the unmistakable essence of her yearning.

Ever mindful of his mission to show her the finer points of the craft, he spoke softly in her ear carefully, purposefully chosen, yet decidedly instructive words of caution, which flowed from his lips much like sensual prose. The warmth of his breath against her ear infused her entire being.

At length, Darcy gently guided Elizabeth towards a smooth release, driving the arrow deep into the target.

Sooner than Darcy would have wished, Elizabeth recalled herself to their surroundings. Rather than wait for Darcy to retrieve another arrow, and thus resume where they had left off, she sat the bow aside.

"I think I had better try another sport, Mr. Darcy," she said, as she proceeded to walk away slowly.

"That sounds promising, my lady," Darcy spoke suggestively, "what sport do you have in mind?"

"If at all possible, one that does not find me in your arms," Elizabeth declared boldly.

"What say you to fencing? The thrusting and pressing, exciting back and forth conversation, it seems a nice change of pace," Darcy recommended.

"I am afraid not, Mr. Darcy. Fencing is not my forte," Elizabeth said, not so innocently, refusing to take the bait but enjoying the repartee all the same.

"That is likely because you have never witnessed its proper execution," Darcy leaned forward and whispered in her ear, before heading over to oversee the remainder of Ben's archery lessons. Ben was eager to demonstrate all he had learnt. Without any help, Ben landed a perfect shot in a target strategically placed a short distance away.

Darcy clapped his hands, "Excellent! You have learnt your lesson well." Ben was immensely proud of his accomplishments and accepted Darcy's commendations with a generous smile. After observing a few other successful attempts, Darcy asked Ben if he would like to join him for a fencing match. Ben was very agreeable.

Together, King Arthur and Sir Lancelot engaged in a challenging match where it was determined the winner would have the honour of teaching the sport to Guinevere. Lancelot proved the victor, thereby forcing his king to step aside.

Alas, poor Darcy stood alone on the side-lines. He suffered as best he could, the exceedingly pleasurable prospect of the woman he absolutely adored, prancing gaily about, armed with a crude, hastily crafted wooden foil in a make-believe match with her son.

The final adventure was the horseback riding excursion. Darcy had one of the jousting horsemen, a groom whom Ben had met the day before, bring forth the pony chosen earlier for Ben's riding pleasure. Ben ran to the lanky young man's side and began smoothing the pony's coat.

Another groom brought a beautiful Chestnut mare forth and handed the reins over to Darcy. Darcy beckoned Elizabeth to come closer, gently reminding her she risked forfeiting the right to bear her chosen appellation should she fail that final challenge.

Elizabeth's courage always rose with any attempt to intimidate her. This dare proved no different. Sooner than even she would have imagined, she found herself in Darcy's arms once more. Standing nearer to her than he would have had she been anyone else, Darcy placed his hands about her waist. He slowly lifted her from the ground and then placed her side-saddled on the mare.

Darcy looked at Elizabeth intently before moving to mount his own stallion. He did not intend they should go very far. Accepting the reins of Elizabeth's horse, whilst the groom did accordingly with the reins of Ben's pony, they all set upon an exceedingly slow-paced ride about the perimeter of the improvised festival staging grounds.

Having returned to their original spot, Darcy dismounted his horse and moved to lift Elizabeth down. As he lowered her ever so slowly to the ground, Elizabeth spoke brazenly, "So, pray tell me, Mr. Darcy, have I passed the test?"

"Indeed," he uttered, "there is no contest where you are concerned, madam."

Ben was not as eager to stop riding as was his mother. He pleaded with his king to allow him to ride a while longer.

Darcy could not object. He approached the groom, giving him specific instructions on where he should lead Ben's pony and advising him not to go beyond the eyesight of the child's mother.

Darcy had much he wanted to say to Elizabeth. He was more than pleased with how the morning had progressed and was eager to establish a means of moving things along. Darcy took a seat beside Elizabeth and reached for her hand. She moved it away within mere seconds of his titillating touch.

Darcy smiled. He recalled his mantra—*discipline and patience.*

"My lady, I wish very much for the two of us to resume where we left off that late night at Netherfield Park."

Elizabeth knew exactly the night of which he spoke. The intense fire he had unleashed inside her was such that she might never forget it. Still, she was not apt to confess that to him. She asked coyly, "To what night are you referring, Mr. Darcy?"

"That late night when I stood just outside your bedchamber door, after having waited for what seemed like forever for you to leave your sister's side. The night when no one else moved about the darkened corridors, save you and me. The night I took your lovely hand in mine," Darcy reached for her hand again and raised it to his lips, "and softly kissed it, like so." Once again, he demonstrated, allowing them both to drift back to the fascination of that mutually cherished place in time.

"I beseeched you for a chance to begin anew," he spoke, at length. Elizabeth slowly withdrew her hand and returned it to her lap. "What are you asking of me, Mr. Darcy?"

"Meet me alone," he tenderly commanded.

Elizabeth was breathless. The passion in his plea threatened to melt every remaining trace of her battered resolve.

"Please, understand me. I love spending time with both you and Ben. However, what I really need is some time alone with you. Time alone, just the two of us, where we might have no thoughts of being interrupted."

Elizabeth could feel her heart pounding, her pulse racing. Her mind filled with sensational possibilities and conflicting sentiments, threatening her equanimity. If she did not speak out, without doubt, it would be her undoing.

"Mr. Darcy, I am not at liberty to do as you suggest, surely —" Elizabeth's trembling speech ceased, halted by the now familiar touch of his fingers on her lips.

"Do not say it. You hardly even know the gentleman," Darcy insisted.

"I hardly know you," she barely voiced aloud.

"I realise that. That is why I wish for some time alone with you. A long walk is all I ask for so you and I might have a chance to talk—to learn more of each other. If you would but say yes, I will endeavour to behave the perfect gentleman."

The irony of his expressed sentiments brought a slight smirk to her lovely countenance. From the moment of their earliest acquaintance, he had managed to ignite profound passion deep inside her with the slightest of touches. He knew it as well as did she. "Do I have your promise?" Elizabeth was compelled at least to ask, for reasons she could not quite fathom, for what if he said yes.

"I promise only to do that which you wish me to do," he offered. "Meet me here, alone, and I will lead you to a place where we will be assured of our privacy."

Darcy and Elizabeth soon noticed the groomsman approaching on foot, leading Ben back to them. Each acknowledged the moment with dissimilar emotions. Discouraged, Darcy needed more time. Relieved, Elizabeth was grateful for the interruption. Her mind and body, she even suspected her heart, were utterly discordant. She rose from her chair.

"Thank you, Mr. Darcy, for arranging this wonderful morning for Ben. I shall forever be in your debt." She began to walk towards her son.

"Meet me!"

Elizabeth chose not to respond to Darcy's appeal. Rather, she took Ben by the hand and told him they would be missed if they did not return to the parsonage house post-haste. The three of them said their good-byes and Elizabeth and Ben took their leave, rushing off whilst Darcy stood there watching until they were completely out of sight.

Chapter 14

Geoffrey Collins was beside himself with worry and pacing the floors back and forth to the general discomfort of his brother and sister-in-law. *Where is she?* The last he had seen of her was the night before when she had pleaded a headache, thus, unable to share the evening alone with him after everyone else had retired. When she did not come downstairs for breakfast, he feared she might be ill still. His sister Charlotte reminded him that Elizabeth had spoken of her plans to spend the morning with her son. She even went so far as to say Elizabeth and her son had awakened at the break of dawn, breakfasted together, and pretty soon afterwards set off on a lane leading towards the village.

Collins took some measure of comfort in that. Persuaded that she and her son might return shortly, he sat down to the breakfast table to read his paper. Upon skimming the pages that held no interest at all to him in the wake of Elizabeth's unpredictable behaviour, he ventured to the small parlour room in the back; the one Charlotte normally reserved for her own personal use but graciously allowed the girls during their extended stay. He found them there, each contentedly reading their books. He spent a scant amount of time with them and left them with a promise that Elizabeth would visit with them upon her return.

"Where have you been all this time? I have been most anxious over your lengthy absence. I have waited hours for you to return," Geoffrey Collins demanded as soon as she walked into the door.

Elizabeth handed her bonnet to the servant and beckoned her son to go to his room and wait for her there. She answered, "I am sorry you worried, but why did you, pray tell? I am known for my penchant to take long morning walks."

"Yes, my sister-in-law kindly reminded me of that fact. Although, I find it hard to imagine after your complaint of a headache last evening, you would have suffered no lingering after-effects this morning. I was most eager to spend time with you. Moreover, Gillian and Emily have been asking for your company. They, too, were disheartened by your lengthy absence. I promised them you would spend time with them this morning."

"Why would you do such a thing without first conferring with me, Mr. Collins? Did I not make it clear I intended to spend today with my son?"

"Does spending time with your son preclude you from enjoying that same time with the girls?" Collins asked impatiently. "As we are to become a family in a matter of months, we need to use our time here in Hunsford to our advantage by becoming intimately acquainted. I expect you to be as much a mother to my daughters as you are to Ben. Likewise, I will be as much a father to Ben as I am to Gillian and Emily.

"It is incumbent upon both of us to do our part. I will start by taking Ben under my wing. I expect you to begin spending time with the girls."

Slowly, Elizabeth counted. *One, two*—surely, the words he spoke in and of themselves were not refutable, but the officiousness inherent in his tone had by then worn dreadfully thin. *Nine, ten*— Elizabeth managed a slight smile.

"As you wish, Mr. Collins," replied she with all the patience she could muster. "Now, if you will pardon me," Elizabeth curtseyed. Before she was able to ascend the stairs, he reached for her hand and encircled it in both of his own. Elizabeth was startled by his touch.

"Is this not your wish, as well, Elizabeth?" The apprehension in her demeanour did not go unnoticed by him. He let go of her hand. "Do you have another idea how the five of us might become better acquainted during this time?"

"I have no objections to your scheme, Mr. Collins."

"Excellent! I felt strongly you would recognise the advantages of my proposal."

"If you will pardon me then, I wish to look in on my son, as I promised I would do."

"Of course, afterwards look in on Gillian and Emily and make your apologies. They are waiting for you in the small parlour room." Elizabeth's eager ascent of the narrow stairway was halted once more. "My brother informed me Lady Catherine expects us later this afternoon. See that Ben is well-groomed and fit to be received by her ladyship."

One, two, three—

Having seen to Ben, Gillian, and Emily to everyone's satisfaction, Elizabeth made way to her room. *Finally—a moment of solitude.* She locked the door behind her, leaned against it, and rested her head thereupon for a second or two to catch her breath.

It was during such times when she missed her life at Camberworth most. She was a tense mixture of emotional and physical feelings, brought on by the combination of the pleasurable moments spent with Mr. Darcy, the contentious conversation with Mr. Collins in the hallway, the challenges of getting Ben cleaned up for his visit at Rosings Park, and finally sitting with the girls. What she longed for was a long hot, relaxing bath. Alas, such a luxury was entirely out of the question in the tiny confines of her chamber, not that she would even think to burden the few household servants with such a selfish request.

Wanting nothing more than a moment or two to indulge in the pleasurable memories of her morning, Elizabeth fell back upon the small bed and closed her eyes. She imagined herself back in another place and time, at home at Camberworth, with hardly a care in the world. Such pleasant thoughts enveloped her as she drifted into a calm peaceful state where satisfying imaginings of HIS touch flooded her senses. The sound of footsteps just outside her door interrupted her light slumber. In no time at all, reality encroached on her life once more. Soon enough, she would find herself once again in his company. Having allowed him such liberties that morning, having assuaged her rekindled aching desire for him in the solace of her room, she reflected upon the rest of her day. *How will I bear to see him again—so soon?*

As the weather was fine, they eschewed the offer of Lady Catherine's carriage and had a pleasant walk of about half a mile across the park. It was all Ben could do to contain his joy over his visit to the castle, which he steadfastly referred to as Camelot in his mind. He did not need the evil Meleagant to remind him yet again that the magical place was to be referred to as Rosings Park. When they ascended the steps to the hall, Ben's excitement was every moment increasing. He did not know what he might expect to find inside but the thought that he might see his king spurred him on without trepidation.

From the entrance-hall, they followed the servants through an antechamber to the room where Lady Catherine, her daughter, and Mrs. Jenkinson were sitting. Her ladyship, with great condescension, arose to greet them. Ben observed the tall, large woman, with strongly marked features, which might once have been handsome, and wondered at the possible connection of the regal personage to his king. She spoke in an authoritative a tone, as signified her self-importance.

"So, you are young Bennet Carlton."

"Yes ma'am, I am. Thank you for inviting me here this afternoon."

Lady Catherine observed the child with some measure of admiration. She noted he was well-mannered. She was exceedingly pleased. Everyone was invited to sit. Collins and Ben elected to sit on either side of Elizabeth. Her ladyship embarked on a lengthy discourse, speaking to Ben of his grandparents and the family resemblance, even as she remarked that he was decidedly his mother's son in describing his eyes. Ben was delighted to hear talk of his grandparents and his heritage. Other than his mother, no one ever spoke to him of the proud Carlton family.

The barrage of ensuing questions, however, was not particularly enjoyable. Even Ben could surmise the elderly woman bordered on being meddlesome. He soon began fidgeting with his neck cloth, the one Mr. Collins had insisted he wear, and he commenced shifting restlessly in his seat.

Less than a quarter of an hour passed before their party was extended.

"Kin—Mr. Darcy!" Ben shouted, immediately correcting himself, upon recalling his mother's earlier gentle admonishment against referring to the gentleman as such in the company of others. Ben raced unceremoniously to his side.

"Ben! Fancy seeing you here," Darcy exclaimed with a bright smile, as he relaxed the haughty stance he typically preferred in the presence of his stern aunt.

"Indeed! It is a surprise to have been invited here. Are you surprised to see me?"

"I confess to having some knowledge I might see you this afternoon."

The familiar exchange caught Lady Catherine utterly by surprise. She had not witnessed such a cordial display from her nephew to anyone, save his younger sister Georgiana. "You know my nephew, young man?" her curiosity begged.

"Yes ma'am. He is my best friend in the whole world!" Ben affirmed without hesitation.

"That is rather strange," uttered Lady Catherine. Her ladyship's countenance bore a befuddled look.

Elizabeth noted the grand lady's confusion. "It seems they formed a close alliance whilst Mr. Darcy visited in Hertfordshire, your ladyship," she began. "I only became aware of it yesterday."

Darcy directed his full attention to Elizabeth. Although she had spoken the words for Lady Catherine's benefit, her eyes were trained on him. "It is a pleasure to see you again—so soon, madam."

Elizabeth smiled daringly, wondering at his boldness. *Does he actually intend for everyone to know we spent the morning together?*

Darcy aimed his focus towards Geoffrey Collins, who had shifted his position to move a bit closer to his intended. Both men merely nodded. Ben tugged at Darcy's hand. "May I have a tour of the castle?"

"I see no harm in that, if your mother is agreeable," Darcy responded.

"May I, Mama? You are welcome to come along!"

Darcy stared at Elizabeth intently, with thoughts racing through his head of what a tempting prospect that would be.

Collins interrupted, "Why don't we all have a tour of Rosings Park?" The light touch of his hand discreetly placed along the small of her back, effectively released her from the grasp Darcy seemed to hold over her imagination from the moment he had entered the room.

"Thank you, son. Yes, you are permitted to go with Mr. Darcy, though I am afraid I must decline. However," said she as she shifted a bit to put a stop to his surreptitious touch, "Mr. Collins must speak for himself."

"I believe my place is here with you," Collins said, with a pointed look at his adversary.

Darcy was not impressed. "Pardon us, everyone." He accepted Ben's proffered hand and led him from the room.

Lady Catherine observed the goings-on of those around her with an odd mixture of curiosity and consternation. For once, she found herself at a loss for words. Her nephew seemed quite taken with the young child, but that was not what puzzled her. She wondered if her nephew did not show a little too much interest in the young widow Carlton, as well. *A mutual regard, no doubt.* She did not want to speak on it to the embarrassment of Mr. Collins. Nevertheless, she would speak on it.

"Mr. Collins, young Bennett seems far more fascinated with my nephew than he is with you. And YOU, about to become the child's stepfather," she voiced aloud. *As does your intended* her silent thoughts insisted. "How do you intend to correct that?"

Indeed, Collins had his own thoughts on how he would right the situation, though none that he cared to discuss with her ladyship. The spectacle of the haughty man whom he was learning to disdain, leading his future charge from the room, usurping his own role as the father figure for the young lad, and slighting him whilst speaking brazenly with his intended before his very eyes, vexed him exceedingly.

The commanding voice of his hostess, dispensing her own strong opinions on the matter, snapped him from his increasingly incensed reverie.

After an adventurous tour of the entire main level of the great manor, complete with fanciful embellishments befitting such a grand *mediaeval* castle, Darcy and Ben eventually made their way to the large, rambling kitchen. They found the staff busy going about the business of preparing for the evening's dinner. Not since Darcy was a young lad himself had he ventured there. After nearly two decades, none of the faces was familiar to him. Everyone certainly knew who he was and, therefore, endeavoured to allow him whatever unimpeded access was necessary to carry out his undertaking.

Darcy directed Ben to the large wooden table where the scullions and other kitchen domestics normally took their meals and told him to have a seat whilst he prepared a light fare. Ben laughed aloud at Darcy's haplessness in securing the necessary provisions. The butler, who had been made aware of the highly esteemed Mr. Darcy's presence in the kitchen, arrived nearly out of breath.

"Mr. Darcy, may I be of service?"

"Yes, Mr. Henry. My guest and I would like—" he looked at Ben with uncertainty.

"Cake!" Ben shouted.

"Yes, cake, that would be nice. Is there anything else?"

"Milk!"

"Of course. Mr. Henry, my guest and I would like two slices of cake and two glasses of milk."

"With pleasure, Mr. Darcy."

As the two friends were enjoying their refreshments, the army of kitchen staff, including the ill-humoured chef, having recovered a bit from the prospect of their mistress's venerated nephew in their midst, were thrown in a tizzy once again by the entering of yet another esteemed visitor.

"Darcy, I have been commissioned by Lady Catherine to seek out and recover the two of you. I might have known I would find you here." He slapped Darcy firmly on the back in recollection of the days of their youth. "Introduce me to your young friend."

Darcy picked up the fine linen napkin to dab his lips before acceding to the older gentleman's wish. Ben did likewise. "Ben, I would like you to meet my cousin, Colonel Richard Fitzwilliam. Richard, this young man is Bennet Carlton."

Richard bowed and encouraged Ben to remain in his seat. "So this is the young man whose story was so broadly spoken of last evening. It is a pleasure to make your acquaintance."

"It is my pleasure as well, sir."

"Pray tell, young man, how do you know my friend?"

"Your friend?" Ben directed a quizzical eye towards Darcy. "You said he was your cousin!"

Darcy smiled widely. "Indeed, Ben. He is my cousin AND my friend. The two are not mutually exclusive, you know."

"If you say so—as long as he does not suppose he is your BEST friend," Ben affirmed adamantly.

"Oh no! I believe you have firmly staked that honour for yourself." Darcy could not help laughing at Ben's possessiveness when it came to such matters.

"Indeed! But I suppose since he is YOUR friend, he might be MY friend as well," Ben said as he leaned a bit closer to Darcy as if speaking confidentially.

"I believe you will find him quite worthy," Darcy replied with certitude.

"But what shall we call him?" Ben asked Darcy as if it were the weightiest consideration they had yet faced.

Richard had had enough of being ignored by the two of them. "I must insist upon having my share of this conversation." Darcy said, "I am afraid there is something you must know about the two of us." He looked to Ben for confirmation. Ben nodded his approval. "You see, I am truly King Arthur and this young man is my brave knight, Sir Lancelot. The two of us are conferring to decide who YOU might be."

"Ah, King Arthur and Sir Lancelot, you say!" Ben eagerly responded, "Indeed! Moreover, my mama is Lady Guinevere, and THIS is Camelot," he declared with considerable enthusiasm, his arms stretched wide and nearly matched by his smile.

"I see!" Richard spoke in a tone apt to the seriousness of the occasion. "Then you must allow me to introduce myself as *Merlin*."

"Merlin?" Ben asked Darcy, with a look of uncertainty.

Darcy recalled the many times Richard had been there for him whenever he had needed him most, including as recently as the evening before. He grinned. "Trust me, my young friend; Merlin is a most befitting name."

Chapter 15

Upon observing Darcy's eager attentions to Ben and his mother, Colonel Fitzwilliam had grown increasingly concerned over the matter. *Does Darcy suffer no awareness at all of how this must seem to the rest of us? Not only is he taken with the child, his regard for the child's mother is such that one would have to be blind not to see.*

It had come with some measure of relief that the Hunsford party took their leave without having received an invitation to dine at Rosings that evening. Richard took his cousin aside soon after the guests' departure. Judging by the looks that had passed between his aunt and his Cousin Anne, Richard was certain Darcy was in for a heated lecture. First things first, his aunt's dressing-down could wait. What he needed to say could not!

"Darcy, let me assure you of my willingness to stand as your second, but are you quite certain it is a step you are willing to take?"

"What are you rambling on about now?" Darcy asked his older cousin impatiently.

"Just how do you envision Collins responding to your unmasked regard for his intended?"

"The lady is not yet married. Until such time as she is, she is free to change her mind."

"As is the gentleman's right to call you out," Richard quipped.

"Do not be ridiculous. Duelling is illegal, the last I heard. I expect Collins and I might resolve any differences we might suffer in a civilised manner, if and when the time comes."

"So, what exactly are your intentions towards Mrs. Carlton?"

"My immediate intention is to allow us to become better acquainted with each other. I am convinced she is perfect for me, but first I must persuade her not to accept Collins's hand simply out of misguided familial sentiments."

"I am afraid I do not take your meaning," Richard expressed, his curiosity demanding satisfaction.

"To make a very long and unexciting story short, I am convinced she accepted the man's proposal because her family's home is entailed away from the female line. He stands to inherit the estate upon her father's passing. In accepting his hand, she makes it possible for her mother and sisters always to have a home."

Richard was intrigued and, therefore, insisted upon knowing more of the story. Darcy reluctantly obliged him with more of the sordid details whilst nursing his brandy. Expanding on Lady Catherine's account from the evening before, Darcy also told of his unflattering opinion of her family. By the end of the account, Richard wondered even more of Darcy's intentions.

"From your account of the Bennets of Hertfordshire—their unseemly behaviour, their lowly status, with no wealth, no connections, and nothing to recommend them—I question even more your true intentions towards the lovely Mrs. Carlton."

"Trust me. She is nothing at all like the rest of her family. I would be honoured to have her in my life," Darcy adamantly affirmed.

"If you insist, my friend, I have little choice other than to accept you at your word. Again, my offer to stand in as your second remains, but I rather urge you to be more guarded in your approach so it does not come to that."

True to his word, Geoffrey Collins immediately set about taking young Ben under his wing. He and his brother had a habit of driving out in the gig and seeing the country in the mornings. Ben was made to accompany them, much to his dismay, for he had thought to spend the mornings with his best friend, just as they had done whilst in Hertfordshire.

The rest of their daily time together, Mr. Collins and Ben spent working with their hands, out of doors, either in the garden or crafting small wooden objects, a particularly favourite pastime of the elder man and one which might have captured young Ben's fancy as well, would his tutor have displayed a semblance of patience. Ben soon likened his part to looking but not touching.

Gillian and Emily were not early risers; therefore, with Ben relegated to Mr. Collins's supervision, Elizabeth was at liberty to enjoy her solitary rambles on her favourite path along an open grove which edged the side of the park where there was a nice shelter that no one seemed to value but herself. That was in the beginning. Somewhere along the way, it seemed, Mr. Darcy also had gained a fondness for the sheltered path. Day after day, she would come across him.

She had often asked herself what might be his purpose. His behaviour had been quite bewildering. He had seemed changed, unfamiliar, and at times somewhat aloof, or perhaps it was her own determined effort to appear completely unaffected by him that had altered her perceptions of his demeanour. Elizabeth had not met him privately on the morning after their *mediaeval* adventure, as he had requested. It was not that she did not want to meet him; rather, it was only after long and careful deliberation that she had decided against it.

Elizabeth continued walking along the path, in recollection of her earlier struggles that had led to her decision not to meet him alone. She had accepted the fact that the two of them would never be able to act on their mutual desire. Still, those magical times when it seemed as if time stood still when they stared into each other's eyes, would linger on in her mind for eternity.

Furthermore, she had resolved she would not allow herself to indulge in such flights of the imagination again. No amount of lingering kisses to the back of her hand, longing looks, nor silent beckoning pleas would persuade her otherwise. Endeavouring to rid herself of any notion of guilt, she began to view their past interludes as little more than harmless flirtations. In point of fact, that was really all it had been—all it would ever be.

Why then was it that every look, every gesture, every touch was etched in her mind? Why was it that whenever Elizabeth considered her intended's touches, she could not help comparing them to Mr. Darcy's? Alas, her intended was found wanting time and time again.

She reckoned she simply was not being fair to the man whose hand she had accepted. Not fair to him, not to herself, not to Mr. Darcy, and not even to her son. Mr. Collins was offering her a home and a future whereas Mr. Darcy merely offered her a chance to escape the miserable path she had set upon—a chance to feel alive once again, but little more, as best she could tell.

Mr. Collins had invited her to Hunsford for the sole purpose of becoming acquainted with her, to woo her, as it were, before meeting her at the altar. She owed it to him to allow the process to unfold—not just go through the motions accompanied by thoughts of trepidation whilst dreaming of being in the arms of another with thoughts of ecstasy. Surely, she owed him as much.

Elizabeth then recalled how her resolve had not been of a long standing before being tested. Mr. William Collins, who had made it a habit of calling on Rosings with some regularity, returned from one of his near daily visits accompanied by Mr. Darcy and Colonel Fitzwilliam a few days later. It appeared to her all her heartfelt soul searching, and her subsequent decision to keep up distance with the gentleman had been for naught. Whilst Colonel Fitzwilliam entered into conversation with everyone directly with readiness and ease, including a most enthusiastic debate with

Geoffrey Collins, his cousin, after having attended to the pleasantries incumbent upon morning callers, sat for a time without speaking to anyone until soon the gentlemen went away.

Elizabeth certainly had not been a stranger to Darcy's changeable moods, having recalled their earlier encounters during their initial acquaintance in Hertfordshire. Still, she could not help wondering what, if any, influence her decision not to meet with him in privacy had had on his altered behaviour.

That was then. Once he had made a beginning, not a day went by, barring unpleasant weather, that he did not happen along the secluded path. It all was arranged so amiably Elizabeth could hardly complain of any sort of impropriety. None of the heated dialogue, the soul piercing looks, or the stirring touch of his hands had a part to play in their exchanges. Rather their conversations tended towards innocuous, even mundane subjects. Darcy inquired of her thoughts of Kent, her attachment to Hertfordshire, her parents, her sisters, and even the conditions of the roads, and expenses of travelling. They exchanged accounts of their favourite authors, and of music and art. Darcy was most animated when he spoke of his younger sister, how he adored her, and how he would welcome a chance to introduce Elizabeth to her.

On one morning, Elizabeth noticed Darcy seemed to be particularly troubled. He was not at all the affable, conversant walking companion she had come to know. She rightly attributed his demeanour to the scene that had unfolded at church the day before. Mr. Collins had insisted Ben sit beside him during the sermon, much to Ben's consternation, for he dearly wished to sit with his friend whom he had not seen in days. Standing outside the church before the sermon began, Ben deliberately ignored Mr. Collins's stern rebuke and appealed directly to his mother for permission to sit with Mr. Darcy and Colonel Fitzwilliam. Awkwardly, Elizabeth sided with her intended. The proud gentleman made no pretence of containing his satisfaction as he led the child and his mother inside. The sight of the two people who had come to mean everything to him being led away by another man was more than he wished to bear and yet, there was nothing Darcy could say or do to alter things.

Darcy who, indeed, had been rather subdued since their initial greeting that morning caught Elizabeth wholly unawares with the intensity of his plea.

"In vain, I have struggled not to act upon our undeniable attraction to one another, but rather to allow us to become better acquainted without crossing the boundaries of your ill-judged arrangement with your cousin. It will not do.

"It was all I could do not to take you and Ben by the hand and lead you from the church yesterday. It is increasingly heart wrenching to see just how miserable Ben is under the gentleman's tutelage. It is equally tormenting to witness your suffering, as well."

Darcy moved nearer to Elizabeth and took her into his arms, as though it were the most natural thing in the world. "I want you, Elizabeth, with every fibre of my being. I want you. You and I belong together. I long to be by your side, I want you to be mine."

His lips met hers for the very first time. Warm, moist, and inviting, it was all he dreamed it would be and more. He was beyond pleased. Darcy knew in that moment this was the woman with whom he would spend the rest of his life.

Her passionate response confirmed that which he already knew, she desired him just as much as he desired her. Moreover, he would have her. The very thought he would have her brought him back to the stark reality that she was not his—not yet.

Darcy ceased his amorous attentions to her lips.

"Please, forgive me—for my trespass against you. I had no right. I can offer no excuse other than to confess you mean the world to me. There is not a day that goes by that I do not wish to be with you. I want you in my life; please say you will share the rest of your days with me."

The abrupt cessation of his lips on hers brought Elizabeth around to her right mind, as well. Enveloped in his arms felt wonderfully fitting. Yet, how could it be? Fighting against her body's own aching desire and her lonely heart's ardent pleading, she pulled herself from his gentle embrace, turned, and walked a few steps away.

"That is hardly a persuasive plea Mr. Darcy. Do you really expect me to turn my back on a decent and honourable man for a chance to be your mistress?"

Darcy went to her, reached out, and took her hand. "My mistress? You ARE my mistress—the mistress of my heart. Moreover, yes, for I am offering you more—to be mistress of my home, mistress of Pemberley. I love you, most ardently. Please do me the honour of accepting my hand."

The look of unsuspecting surprise that overspread her lovely countenance urged the resumption of Darcy's heartfelt proposal.

"I wish to be the one who takes care of you and your son. I want the two of you in my life. I will honour and protect the two of you. If you will but trust me and come away with me today, you will have no cause for regret."

"Surely, you see the fault in your proposal, Mr. Darcy. The reality of our situations is that we BOTH are spoken for, regardless of whether you choose to acknowledge the truth of the matter."

"I will NEVER marry my cousin! I am in love with you. I intend to devote my life to you."

"Does Miss Anne de Bourgh know that?"

"Let us not speak of Anne. That matter is easily settled. It is your encumbrance, alone, that stands in our way. Deny him. Forget him. Break your arrangement with him today, so we might leave here together. You need not return to Hertfordshire and suffer the disappointment of your family. I want you and Ben with me.

"Come away with me. I wish to be the one who takes care of you and your son." He stroked the back of her hand tenderly.

"What is the purpose? I have made my choice for my future and that of my son. Sadly, it does not include you." The disheartened look in her eyes instilled in her words a sense of hopelessness. "How would I find happiness with you when I know it comes at the expense of a decent and respectable man and his two young daughters?"

Elizabeth removed her hands from his. Speaking the words destined to cause both of them enormous pain, she continued, "If you love me half as much as you profess, I beseech you to let go of this undeniable hold you have over me. If you love me, let me go."

"I do love you! But if you insist upon staying the unwise course of this path you have chosen for yourself, I will not interfere." Darcy paused and put some distance between them. "I will not stand by idly and watch as you throw your life away—commit yourself forever to a man whom you do not love."

A blaze of thinly disguised annoyance ripped through him. Reluctantly and painfully conceding the fact that she needed time to see for herself that which was abundantly clear to him already, as well as the fact that he could only be in the way, Darcy resumed his portentous speech. "Collins is not the man for you. However, I will leave Kent, thereby allowing for no further interference in your courtship, if it is what you want. Is this indeed what you truly wish for, Elizabeth?"

"I do. I made a promise to Mr. Collins. I intend to honour it, and not because of some misguided notion of loyalty to my family, but because he is a good, upstanding man who deserves nothing less than the trust he has bestowed in me by offering his hand and bringing us all together to become acquainted with one another before becoming a family. He has done everything to live up to his part of the arrangement and has asked nothing more of me than I give us a chance.

"All I ask of you is to allow me to do just that."

"Very well, madam. I will honour your request. I will return to town on the morrow. I do love you—enough to let you go your own way, to discover without further interference from me if he is the man for you.

"What I would ask of you is to allow me to see Ben before I go. I wish to be the one to impart the news of my departure." Their eyes met. Darcy drew in his lower lip whilst awaiting her response. Elizabeth's heart turned somersaults.

Deeply attuned to his hurting, for she suffered it as well, she spoke softly, "Have I ever purposely set out to keep the two of you apart?"

"You have not. I thank you for that." Heart-wrenchingly silent moments later he continued, "There is only one other thing I would ask of you." Darcy took Elizabeth's hand in his. "Do not find yourself in a position where you need anything at all and be unwilling to turn to me. I will always be there for you." Darcy reached out to caress her face for what he prayed would not be the last time. He stared deeply into her eyes and uttered softly, slowly, "Always."

Chapter 16

I f Elizabeth would but admit it, even to no one but herself, she would confess she had come to look forward to her early morning encounters with Mr. Darcy along the sheltered path. Following his going away, what had become her favourite pathway suddenly seemed desolate and lonely. The warmth that infused the air when she had first glimpsed his fine stature approaching her from a distance was no more. The weather somehow had turned cold; the skies, at first bright and promising, now seemed dark and forbidding.

In the wake of such quiet isolation, the only sounds she was aware of were the chirping of the blackbirds inhabiting the trees, the sole witnesses to the scene that had just occurred—yet another act in the tragedy of timing that was her life.

Mr. Darcy offered his hand in marriage. He is in love with me, most ardently. How painfully sad it is to be promised to someone else when the perfect one comes along.

Utterly forlorn, Elizabeth walked along, tightly cradled in her own embrace as if the whole world had turned its back on her. She knew it would be quite a while before she headed back to the parsonage. What she needed was time; time enough to persuade herself she had done the honourable thing in refusing Mr. Darcy. Even as she silently recited the motives for her selfless actions, she could not satisfy the unabated questions of her heart. *Indeed, my decision was the right thing to do. Why then does everything feel so wrong?*

Mr. Darcy—in love with me! So much so he would honour my wish to allow me to pursue my own path. Such was the only comforting thought she could muster as once again, Elizabeth outlined the many reasons her decision to push Darcy away was the right thing to do. Her own sense of decency and propriety aside, she thought of her family back in Hertfordshire. To throw caution to the wind and follow Mr. Darcy, very well meant disappointing her family's hopes. Having defied her father once, to have accepted Mr. Darcy's proposal would have been tantamount to defying him yet again. She had not yet regained his good opinion. Did she want to sever any lingering possibility she might reclaim his esteem?

The scandal of a broken engagement which would have ensued might be a cause for concern as well, although not so much for Elizabeth, for the worse she would suffer was to be labelled a jilt. Whilst she could bear it, what of the consequences for her four sisters, all of whom had decidedly poor prospects already? Did she wish to endure such guilt?

By the end of her ramble, she had managed to convince herself she indeed had done the right thing in ignoring her heart and listening to her head; albeit, not without some cost. Already, she sensed her independent spirit waning as she reached to unlatch the parsonage gate. Elizabeth managed a weak smile which would continue to grace her countenance as she went through the motions of her day—surrogate mother of the twins, extended houseguest of her dear friend Charlotte, and dutiful betrothed of Mr. Geoffrey Collins. Her life as devoted mother of her beloved son was the sole thing she embraced. It was, in fact, the very reason for her being.

Darcy found Richard in the stables, the latter having just returned from a strenuous solitary ride about the countryside. Richard sensed something was not quite right, for Darcy had not looked so forlorn since before his discovery that the lovely Mrs. Carlton and her young son were in residence at the parsonage.

"Pray tell Darcy, you look as though you have lost your best friend in the world. What has happened to bring about this change? Did Collins decide to run off with Mrs. Carlton to Gretna Green before you could persuade her against the marriage?"

"Not exactly, wise old man. I came down here to tell you of my decision to leave Kent tomorrow."

"This is rather sudden, is it not? What happened to your plans for Mrs. Carlton? What prompted you to change your mind?"

"I have not changed my mind. Elizabeth and her son mean everything to me. In fact, I made her an offer this morning, which she refused."

"An offer? What sort of offer does a man make to a woman who is already promised to another?" Richard asked, hoping Darcy had not proposed the foremost thing in his own somewhat world-weary mind.

Darcy paused for a moment before responding to his cousin. *Is that why Elizabeth asked if I were offering to make her my mistress? Have my intentions towards her of late been so unclear? Since that wonderful morning spent with Ben and her, I have not as much as placed my hands on hers. I have done everything in my power to keep up a respectable distance between us and to regard her as would a gentleman who was not violently in love.*

Richard cleared his throat to gain Darcy's attention. "Have you heard a single word I have said?"

"Suffice it to say I offered her all I have, and she refused me. She is honourable. I cannot fault her decision. It is who she is, and a part of why I am so in love with her," Darcy responded.

"Then you have given up and chosen instead to leave."

"I am honouring her wish by doing the only thing she has ever asked of me."

"Be that as it may, I do not imagine Lady Catherine and Anne will be very pleased with your decision to take your leave, especially since you have yet to satisfy their wishes."

"Believe me when I say that pleasing either of those two is the farthest thing from my mind, from this point on. I intend to make that clear this evening. My greatest concern now is for Elizabeth and Ben, and how I might be there for them should they ever need me. I fear she is as stubborn and proud as she is honourable and loyal. She might not reach out to me, should it ever come to that." *Somehow, I must find a way to let her know I will always be there for the two of them,* he silently voiced.

Some time had passed since the Hunsford party was last invited to dine at Rosings. Lady Catherine was determined not to put her nephew in the company of the beautiful young widow, whom he could not manage to take his eyes off for more than a few minutes at a time. Subtle words during dinner regarding his inattention to Anne over the past weeks and his preoccupation with the entertainment of young Bennet Carlton, even at the risk of usurping Mr. Collins's rightful place, turned into full-blown admonishments after dinner when the family gathered in the drawing room. After fifteen minutes or so, Darcy had heard enough and determined to put an end to the harsh discourse, for the last time.

"Lady Catherine, you have insulted me in every possible way. You can now have nothing further to say. In spite of the considerable pain, I must inform you of my decision to break all ties with both Anne and you." Darcy turned to face his cousin. "I never wished to hurt you, Anne. However, you know, as well as does Lady Catherine, I never intended to marry you. I never offered you my hand, and the carelessly spoken words I uttered last autumn were nothing more than an inane attempt to revive you from what I then believed to be death's door. I shall leave Rosings tomorrow. I am sorry if this distresses you, but I shall never cross its threshold again."

Anne grew even paler in the wake of her cousin's harsh words. She quickly arose from her chair, threatening to collapse from the shock of it all. Before she could raise her hand to her head to swoon, Darcy declared, "Give it a rest, Anne! I am exhausted by your convenient malady. Fall sick again if you will, but you will sooner see death than you will see my face again."

Lady Catherine's mouth shot wide open! She was appalled. She walked over to Anne's side and placed her hand on her shoulder. "Leave us now, daughter, whilst I speak with your cousin," said she. She then directed her attention to Mrs. Jenkinson, Anne's companion, "Please return with my daughter to her room and see to it she rests."

Grateful to escape the unpleasant scene unfolding before her eyes, Mrs. Jenkinson did as she was told by offering assistance to Anne, who brokered no argument. The moment they were outside the room, Anne stationed herself near the doors, which she had left slightly ajar, especially for the purpose of bearing witness to the stern reproach her cousin was destined to receive.

"How dare you speak to your cousin in such a despicable manner and utter such idle threats?" Lady Catherine demanded. "To do as you suggest would surely dishonour your own family."

"My decision is no more dishonourable than your threatening to announce in the papers that Anne and I are engaged when you know it to be a falsehood. Though it is one thing for members of my family to consider it a possibility in light of my late mother's own wish, it is entirely another to have such foolishness widely circulated amongst society."

"Heaven and earth! You are a grown man of eight and twenty with responsibilities to uphold as master of Pemberley. Do you not think it is beyond the time you consider marriage? Why should you not marry Anne, just as well as any other?"

"The answer is simple. I do not love Anne, not in the way a man should love his wife. I have been in love. Hell, I AM in love! I will not settle for anything LESS than love!"

Lady Catherine paused long enough to consider his words. *His father's son*, she surmised as she recalled how the late Mr. Darcy and her sister, indeed, had enjoyed a love match. She could no longer deny that regardless of the agreement between two sisters so many years ago that their offspring would one day be joined in wedlock, Lady Anne, if she were alive, would not want her son to do what she would not do herself. Lady Anne would not wish to see her son marry out of family obligation rather than follow his heart.

"I have heard quite enough, young man. I do not wish to see you take your leave of Rosings with the prospect of you never returning. I have lived with the notion that you and Anne would be married for so long, the very thought of it has consumed me. You are correct. I obviously cannot force the matter, otherwise you two would have been married years ago, and we would not be having this conversation."

Darcy glanced over to his cousin Richard, and the two cast looks of utter disbelief mixed with apprehension. Flabbergasted, both silently asked the other had their aunt taken leave of her senses.

The dubious looks that passed between the two gentlemen did not go unnoticed by the elderly woman. "Why are the two of you looking at each other thus?" Lady Catherine began. "I know what I am about."

Still poised just outside the door, Anne could not believe what she had heard. All her life, her mother had insisted she would marry Darcy, even against her own misgivings, and now she was conceding the marriage would never be. She had heard quite enough for one evening. Anne angrily stormed towards the stairway. Without help from Mrs. Jenkinson, she made her way up the long spiralling steps. *We shall see about that!*

Violent rains had persisted throughout the night, but the morning came filled with the invigorating scents of the welcoming spring air. Elizabeth saw to it her son was free to meet with Mr. Darcy and the two of them set out early. She led him along the sheltered lane which now held such bitter-sweet memories.

Over halfway there, she paused. "Run along ahead, Ben. Mr. Darcy is expecting you," she kindly instructed her young son.

"Are you not planning to join us, Mama? It has been far too long since our last adventure with King Arthur!"

Elizabeth knelt before her son and straightened his collar. "I am afraid not." She gently informed her young son Mr. Darcy wanted to speak with him, man to man. Ben's eyes widened. The prospect was pleasing to the young lad, for he, too, had wanted a chance to do just that for some time. The eager smile spread across his innocent face tore at Elizabeth's heart. She prayed the trust she had placed in Darcy was not misguided, that he would know exactly the right words to say to protect her child's sensibilities.

"Do not keep Mr. Darcy waiting," said she. "I shall see you back at the parsonage."

"But you cannot leave just now. I need your help with another adventure!" Ben exclaimed, upon hearing from his friend that he would be returning to London that same day.

"What sort of adventure do you have in mind?"

"Well, you know the evil Meleagant intends to marry my mama."

"I take it you are referring to Mr. Collins, Ben," Darcy gently rebuked. The young man nodded affirmatively. Darcy continued, "Then I would say yes. I have been reminded on more occasions than I care to recall of the gentleman's intentions."

"I say we save my mama!" Ben avowed eagerly.

"Save her? How do you propose we do that? In the end, is it not your mother's choice whom she marries?"

"Well yes, but perhaps if we rescue her then she might marry you. I know she likes you better."

"You think so, do you? How do you suppose that to be true?"

"She laughs whenever she is around you. She never laughs around the evil Meleagant."

Out of the mouths of babes, Darcy thought. "Ben, you and I must talk about your attitude towards Mr. Collins. It is of some concern to me. Suppose he does marry your mother," Darcy voiced aloud even as his thoughts sang out, *Heaven forbid!* "Then, you must not refer to the gentleman as evil. I am sure he is a decent fellow, and not at all evil."

"But he is not very amiable. He is harsh and forbidding, and he has no imagination whatsoever."

"Is he not a good father? Do his daughters not revere him? Should he become your stepfather one day, then you too must revere him."

"How do I go about doing that? I do not like him at all, and I suspect he does not like me either."

"You do not have to like him, though I would encourage you to try. However, he is your elder, and you must show him the proper respect. The best way to start is to stop thinking of him as evil. Do you not agree?"

Darcy and Ben continued to discuss the matter at length, each with a measure of give-and-take, until they were as close to one mind as could be, considering such varying sentiments. In the end, Darcy only wanted what was best for his young friend. Ben trusted his older, wiser friend enough to know he would not counsel him fool-heartedly.

That resolved, Darcy imparted the words he would never have wished to speak to his friend as short a time ago as the day before, words of farewell mixed with comforting reassurances.

"Ben, because divine providence brought us together again, I contend our friendship is meant to be. Even as you and I are about to embark on paths that will find us miles and miles apart, we are best friends, are we not? I shall always carry you here," Darcy lifted Ben's small hand and placed it so, before continuing, "in my heart. Moreover, I will not say good-bye, but rather so long, for I strongly believe this is not the end."

Saddened and yet ever inquisitive, Ben asked, "How shall I ever contact you—in case I need you."

Darcy reached into his pocket, secured a finely embossed card with his name and address, and handed it to Ben. "Here is my London address. For now, I suggest you put this in a very safe place. Should you find yourself in town and in need of a friend, do not hesitate to call on me."

Ben looked at the card intently and slowly read, "Fitz-william Darcy. FITZWILLIAM, is that your name?"

Darcy smiled. "Yes, is there something wrong in that?"

"No, no, it is just that Fitzwilliam is your cousin's name, just as Bennet is my grandfather's name."

"Yes, yes I know, Bennet is also your mother's maiden name, just as Fitzwilliam was my mother's maiden name."

Ben was encouraged by that bit of information, for there was another thing the two of them shared. Reluctant to part, Ben began to list the other things they had in common until some time had passed and Darcy was obliged to send the young lad on his way.

Darcy stood and watched his young friend move farther and farther away with a muddled mixture of sadness and gladness. He felt sadness because once again he found himself having to say good-bye, but gladness because Ben did not appear to suffer the imminent separation as painfully as he had in Hertfordshire. Ben continued to amble along the path, occasionally looking back over his shoulder, quietly reassured to find his trusted friend still standing there. When at last, they were far enough apart that Ben could no longer see his friend, he ran off, saddened, of course, and yet heartened by the hope of one-day being in Mr. Darcy's company again.

Chapter 17

D arcy was well on the road to London before he could completely disregard his cousin's odd behaviour. Never before
had she accompanied his cousin Richard and him to their carriage
when they took their leave of Rosings Park. Her ominous last
words, spoken for his ears alone caused the hairs on the back of
his neck to stand. Applying a bit of pressure to his proffered hand,
her hushed tone prompted him to lean in closer, "This is not over
until I say it is over."

Nearer to town, haunting thoughts of Anne were pushed aside
by thoughts of the two people he had learnt to care about, uppermost in his mind. The two people he had left behind. *Will I ever
see them again? If ever again, should Elizabeth choose to go
ahead with the marriage, will I even recognise her, or will she
have lost her spirit and liveliness pursuant to her marriage to
Geoffrey Collins?*

Darcy endeavoured to shake off such thoughts. He picked up
his neglected book and tried to recall where he had left off in the
text. *I must not think like that. Surely, she will not yield to the
man's strong rule.* In spite of himself, Darcy recalled some of his
most heated exchanges with Elizabeth, where he might have made

mistakes, and what he might do differently, if given a chance. He persuaded himself he had done the right thing by her in leaving Kent. *She needs to see for herself how her life would be, how Ben's life would be. I have faith in her judgement. Even if she is not in love with me, even if she feels duty bound, a sensible, lively, and passionate woman such as she, will not settle for a life of submissiveness.*

The manner in which she railed against any act of officiousness on my part is proof enough of that. It is but one of the less than amiable qualities that particular gentleman possesses in spades. He gives the term officiousness an entirely new meaning.

In the ensuing weeks, the Hunsford party fell into a rather comfortable, though sometimes awkward routine. Regular invitations to Rosings resumed as Lady Catherine sought to overcome the sense of loneliness brought on by her nephews' departure.

It was a beautiful day for a picnic and in keeping with her promise to the girls the day before, that is just what Elizabeth and the girls set out to do. They found a lovely spot that offered a splendid view of Rosings Park. After an hour or so, their delightful party of three was interrupted by the addition of a fourth, Mr. Collins. The girls were eager for the chance to spend time with their father, especially in their future stepmother's company, for he displayed signs of light heartedness and gaiety theretofore not attributable to him.

After a moment or two, he glanced about to survey the environs. "Where is Ben?"

"He was eager to go out after breakfast," responded Elizabeth. "I reminded him he was not to venture too far," she quickly added, reminded of his earlier rebukes against Ben's wont of scampering about on his own.

"I shall look for him, then. I thought we might take a ride in the country this afternoon," Collins replied, before rising to his feet.

Ben was off planning a surprise. He had often recalled old tales of lore as recounted to him by his mother, who as a child likely heard it from her own mother, who heard it from her mother, no doubt altered in translation through the generations; tales of princes, and princesses, and far-away kingdoms and the like.

His soon-to-be sisters, rather stepsisters, as he was always known to voice aloud, were the closest approximation of princesses he could imagine. What with the way they sat around at leisure, wasting away the day in one frivolous pursuit or another, having tea, fussing over each other's hair, dressing up, and staring into looking glasses. The only time they even deigned to allow him in their court was when they needed a jester or a servant, or so it seemed to him. Imagine, *Sir Lancelot* standing attendance to two haughty princesses, when there were wars to be waged and fierce battles to be won. On the other hand, two haughty princesses were far better companions than the loneliness that beset him in the wake of King Arthur's leave-taking.

"Princess Gillian, Princess Emily!" he shouted eagerly as he joined them on their outing. Ben had blessed them with that regal appellation as a means of teasing them. Alas, addressing them so had become the only way they would recognise his presence. "I have a wonderful surprise for the two of you! Come see what it is."

The girls had no doubt he had something for them. The excited look reflected on his face was proof enough of that. In addition, he had both hands tucked behind his back. The glances that passed between them were confirmation of their opinion of the status of the youngest as compared to their own.

Gillian, the older of the two by at least thirty minutes commanded, "If you have come bearing gifts, then you must step forward and produce them." Emily confirmed her sister's decree with a slight nod of her head.

"Very well, ma' ladies," Ben humbly replied as he approached. Without further ado, he removed his hands from behind his back and brought his offerings forth. "Your princes have arrived!"

The girls let out two deafening screams, surprising Ben as much as he had surprised them. How could they not be pleased with his gifts? It had taken him most of the morning to capture the two toads!

Elizabeth, it seemed, was the least surprised. Masking her amusement as best she could muster, she managed to say, "Ben!" only to be interrupted by the ferociousness of Geoffrey Collins's voice.

Appearing from nowhere, he grabbed young Ben by his upper arm forcefully. Ben broke away from the man's grip and backed away, stumbling over in the process, shock clearly registering on his young face. Before Ben could right himself, Collins reached for him again. He took him by the shoulder and positioned him before the girls, who by then were just as confused as young Ben, any thoughts of a possible catalyst for the scene that occurred before them, completely erased.

"Apologise to the girls this instant for your unseemly behaviour and promise not to upset them with such foul things as this again."

"NO! I will do no such thing!" Ben insisted. "There is no harm done!"

Collins took hold of Ben's wrists and scolded him. "Return to your room at once, where you are to remain until I arrive and attend to your punishment! You will learn to conduct yourself as a civilised young man who gets along with his sisters and not some wild savage who torments them!"

Cowered by the man's fury, Ben broke free and ran towards the parsonage-house. Elizabeth was appalled. She made no pretence to hide her own anger. She stood to race after her son to offer him solace.

"Stay where you are!" Collins ordered. "You must learn to stop coddling him as though he were a helpless infant. He is a mischievous young boy badly in need of a strong hand!"

Elizabeth looked at Mr. Collins as though he had taken leave of his senses. As irate as she was, she spoke not a word, even as she completely disregarded his admonishment. Rather she considered that this was not the time, not in front of the girls. However, rest assured she would make her way of thinking known. First things first, she raced after Ben to nurse his bruised feelings.

A day filled with tension eventually neared its close when everyone else retired, and it was just Elizabeth and Geoffrey Collins who remained downstairs. That evening, Elizabeth was as eager as was he for the moment to arrive, when it was just the two of them, alone. Elizabeth was set upon firmly taking Mr. Collins to task for mistreating her son as he had. Discipline was one thing, but it was hardly an excuse for his being stern, severe, harsh, and rude. True, she was reared in a house full of females as he was so apt to point out, but she knew enough to know boys will be boys. She had hardly spoken a civil word to him the entire day, and yet it was as though he was wholly oblivious to the fact that she was furious with him. *Just another example of how he views the world. The man, the woman, the child—everyone has his or her place,* she considered.

Collins sat close to her on the sofa with his arms resting atop its edge. "I look forward to our evenings together, which makes what I have to say all the more difficult."

"Pardon me, Mr. Collins, I too have a matter which I can hardly wait to discuss with you."

"If you will allow me, Elizabeth, to express that which is uppermost in my mind first, I am certain it will put to rest any concerns you may have.

"I am most eager to make you my wife, to share your passion. You and I have made such progress over the past two weeks. I am convinced we should not wait any longer." Collins moved nearer to reduce any distance between them. "I know it will be some time before the marriage will take place, but the sooner we make it publicly known, the sooner we will be united. I plan to return to my home to have the Banns read, for it is there, in my own parish that I intend for us to wed.

"Does that not sound wonderful?" Mistaking the incredulous look on her countenance as elation and interpreting her silence as acceptance, he leaned forward to kiss her lips. Elizabeth turned her face in time enough for his lips to render a scant brush against her cheek. It seemed enough for him as he drew her closer and rested her head against his shoulder. Even as she resisted his embrace and put some distance between them, he uttered, "Tell me you are as excited for us to begin our life together as am I."

Elizabeth would not utter the words he wished to hear; she could not. He raised her chin to look into her eyes.

"What is it, Elizabeth?"

"Mr. Collins," she began, after finally freeing herself of his touch. Upon walking away towards the window, she turned to face him. "I am sorry if what I am about to say is a cause for pain, to you, as well as to Gillian and Emily. However, I cannot go through with it."

"What are you saying? You have accepted my hand already. The only thing that remains is the formalities."

"No, I will not marry you. I must confess that I, in good faith, shall not pretend to have feelings for you such as you want and admittedly deserve. While I believe you might be a good husband to someone, you cannot possibly be a good husband to me, and I surely will not be a good wife to you. Everyone deserves some measure of happiness. All either of us would offer the other is misery. Of this I have no doubt. Your dogmatic approach to wedded life is in every way offensive to me. You sir, do not want a wife! You want a subservient creature, one who submits to your every dictate. I know myself well enough to know I would be in grave danger of an unhappy alliance should I pretend to be that person."

"Elizabeth, I confess to having very established views on matrimony. I know I have a tendency to come across as harsh and demanding at times. I am not unreasonable. I am quite agreeable to change my ways, if that is what I must do. I have already begun to take a different view on many things since becoming acquainted with you."

"It is more than just your rigid expectations of me, and you know it!"

"What other objections have you to our marriage?"

"Do you think I would be tempted to marry someone who has been the means of such heartache and pain to my son?"

"Do not discard the security I offer you and your son just because you fear I mean your son harm. You and I have a difference of opinion on what is best for him, is all. Elizabeth, you must trust me to know what is best in such instances. You are a young woman. Moreover, you were reared in a household of silly females. What do you, a mere woman, know of what it takes to raise a man?"

"I wager there are better ways to rear and discipline a child, regardless of its sex, than to resort to harshness and oppression!" Elizabeth spoke in raised tones. "You may be an excellent father to your own daughters; however, your ideas for Ben, in every way, are opposed to my own views on how my child should be reared."

"Granted, I may at times have appeared a bit severe when speaking to Ben. Again, I am willing to change in that regard, if you will but allow me the chance."

"It is much too late for that. In the face of your callous treatment of my son, your self-righteous views on what is best for Ben, what is best for us, you sir, are the last man in the world whom I could ever be prevailed on to marry. I would sooner take my son and live in the streets, than I would subject him to your harsh and bitter treatment ever again!"

Collins stared at Elizabeth with an expression of mingled incredulity and mortification. How on earth could he have been so mistaken about her? He walked with quick steps across the room in a futile attempt to rein in his temper. It would not do. Did he even know her? He halted abruptly and faced her. Speaking with utter contempt, he declared, "Spare me your sanctimonious speech about my treatment of your precious son! You and I both know what this is about!"

"What on earth signifies more than what I have conveyed?"

"Your change of heart has little to do with your son and everything to do with your feelings for Fitzwilliam Darcy! I warn you of the foolishness of this path you have chosen. He is the type of man who wants that which he cannot have. Be forewarned, the sooner you are free, the sooner he will take what he can get from you and then move on. He would be a fool not to marry his cousin, especially when he can marry her and have the likes of you as a mistress on the side."

"You are quite mistaken. My reasons are just as I have expressed. This has nothing to do with Mr Darcy and everything to do with you and me. A marriage between us would prove a grave mistake."

"Do you think for one moment you would find happiness with him? The mere fact that you were able to marry above your sphere once by no means suggests you might do so a second time, that you might ever be so fortunate again. It is one thing to marry a naïve young man from a wealthy family, but *your* Mr. Darcy is no doubt a worldly gentleman of sense and education. He will never marry someone such as yourself, someone who is so far below him in consequence it is laughable."

The realisation of his worse fears since first laying eyes on Darcy and Elizabeth in each other's company finally having come to fruition, Geoffrey Collins would not be persuaded by what he perceived as her feeble attempts to deny the undeniable truth.

"Elizabeth, no pardon me, *Mrs. Carlton*—at least give me some credit for recognising lust when I see it, rather than continue to question my understanding. This has everything to do with HIM. For you to continue to deny it renders you all the more foolish, dare I even suggest duplicitous.

"In the end, it is for the best we do not marry, for if he has not staked his claim on your body as of yet, from what I know of his kind, it is merely a matter of time. Better, it should be with HIS mistress than with MY wife!"

"You have purposely misread my meaning to suit your own selfish reasons. I implore you to be less condemning. We remain as family and our paths are bound to cross yet again. You shall see. My decision has nothing to do with Mr. Darcy!"

"Yes, our paths no doubt will cross again, which is why I ask you one thing. Admit the reason for your change of heart has everything to do with your feelings for this other man, and I will release you from this engagement with no accusations of breached promises or the like."

Elizabeth stood firm, unmoving, speechless. It WAS more than that. He had to see it, even if he sought to assuage his hurt pride by wounding her own. Unforgiving looks on both sides quickly gave way to loathing, neither of them willing to bend.

Finally, Geoffrey Collins conceded. "You disgust me! You both disgust me! You two deserve each other!" He turned to quit the room but just then stopped and turned to meet with her unrelenting posture.

His thoughts by then were of how he had grown to care for her. What a disappointment she had been, forfeiting her promise, letting him down, and destroying his daughters' hopes for a mother's love. He had thought of her as an intelligent, sensible woman. He asked himself yet again how he had been so wrong.

"I shall take my leave of Hunsford at sunrise. Furthermore, I shall not upset Gillian and Emily with an abrupt uprooting of their stay. I will leave with the excuse of bringing their governess here to look after them. Mind you, when I return in four days hence, I shall not expect to find you here. Make whatever excuse you deem as necessary upon your departure."

With that, he turned away once more, and upon quitting the room, closed the door forcefully.

Frozen there, it was as though time stood still before her, as Elizabeth considered what had become of her life and the uncertain, immediate future. Fragments of intense emotions abounded

—alarmed and yet relieved, unsure and yet hopeful. At last, she was free.

Chapter 18

*B*y now, my father will have read the letter conveying the news of my decision not to go through with the marriage to Mr. Geoffrey Collins, she thought as she cradled her sleeping child in the public carriage on the road to London. Pursuant to her actions, she wondered if she might ever see her childhood home again. Having overseen the packing of all her worldly possessions in anticipation of the wedding, all that remained was to have her sister Mary arrange for her belongings to be sent to her new home.

My new home, she silently deliberated. *Wherever that might be.* It was one thing to arrive unexpectedly at her Uncle and Aunt Gardiner's doorstep, seeking temporary shelter; surely, she could not expect to reside there for any extended length of time. Jane, who had travelled with them to town just after Christmas, had decided to remain with them indefinitely. In fact, Elizabeth understood from her correspondence from her eldest sister, that she was effectively the Gardiner children's nurse and governess. She had no idea what had led to that particular arrangement, though she was destined to find out.

Elizabeth sat in her uncle's study intent on apprising him of her plans for her future. Right away, she could tell something was amiss. Never before had she witnessed such turmoil in her uncle's face. He had borne a troubled, weary smile from the moment he walked into the door after a long, laborious day in his warehouse.

"Uncle, I appreciate the hospitality both you and my aunt have shown in allowing Ben and me to stay here. I want to assure you it is but a temporary measure for I intend to use some of the funds I have entrusted to your care as a means of securing a modest house in town or a small cottage in the country."

"Lizzy, my dear," he began. "There is a matter I wish to discuss with you; one I had wished to avoid altogether. Alas, in light of your appeal, it is incumbent upon me to inform you of the details of my handling of your funds.

"You see, my dear, an exceedingly lucrative venture was presented to me a while back, coupled with a chance to increase my stake, a little more than six months ago." Mr. Gardiner went on to explain the intricate nature of the investment; not only had he invested the greater part of Elizabeth's capital assets in the speculative venture, he had invested a significant portion of his own funds as well.

"It is not as bad as it sounds," Mr. Gardiner explained. "You will see a substantial return of your investment. It is just a matter of timing. To liquidate your stake now would result in a significant loss."

"What exactly are you saying? When do you anticipate a return of my investment?"

"At least five years hence. Mind you, my dear, your purpose in saving has always been to secure your son's education. My intentions were based on your plans to marry Mr. Collins, thus rendering no need for ready liquidity."

"I beg your pardon, Uncle, but I beseech you to speak honestly. What is the true state of my holdings, this investment notwithstanding?"

He opened his ledger and pointed out her worth. Elizabeth's heart sank. She was no better off financially than she was when her father-in-law had passed away. Far from penniless, she was hardly in the position of providing for her son in a manner befitting the young heir. All of those years of living frugally, sacrificing, and saving the bulk of her meagre monthly stipend in anticipation of her son's education were for naught. *What if my uncle is mistaken? What if the speculative investment fails?*

"Fear not, Lizzy," he said as if reading her mind. He took her into his embrace. "Though my finances are as tenuous as yours at the moment, I will not see you and Ben go without. I bear full responsibility for your current straits. I will do whatever I must in supplementing your monthly stipend to allow you and Ben to live comfortably—regardless of the sacrifice to my own wife and children.

"There is no need to rush into anything just now. Ben and you are free to live here for as long as you wish." Five children, four adults, and only one remaining servant, as best as she could tell, residing in overly crowded conditions in a home less than a third the size of her childhood home, scarcely a tenth of the size of Camberworth. While it might do for Elizabeth, it was hardly the childhood she had envisioned for her son. In light of her drastic change of fortune, what other choice had she?

Elizabeth allowed herself the comfort of his arms for only a moment before she pulled away from her uncle. "If you will allow it, I fear I need some time to myself to comprehend fully all you have said."

"Of course, I will leave you for now. Take as much time as you need." Her uncle slowly moved towards the door, as Elizabeth walked over to the window to peer into the darkness of night. Mr. Gardiner regarded her with a heartfelt look of apology, one she did not observe, then slowly closed the door behind him.

Hours later, in the loneliness of her uncle's study, lit only by a single candle, Elizabeth wondered if she had made the best decision in rejecting Mr. Geoffrey Collins, after all. Had it not been for her friend Charlotte's generosity in offering her all the excess pin money she had managed to amass, Elizabeth would not have been able to arrange the expeditious departure from Hunsford. A young woman and her son travelling by post, departing in much the same manner as they had arrived, yet not quite the same as regarded the prospects for her future. Her arrival in Hunsford was marked by resignation to a certain fate. Her departure was marked by a steadfast determination to make her own way in life.

The wounded looks from the girls had been countered by the disdainful looks from Mr. William Collins. To his great contentment, the matter of her broken engagement and hurried departure had all been managed in a way that caused no diminishing of his noble patroness's esteem towards himself.

No, she would not second-guess her decision. Recalling her hastily spoken words that she would sooner live in the street than subject her son to Mr. Collins's tyranny, in her heart she knew it would never come to that. Surely, she could scrape out a modest existence for her son, even if it meant letting a small place and relying on her meagre monthly stipends to carry them through. As the daughter of a gentleman, and the mother of a gentleman as well, the last thing she ever intended was to reduce Ben's prospects one bit. In removing him from the Carlton family estate, she had sought to raise him in an atmosphere free from debauchery. He was heir to his late grandmother's fortune, a substantial fortune held in trust until he reached majority.

Try as she might to not find fault in her uncle's handling of her finances, she could not help feeling a measure of resentment. She had been saving her money to pay for Ben's education. His grandfather, as well as his father, had been educated as proper gentlemen. She wanted nothing less for her son. She prayed it was destined still to be.

For all intents and purposes, Elizabeth had commandeered her uncle's study, as day after day, she would sequester herself inside.

When she did venture beyond the room, it was to offer whatever assistance she could provide to her aunt and to tend to Ben's needs. She did not intend either of them would be an added burden. She had very little of meaning to say to anyone, sensing, as she did, an ever widening gulf between her sensibilities and those of her eldest sister Jane. Too much had happened since she last shared confidences with Jane. How might she explain her decision to reject the hand of not one, but two respectable men in the course of a few weeks? Certainly, Jane could not be expected to be sympathetic, having never received a single offer of marriage. With all of her angelic beauty, at six and twenty, Jane seemed contented to spend her life as the unpaid nurse and governess for her uncle and aunt's four children. Perhaps her Aunt Gardiner might understand, but Elizabeth did not trust herself not to speak candidly on her true feelings over the repercussion of her uncle's investment schemes on them all.

Feeling dismayed, she endeavoured to recall all her uncle had done for her over the years. Without doubt, he did not intend her any harm, she reckoned. *It is enough that he will have to live with the shame of his deeds.* Besides, she had ceded control over her finances to him because she had a deep abiding trust in his judgement. She would forgive him.

Again, it was just another example of the failings on the part of the men in her life; first, her father for not doing his duty in making sure she had a proper marriage settlement and secondly, her father-in-law for his apparent belief in his own immortality. However, she would not blame him too much. At least, he had arranged for her to have a lifetime annuity, pursuant to her husband's untimely passing, though hardly enough to keep Ben and her in the style to which they were accustomed. He had thought they always would reside at Camberworth.

How I wish I had not ceded all matters of finance to my uncle. Would that I could have inquired more into the state of my own financial dealings?

Thoughts of the men in her life drifted from one to the other and eventually tended towards Mr. Darcy. *He promised me he would always be there for me. Were those just words? Even if he spoke in sincerity, what right have I to lay claim to those words after having rejected his offer of marriage in favour of another?*

Though he did not know exactly what was afoot, Ben knew enough to know all was not right. The smile he so treasured in his mother's face, no longer shone in her eyes. It had been that way for a while. He sensed his mother was quite disheartened. Having children of his own age to play with was a novelty for young Ben. Unlike the twins, he liked his cousins very much. However, if his mother was not happy, then he was not happy; even though he tried his best to put on a cheerful face whenever he was in company, as did she.

Throughout each day, he would seek her out and endeavour to distract and amuse her from her steady perusal of the papers, as though she was in search of something. Though what that might be, he could not imagine.

"Are you happy, Mama?" Ben asked one day, as he brushed his tiny fingers along her face.

"Of course I am happy, Ben," she began, setting the papers aside to welcome him into her lap. "I shall always be happy, as long as I have you."

"But you do not seem very happy. You have not seemed happy since King Arthur left Camelot."

"You mean to say, since Mr. Darcy left Kent?" Elizabeth corrected her son.

"Yes exactly. You know Mr. Darcy lives here in town, do you not?"

"Indeed, it is a fact that I can hardly contest, seeing as how you have chosen to remind me almost every day since our own arrival in town."

"I miss him dreadfully. Surely, you must miss him as well," he declared wistfully. "What say you to the two of us calling on him in the morning?"

"Aside from the fact that it would be a grave impertinence for an unescorted single woman to call on a gentleman, I have no idea where he lives. I suspect his home is far, far away, way across the other part of town."

Ben scurried down from his mother's lap, "Wait here for a moment. I shall only be a short while."

Soon enough, Ben returned to the study and handed his mother the card his friend had given him. Elizabeth took the card in hand and looked it over. She made a mental note of the illustrious address. "Where did you get this?"

"Mr. Darcy gave it to me. You see, Mama, we have an invitation to call on him. He will not view it as impertinence, for you will not be unescorted. I will escort you!"

Elizabeth handed the card back to her son. "I grant you Mr. Darcy was simply being kind, and he offered his card to you as a keepsake. It would be most inappropriate for either of us to call on Mr. Darcy, for reasons I fear you are too young to comprehend."

Elizabeth suspected something was amiss, for the household was unusually quiet for that time of the day. "Where is Ben?" began she. "I am surprised not to have seen him since breakfast. He is not with his cousins," she informed her aunt, after having checked to find the other children in their rooms. "Would you happen to know of his whereabouts?"

"Did he not accompany you to the park?" Mrs. Gardiner asked, looking up from her mending. "When I did not find him with the other children earlier, I reckoned he must have been with you."

"No, he did not join me on my walk. I, too, was of the mind he was enjoying himself with his young cousins, and I did not wish to interrupt." The alarm that rang out in her voice was accompanied by a tightness in her chest. "My God, what if he has gone missing?"

"Lizzy, please calm down. He has to be around here somewhere. We shall find him," her aunt beseeched.

After an hour or so of searching the house from top to bottom, every room, every nook and cranny, and then some of his favourite out-of-door spots, Elizabeth's anxiety heightened. Ben's propensity to go off on his own while they resided at Longbourn Village had never been a matter of true concern, for he never ventured beyond the estate and was well-known enough that she was comfortable of his safety. Even his habit of venturing as far as Rosings Park during their stay in Hunsford had been of no great concern. It suddenly dawned on her that Ben had spoken of little else since learning they were coming to town than his desire to see Mr. Darcy. *Would he actually endeavour to discover Mr. Darcy on his own?*

Now panic-stricken, the prospect of her young child, not yet six years of age wandering the streets of London alone, struck her as forcefully as a bolt of lightning. The darkness that promised to blanket the sky did nothing to bring to mind notions of impropriety, or concerns for her own safety. Without giving a thought to anything, other than her son out there alone and afraid, Elizabeth donned her coat and headed for the door. She ran down the steps, and raced up the street, not bothering to stop and catch her breath until she had managed to hail a hackney coach.

Chapter 19

Anxiously, Elizabeth sat perched on the edge of the shabby, badly worn cushions with her eyes trained out of the windows of the rickety hackney coach. That way she felt as though she was doing something of meaning. Otherwise, she might surrender to the tears threatening to consume her, to cloud her judgement, and cause her to blame herself for her son's going missing.

Any sign of a young child on the passing street corners and she knew she would take flight from the coach without a second thought. Lurking about on poorly lit streets teaming with filth and garbage were hordes of nefarious characters—beggars, folks of ill-repute, and the like. Silent blessings abounded as none of them turned out to be small children.

Elizabeth's heart overflowed with despair. By comparison to all those people, she and Ben had enjoyed a sheltered and privileged life. *People actually live this way.* The prospect that her son, her heart and soul, was now lost amongst that world, alone and helpless, was too much to bear. Elizabeth cried.

Another long and uneventful day was shaping up to be yet another long and uneventful evening for Darcy. Rarely did he venture farther than his sister's establishment since his return from Kent. The Season was well underway, but rather than revel in it and take advantage of all the excitement it offered, Darcy felt an overwhelming sense of dread. Inevitably, when he felt that way, his thoughts tended quickly towards Elizabeth and her refusal of his hand.

Another Season meant another year on display for all the scheming mamas and their eager daughters. *Might any of them even compare to Elizabeth?* Darcy wondered. He doubted it was possible.

The rich echo of his austere butler's sonorous voice interrupted Darcy's reverie.

"Miss Caroline Bingley," he announced, as she sashayed into the room, adorned in the latest fashion of the Season and looking quite fetching, a fact that Darcy would not deny, if pressed.

The butler, who quickly made his escape from the room, had no sooner closed the door than Darcy crossed the room and opened it. He looked up and down the hall, before returning his attention to Caroline. "Where is your brother?"

"Am I my brother's keeper, Mr. Darcy?"

"I suppose not," he uttered, nonchalantly. He walked over to take a seat at his desk and commenced composing a letter to his steward, hardly giving a thought to her presence. He looked up to find not only had she closed the door, she also was hovering on the edge of his desk.

"There are several chairs about, if you would care to choose one," he offered.

"No thank you, sir. I am quite comfortable here," she waxed, coquettishly. Caroline eased herself atop his desk and proceeded to smooth the indiscernible wrinkles in her gown.

"I warn you, Caroline, if you do not take care to mind your reputation, I certainly shall not."

"That sounds promising."

Darcy yanked himself from his chair and stood to give Caroline a hand down from his desk. Leading her over to the settee, he urged, "Please, have a proper seat."

"If you insist, Mr. Darcy," she said. Caroline patted the empty space next to her. "Will you join me?"

"What brings you here, Caroline?" Darcy asked, ignoring her wanton invitation and moving instead to pour himself a drink. He took a long swig and eyed her intently.

"I was most eager to see you."

"You were? Whatever for? What is it you want?"

"Have I not made myself abundantly clear," she purred as she eased from her seat and flounced towards him.

"Please, not that again, Caroline."

"For Heaven's sake, Mr. Darcy, when do you intend to stop this game of cat and mouse?"

Darcy regarded her with an incredulous look, one that served to spur her on further. "You persist in leading me on. You speak to me as tenderly as you look at me. You even address me by my given name!" Caroline accused.

"That was only at YOUR insistence. I see now what a mistake that was. Surely, you must know there is no chance for a meaningful future between us, and I refuse to take advantage of you."

"No, I refuse to believe it. I am exactly what you need, if you would but give us a chance," Caroline exclaimed as she threw herself into his arms.

Gingerly, Darcy took both her slender wrists into his hands and tried to release her hold on his body. At that very moment, a knock at the door summoned his attention. Taking note of the compromising position, he urged her apart from his person. "Please, get a hold of yourself." Allowing a few seconds to pass for her to compose herself, he called out, "Enter!"

His command went unheeded. There was yet another knock. Annoyed, Darcy walked over and flung the door open. "What is it, Mr. Brooks?"

"Pardon me, Mr. Darcy. There is a young woman here to see you."

"Why did you not show her inside?"

"Your other guest insisted the two of you were not to be disturbed." Darcy looked at Caroline, silently questioning her presumptuousness with his staff. She did nothing to dispute the butler's claims but rather confirmed it with an unapologetic smirk.

Thoroughly exasperated, Darcy returned his attention to his butler. "Did the young lady give her name?"

"Yes. She is a Mrs. Carlton."

"Mrs. Carlton?" Darcy stepped into the grand hallway and espied Elizabeth standing a few feet away.

"Eliza—Mrs. Carlton, I beg your forgiveness. I pray you have not waited long. Please, come inside," he offered as he stepped aside to allow her to enter the room before him.

"I am so sorry to intrude, sir," she began immediately. "Your butler said you were not to be disturbed, but I insisted. Please forgive my intrusion."

"Do not concern yourself. You are always welcome in my home," he started. A closer look gave him to know she was merely putting on a brave face. Something was terribly wrong. "You remember Caroline, pardon, Miss Bingley."

Her initial astonishment was met with Caroline's unwelcoming countenance. Elizabeth immediately questioned if she had done the right thing in coming. The two women merely nodded at one another in feigned politeness.

Taking note of the tension, Darcy interjected, "Yes, well, Miss Bingley was just leaving."

"Was I, Mr. Darcy?"

"Indeed, you were." Refusing to grant her any cause to linger, perhaps to discover the purpose for Elizabeth's visit, he declared, "Come, I will see you to the door. I shall only be a moment, madam," said he to Elizabeth, before coaxing Caroline from the room.

Darcy returned a few moments later and apologised to Elizabeth that she was made to wait. The emotions she had fought to contain, after succumbing earlier in the hackney, now flowed with unbridled abandon. Through unrelenting tears and muddled words, she cried, "Mr. Darcy, it is Ben. He has left my aunt and uncle's home in Cheapside. It has been many hours since any one last saw him.

"He has been asking to visit you. My immediate thoughts were he may have tried to venture here on his own."

"I am sorry to say he is not here, but I will do all that is within my power to see you two reunited." Darcy took Elizabeth into his arms to offer her some measure of comfort. A moment later, he continued. "First, I will notify my staff to be on the lookout for his possible arrival, and then I will accompany you back to Cheapside. Pray to God he has returned by then, but if not, I will organise a rescue party to scour the city in search of him.

"Please have a seat, whilst I pour you a glass of wine. It might help you relax whilst I summon my carriage."

No sooner had Darcy helped Elizabeth to her seat, than the doors swung open, and in walked Colonel Fitzwilliam, with young Ben cradled in his arms.

He did not expect to see Elizabeth, of all people, there; yet, he whispered silent gratitude that she was. "Fear not, madam. The lad is merely sleeping. Exhausted, he wants for nothing more than a good night's rest in a comfortable bed."

"Praise the Lord," Elizabeth uttered, crossing the room faster than even she could fathom, to gaze at her son. She smoothed his dark, unruly curls from his forehead and placed a light kiss thereupon.

Darcy quickly joined his cousin and Elizabeth, and accepted Ben into his arms. "I cannot thank you enough. Wait here until I return; there is an urgent matter I wish to discuss with you once I have settled this little fellow in a comfortable bed upstairs."

Upon entering the hallway with Ben in his arms and Elizabeth by his side, he asked his butler to seek out his housekeeper so he might speak with her to arrange suitable accommodations for his guests and a nurse for Ben.

"Do not go to the trouble. I shall tend to my own son," Elizabeth cried.

"This is no trouble at all. It is no less than I would expect that you wish to see to your son. However, you too are tired. You have suffered a horrid ordeal. I expect you to get some rest, as well, once you are assured of your son's comfort."

After settling Ben into bed in a comfortable apartment directly across the hallway from his own, Darcy spoke to his housekeeper with directives on how best to accommodate his unexpected guests. He then went in search of his cousin, whom he found helping himself to his best brandy.

Upon accepting the offering of a generous drink, Darcy said, "I did not wish to alarm Elizabeth by being overly cautious, but I have taken the liberty of summoning my personal physician to take a look at Ben. It may be excessive, but it will certainly give me peace of mind.

"It may very well be only a matter of exhaustion. On the other hand, there is no telling what Ben may have experienced wandering about alone and vulnerable for the greater part of the day. I am unwilling to overlook anything where the child is concerned."

"I say that is a good idea. I did not wish to alarm her either, but the truth is some of the men in my regiment came across the child in a precarious situation." Richard went on to explain how Ben had been involved in a scuffle with three or four older boys who all ran off when his men came across them. "Ben appeared to have been unscathed. Nonetheless, you are correct, one never knows, especially seeing as how he did not even stir when I attempted to rouse him to quit the coach, and he remains asleep even now."

"How did your men know of a possible connection between you and the child?"

"As they were donned in their regimentals, young Ben asked if they knew of a Colonel Fitzwilliam. He even brandished your card to prove his connection to me by way of you."

"I am eternally grateful to your men. You must bring them around to my club, as my special guests, so I might reward them."

Richard was not apt to argue with Darcy's gesture of gratitude. They sealed the deal with a handshake. Darcy's thoughts immediately returned to Ben's health. On a more sombre note, Darcy continued, "Pray tell, how was Ben's behaviour when you and he first were united? Were there any signs of lethargy?"

"No, none at all. In fact, he was overly excited, giving me a full account of his adventure from way across town. He mentioned he had come from Cheapside, but he was unable to recollect which street or even the direction whence he had ventured. Judging from the location my men came across him, I would say he had walked at least a mile, possibly two. He was a little spitfire, racing about the quarters by all accounts, only to fall asleep once we entered the hackney coach to come here."

"Again, I am indebted to you. There is another matter I wish to discuss with you. I need you to grant me a favour."

"Would this have anything to do with Georgiana?"

"Indeed, you are correct in your assessment. I need her to come here to act as hostess in my home whilst Elizabeth and Ben are residing under my roof."

"It is only proper," Richard began, "but what of her engagement to Mr. Geoffrey Collins? Do you not imagine he will object to her being here?"

"That gentleman is the least of my concerns. I only pray that the arrangement has ended. I can think of no other way to explain her presence in town. However, answers to such questions can wait. Ben's safety is uppermost in my mind." As Richard prepared to take his leave, Darcy added, "There is also the matter of informing Elizabeth's family of what has occurred—a Mr. and Mrs. Gardiner. They reside in Cheapside, though I have no knowledge of which street."

"Enough said, I shall take care of it," Richard promised.

A quarter of an hour later, Darcy and the physician ascended the long staircase, headed for the room where Ben slept quietly. Darcy's soft knock went unanswered, so focused on her son was Elizabeth.

"Pardon me, Mrs. Carlton," Darcy spoke quietly as he approached Elizabeth's side. "I have asked my physician to have a look at Ben."

Elizabeth felt a wave of emotions threatening to overcome her. He placed his hand lovingly on her shoulder. "Do not be alarmed, please. After Ben's ordeal, I simply wanted to make certain nothing is overlooked, that he is perfectly safe and unharmed."

"Mrs. Carlton, I am Mr. Darcy's personal physician, Mr. Everett. If you will allow, I wish to examine your son."

Once again, Darcy placed a calming hand on Elizabeth's upper arm to reassure her, settling her almost immediately with his gentle touch as they stood by whilst the doctor examined Ben. His scrutiny of the young child's arms and legs revealed a minor scratch or two; no such evidence existed on his body. Though there were no clear signs of a head injury, the physician recalled Colonel Fitzwilliam's words that there had been a scuffle, upon his arrival. He suspected should the child have suffered a blow to the head or blow to the body, it might be the cause of his deep slumber.

In endeavouring to explain the nature of Ben's malady, the physician gave his prognosis and recommended quiet rest and vigilance.

"I appreciate your advice. I will adhere to every word you have said, most diligently. However, pray tell, how long shall my son remain asleep? When might we expect improvement?"

"There is a possibility your son may have suffered what is known as a concussion. With that being the case, then only time will tell. It might simply be a matter of hours. Prepare yourself madam. Though your son seems healthy and strong and he may recover quickly, there is a chance he may not."

Elizabeth went weak in the knees with that dire prognosis and was forced to rely on Darcy's arm for support.

"Please forgive me my bluntness, madam, Mr. Darcy."

"What must we do to guarantee he does awaken?" Darcy asked.

"Much the same as you are doing already, is my advice. Continue doing all you can in assuring his comfort."

The physician directed his attention to the nurse whom Darcy had hired, who by then had joined them at Ben's bedside. He gave further instructions for the next several days. She then went away long enough to gather the necessities for Ben's care. Taking over for the nurse, Elizabeth immediately reached for one of the moistened linen cloths. In spite of the silent tears etching their paths down her face, Elizabeth sat next to her son on the bed and dabbed the cloth on his forehead.

The early morning hours found Elizabeth at Ben's bedside. Her own eyes closed in silent prayer, curious eyes regarded the evidence of her fallen tears intently.

"Why are you crying, Mama?"

"Ben, you have awakened! Thank Heaven! I could not have imagined going on without you." She stood to climb next to him on the bed and gathered him in her arms. Ben then noticed a beaming Mr. Darcy, who, despite his eyes filled with unshed tears, smiled as widely as the joyous occasion warranted.

"King Arthur!" Ben shouted, nearly breaking away from his mother's embrace. Elizabeth held him tightly, not quite willing to relinquish the overwhelming bliss of her son in her arms.

Darcy knelt beside the bed and took Ben's hand in his own. "Yes, I am here. How are you feeling, my young friend?"

Ben smiled as widely as did Darcy and eagerly declared, "I am famished!"

Chapter 20

"Pardon me, ma'am. The Master wishes to know whether you will be dining downstairs, or if you would like a tray sent up. I am to sit with Master Ben, along with the nurse, should you wish to take your meal downstairs. I will be able to fetch you at once should you be needed."

Elizabeth did not respond straight-away, even though she looked intently at the timid young girl who barely spoke above a whisper. Everyone in Mr. Darcy's household had regarded her with such deference since the frightful incident involving her son began.

"I suppose I might join my host for breakfast. Do you know whether Mr. Darcy and I will be dining alone," she asked, wondering if his cousin Colonel Fitzwilliam might be joining them, as well.

"No ma'am. You will be dining with Mr. Darcy and his sister, Miss Darcy."

Elizabeth brushed her fingers through her unkempt hair. In the aftermath of the excitement of the previous day, she had given precious little thought to her appearance. Moving her hands to smooth her dress, she suddenly realised she wore the same clothes she had worn when she had arrived at Mr. Darcy's town-house the day previous. Her appearance was utterly lacking. It would not do to meet his sister in such a state, yet she had nothing more than the clothing on her back.

"What is your name?" Elizabeth thought to ask.

"I am Agatha, ma'am."

"Agatha, please tell Mr. Darcy I shall be delighted to join him for breakfast. I only require a half-hour or so." Elizabeth surmised it would take at least as long to attend to light toiletries and to freshen her attire.

"Certainly, ma'am, my Master figured you would be wishing for some time. I am to show you to your apartment."

Thinking the room he had arranged for Ben was more than adequate accommodation for the two of them for whatever time they would remain there, Elizabeth interjected, "My apartment?"

"Yes, ma'am, if you will follow me."

Elizabeth lightly placed her hand on Ben's shoulder and brushed a gentle kiss atop his head. The child did not stir. A reassuring nod from the nurse sent Elizabeth comfortably on her way.

Upon entering the grand apartment across the hall, two doors up, Elizabeth was convinced there had been some sort of mistake. After opening the door and quickly stepping aside to allow Elizabeth to pass, Agatha bid a hasty retreat down the long hallway. Decidedly feminine, the room was bright and airy, pleasingly decorated in a medley of soft pastels. Warm fragrances of spring filled the air. She noticed the large bouquet of freshly cut flowers in the vase on a beautiful mahogany vanity table.

"Pardon me, I fear I am in the wrong room," said Elizabeth to the young woman who busily arranged gowns in the wardrobe. Noticing them to be her very own, she said in surprise, "Are those my belongings?"

Caught unawares by her presence, the young woman immediately ceased her activities and rushed to greet Elizabeth at the doorway, where she had remained standing.

"Yes, ma'am," she eagerly spoke whilst bobbing politely. "It is my pleasure to meet you. I am Hannah. I am to be your new maid."

Incredulous, Elizabeth repeated, "My new maid?"

"Yes, ma'am, I have taken the liberty of preparing your bath and laying your clothes out for this morning."

"Thank you Hannah, but you need not go to the trouble. I am able to fend for myself."

"It is no trouble at all, ma'am. It is my job as well as my pleasure to attend you."

Downstairs in the breakfast room, Darcy, Georgiana, and Mrs. Annesley, were enjoying coffee and hot tea whilst waiting for Elizabeth to join them.

"You must allow me to thank you once again, dear Georgiana, for agreeing to stay here in my home and act as my hostess whilst Mrs. Carlton and her young son are in residence."

"I am delighted to be of service to you," Georgiana affirmed with good humour for the third time since her arrival that morning.

"So, how did you find Mrs. Carlton's relatives when you arrived to retrieve some of our guests' belongings?"

"I must say the Gardiners seemed a bit taken aback by the lateness of the hour and our cousin's take charge manner. On the whole, I believe they found my presence somewhat reassuring. Above all, they were delighted to know Ben had come to no severe harm, and both he and his mother were safe."

"At the risk of being crass, how would you describe the Gardiners? What of their home, their living conditions? Does it seem an ideal situation for the Carltons?"

"Brother, I am afraid you raise questions which I am quite unprepared to address. I have yet to meet the Carltons! Mrs. Gardiner did speak of their four small children and how they were all distressed over the news of Ben's disappearance. Oh, I met Miss Bennet, also. She resides with the Gardiners, as well."

"It must be very crowded. Would you say the Gardiners' home in Cheapside is suitable for four adults, five children, and who knows how many servants?"

"I can hardly say, Brother. I suspect you would rather suffer anything than to see the Carltons return to Cheapside when it comes time for them to leave here." Georgiana looked up at him as she sipped her tea, her brows arching. "How would you feel about their being invited as extended guests in my home?"

"You would do that for me?"

"I would do anything in the world for you, Brother. Have you not always felt the same in regards to me?" She reached over and gently laid her hand on his. "Besides, it is no sacrifice on my part. I would wish for nothing more than to become acquainted with the two people who have captured your heart."

Some moments later, Elizabeth was shown into the room. Darcy immediately stood and greeted her with a warm smile.

"I am delighted to see you this morning," he expressed, as though the two of them had not separated mere hours earlier after their nightlong vigil by Ben's bedside. "Thank you for agreeing to join us for breakfast. I wish to introduce you to my sister, Miss Georgiana Darcy."

By then, Georgiana was standing directly beside her brother, in front of Elizabeth. Both ladies smiled brightly and curtseyed.

"Miss Darcy, it is my pleasure to meet you."

"The pleasure is all mine," Georgiana responded. "Come, let us have breakfast whilst we become acquainted with each other." She wrapped her arm around Elizabeth's and proceeded towards the table. "Allow me to introduce you to Mrs. Annesley."

At one point, during a rare lull in the conversation between the two younger women, Darcy explained to Elizabeth his sister would be staying at his town-house with them until Ben fully recovered. Though Elizabeth enjoyed meeting his sister, she was rather uncomfortable with the notion Darcy had invited her there with the expectation she and Ben would be guests at his home for any extended length of time. Knowing how this would look to her family and others once they got wind of it, she had no intention of compounding her transgression of a broken engagement by taking up residence with the one man her former intended had marked as the reason for the alienation of her affections.

Elizabeth had no time to speak freely with Darcy after break-fast. As much as she wanted to express her gratitude on the one hand, on the other, she had some concerns with the manner in which he had taken it on himself to make decisions regarding her immediate future. As disconcerting as she felt his actions to have been, resolving them could wait for proper consideration and discussion. Not only did she suffer a strong desire to return to her son's bedside as soon as could be, Darcy was just as eager to look in on Ben, as well.

Darcy and Elizabeth arrived in Ben's room and found him sitting up in bed. Mr. Everett was just completing his examination.

"How is our patient this morning?" Darcy asked.

"Are you asking me, King Arthur?" Ben interjected.

"Well, no Sir Lancelot, for I have no doubt of what your response might be." Darcy spoke from experience. Both he and Elizabeth had remained with Ben at least an hour after he woke before dawn that morning. At that time, Ben had insisted there was nothing at all wrong with him in one breath, then immediately returned to a deep slumber when Darcy and Elizabeth took turns reading to him.

Dr. Everett, who by then had completed his examination said, "Our young patient is not completely recovered just yet. I detected a slight bump to his head that had gone unnoticed last evening. It is no cause for alarm, as I suspect he is quite beyond any danger. However, I urge a longer period of rest before he resumes his normal routine."

Elizabeth sat on the bed beside Ben, "It will be a while before your next adventure, young man."

Darcy walked into the hallway with his physician. "Have you any lingering worries where the child's health is concerned?"

"As I said last night, he is healthy and strong. I now add to the prognosis that he is quite vibrant and alert. Allow another day or two to pass, at which point you should have no reason at all for further concern."

Whilst Darcy accompanied his physician down the stairs, Elizabeth spoke to Ben about what all had occurred.

"Ben, you gave me quite a scare yesterday. Why on earth did you take it upon yourself to leave my aunt and uncle's home unattended?"

"Mama, I did not mean to alarm you. I went in search of Mr. Darcy because I wanted the smile to return to your face. Ever since our arrival at Cheapside, you have seemed very sad. I hated to see you so. I reckoned if I brought Mr. Darcy back with me, you would smile once again."

"Ben, what you did was wrong. You caused a great many people to worry."

"I am sorry, Mama. Nevertheless, was it not worth the trouble? Are you not happy to be here?"

"Ben, that is neither here nor there. We will remain here only for another day or two at the most."

"No," Ben adamantly expressed, "I do not want to be parted from Mr. Darcy again!"

"Ben, it is not proper—" she began. A light knock on the door that had been left slightly ajar interrupted what she had meant to be a stern speech. Thinking Mr. Darcy was returning, Elizabeth spoke without diverting her eyes from her son, "Please enter."

"Pardon me, Elizabeth. My brother mentioned your son had awakened," said Georgiana as she approached Ben's bedside. "I am most eager to meet the young man who my brother professes to be the bravest young knight in all the land and his dear friend."

If Elizabeth could have used but one word to describe her young son at that moment, she would have chosen *smitten*. Ben, who heretofore never looked at anyone of the opposite sex, who was not also his family, except perhaps to find fault, bore an expression of complete awe. The golden tresses framing Georgiana's face lent a majestic glow to her graceful mien. Having never seen a true-to-life angel, surely he felt himself to be staring into the face of one such heavenly creature now.

Elizabeth happily made the introductions. "Ben, I would like you to meet Miss Georgiana Darcy."

Georgiana curtseyed, "I am happy to meet you, young sir. My brother has told me so much about you."

"You are Mr. Darcy's sister! He has spoken of you to me, as well. I am delighted to meet you, Miss Darcy."

"Indeed, but you must call me Miss Georgiana. I hope to become acquainted with you very well over the coming months."

"Georgiana, you are very kind," Elizabeth began. "As I was just telling Ben, we will soon return to my uncle's home in Cheapside. I do not imagine we shall have many opportunities to see one another once that occurs."

Georgiana witnessed the dismay in Ben's eyes on hearing his mother's words. The younger woman took Elizabeth's hand in hers and said, "Elizabeth, I am sympathetic to the notion that you may not wish to remain in my brother's home much longer, but I hope those sensibilities do not include my home, as well. It would mean the world to me if you and Ben would be guests in my home at least through the end of the Season.

"I am not yet out in Society, but I imagine there are many pleasant diversions we all might enjoy."

Ben's face glowed brightly with enthusiasm. "May we accept Miss Georgiana's invitation, Mama?"

"May I have time to consider your kind offer and its implications before I respond yes or no? I have concerns that I must first address," Elizabeth said.

"Of course, take as much time as you would like. But mind you, nothing would please me more, nor would anything bring greater joy to my brother, for that matter, than for you to say yes. It would be an opportunity for you to get to know both of us better, would it not?"

Later that day, Darcy came across Elizabeth in the library. She was stretched out on the couch, an opened book in hand, soundly asleep. He watched for a moment, taking in the sight of her, her slow even breaths causing her breasts to rise and fall with a gentle motion. He found himself unable to resist the opportunity to approach her and attend to her comfort. The gentle pressure of his removing the book from her hand stirred her. Upon sitting upright, she recalled herself to her surroundings after a moment or two passed.

"I am sorry to have disturbed your peaceful slumber. I know you must be exhausted. Have you had any rest in bed at all? How do you find your room?"

"I should be begging your forgiveness for my unseemly behaviour," she expressed tentatively. "What must your staff think of my falling asleep in your library?"

"It has been a harrowing ordeal for us all. My staff would never think unkindly of you. Besides, you are welcome to fall asleep *anywhere* in my home, at any time."

"Are you flirting with me, Mr. Darcy?" Elizabeth asked, smiling fondly in reminiscence of their irrepressible affection for each other.

"I am afraid you have that effect on me," he declared unabashedly. He seated himself beside her and took her hand in his. On a more serious note, he continued. "Despite how this all came about, you must allow me to tell you how delighted I am to have you and Ben here with me. As much as I would wish to avoid any unpleasant conversations, I must know how this came to be. When last we spoke, you were determined to go forth with your plans to marry Geoffrey Collins. Shall I expect him to barge through my door at any moment demanding what is rightfully his?"

"For better or for worse, that ship has sailed. You see, Mr. Darcy, I am no longer engaged to marry Mr. Collins."

His heart swelled with hope. "Does this mean—" Darcy optimistically began, only to be interrupted by Elizabeth.

"I am afraid it means nothing as far as our situation is concerned, Mr. Darcy," said Elizabeth. Looking away from the sight of the hurt she had inflicted on him, once again, so reminiscent of the look she witnessed their last time together in Kent, she continued. "I am sorry if this causes you pain, Mr. Darcy. I shall be eternally grateful to you for all you have done for both Ben and me. You mean the world to Ben. You mean a great deal to me, as well. It is just that—" unable to continue, Elizabeth stood and moved away from Darcy. She walked towards the window and looked out, paying no attention at all to the sight beyond.

"It is just what?" Darcy approached her from behind and spoke tenderly.

"Mr. Collins accused me of ending the engagement because of an unhealthy and unrequited desire for you."

"You know better than that, Elizabeth," Darcy said, as he gently took a hold of her arm and guided her to face him.

"Well, yes, but I am unable to swear his words are wholly without merit. I confess, he was all wrong for Ben and me, just as you foretold. However—" Elizabeth lost her voice in the wake of Darcy's skilled fingers cupping her chin, willing her to look deeply into his piercing blue eyes.

"Did he harm you or Ben?"

"No...not physically," Elizabeth said, tentatively. Darcy stood mere inches apart from her...so close, the faint scent of lavender brought to mind the first time he had held her in his arms.

"Yet, he wounded you deeply with his words. I understand, I can only imagine the harsh things he might have said to you, especially regarding my intentions. However, surely you must know the truth. I am in love with you. And just in case you have forgotten, may I remind you, gently?" Darcy feathered soft kisses along Elizabeth's cheek that concluded with a gentle brush against her lips. Past spoken words, ever-present hushed thoughts to the contrary, she yearned for the pleasure of his touch. The ensuing cessation of his lips touching hers and the absence of the gentle stroke of his fingertips on her chin prompted the opening of her eyes.

"Have you given Georgiana's invitation any further consideration?" Darcy asked as he gradually moved a respectable distance apart and laced his fingers behind his back.

Before Elizabeth could respond to what had happened, he continued, "I want Ben and you to remain close to me whilst you decide your next step. There is no logical reason for the two of you to be uncomfortable in an already crowded house when Georgiana has more than enough room to accommodate you in a manner befitting Ben and you."

"Did you tell your sister to extend the invitation, Mr. Darcy?" Elizabeth challenged, endeavouring to mask the overwhelming effect of his deep, loving voice on her composure.

"No, it was her own idea. I thought only to have her here to make you more at ease, and hopefully, more willing to stay. Nonetheless, I could not have been more pleased at her initiative. I freely admit my motives are entirely selfish. I want you and Ben always to be a part of my life. You know this. Be that as it may, I will not press you into doing my bidding," he promised. "My mind will be eased considerably knowing you and Ben are safe and comfortable and as near to me as my sister's home.

In no time at all, Darcy had rearranged his life to accommodate his new guests by doing everything in his power to see to their comfort and satisfaction. He wished he might never have to be separated from Elizabeth again. However, the reality of the situation was such that they would be parted before long. Ben had recovered fully after a healthful stay in bed. In but a day or so, Elizabeth and Ben would be obliged to remove to Georgiana's establishment.

One evening, both having bid Ben a pleasant night's sleep, as had been Darcy and Elizabeth's routine ever since her arrival, they stood in the hallway just outside Ben's door.

"Is this goodnight for the two of us, as well?" Darcy asked, hoping Elizabeth might be amenable to the true, unspoken nature of his appeal. One too many innocent brushes of his hand against hers over the course of the evening and chance glimpses at one another whilst turning the pages of Ben's night-time storybook had sparked natural curiosity that begged for satisfaction.

Elizabeth's stomach fluttered. Her silent voice screamed inside, *I wish this night might never end!* "What do you have in mind?"

Darcy conveyed his intentions, not with words, but rather with not so subtle sweeping looks—her eyes, her lips. At length, he bestowed an intimate touch upon her face and was about to follow the earlier path of his eyes with his fingers—if that went well, perhaps even his lips. Elizabeth gasped. His gentle touch was agreeable in every way. She closed her eyes as her imagination of what was to come leapt.

A faint cry interrupted the anticipated bliss. "Mama—" echoed softly through the closed-door.

Elizabeth opened her eyes and read in Darcy's some measure of dismay. "I must see what my son wants," she whispered.

"Must you?"

"I must."

"Of course, you must," he conceded, a bit of reluctance evidenced by his tone. Darcy relinquished his touch. Elizabeth gradually increased the physical distance between them, even if not the emotional embrace, for she did not turn her back towards him until the last possible moment. Upon entering the room, she unhurriedly pushed the door shut with her eyes settled upon Darcy, who remained standing in the same spot with a look of longing as telling as was hers.

Elizabeth enfolded her hands behind her back and rested against the door for a moment. *Breathe*, she reminded herself before going to Ben's bedside.

Chapter 21

Geoffrey Collins could not have been more pleased with himself than he was of late, having visited with Mr. Bennet at Longbourn to give his own account of the broken engagement. What was more, having assured Mr. Bennet he bore no ill will at all towards the Bennet family, he subsequently had arrived in Cheapside armed with a letter from the old patriarch to his eldest daughter Jane.

Therein, her father's words had urged her to receive its bearer with an open mind and to listen to all he had to say. The carefully crafted correspondence told of how Elizabeth had wounded Mr. Collins most egregiously, his only true failing being that he was not the gentleman from Derbyshire, whose name was not to be mentioned. He had spoken of Elizabeth's stubbornness and how she was determined to thwart him at every turn. Though he had made clear Elizabeth would never be received at Longbourn, he had offered some solace, at least to his way of thinking. There was yet another chance for the Bennet family to maintain ties to their beloved home always.

Geoffrey Collins and Jane were returning from an afternoon stroll in the park, when Elizabeth descended from an elegant carriage, followed by her maid. The tension in the air was as thick as the fog hovering in the sky. With all the forbearance of civility that he could muster, the gentleman merely nodded at Elizabeth.

Elizabeth made no secret of her surprise in seeing him there, of all places. Collins and Jane stopped a few yards away. Elizabeth witnessed the cordiality between the two and the manner in which he looked on her sister. *Does he suppose he might cause me to be jealous?* Elizabeth asked herself, as if she truly cared. Soon enough he walked back towards the direction whence he had come, and Jane approached Elizabeth. In silent agreement, the two sisters ascended the steps.

Once inside, Elizabeth seized the opportunity to determine what was afoot. "What on earth was Mr. Collins doing here, Jane? I can only surmise he must have come to see me, but in light of the manner in which we parted, I can hardly imagine what his purpose might have been. I am sorry you had to endure his presence in my stead. Nonetheless, you seem to have managed it fairly well."

Jane regarded her younger sister with a disbelieving stare, one Elizabeth did not discern as she retreated from the window. "Indeed, Lizzy," Jane responded. She sat on the couch and picked up where she had left off in her sewing. "With this being the third day in a row he has called—I would agree. I *manage* it exceedingly well"

Elizabeth considered her sisters words. *Mr. Collins has been stalking about for the past three days.* "What are you saying, Jane? That he has come all this way to see you."

"I am sorry if that displeases you," uttered she, seemingly absorbed in the task before her with far greater concentration than was warranted.

"Then, you believe all this has had nothing at all to do with me?" Elizabeth asked. She had always considered her eldest sister a bit naïve in such matters as this. Her opinion of Jane was fixed by experience; she thought Jane believed everyone was inherently good.

"I confess he has acquainted me with knowledge of your behaviour whilst in Kent, confidences you saw no need to share," Jane said as a matter of fact. Her arched tone suggested anything but naivety. She seemed rather persuaded towards Mr. Collins's point of view.

Elizabeth at that moment wished she had been more forthcoming with her eldest sister, upon her arrival at Cheapside. Then she might not have suffered the disillusioned, disdainful looks and the unspoken accusations.

"Jane, I trust you know me better than to believe the words of a scorned man," Elizabeth pleaded.

Jane sat her work aside and regarded her sister intently. "I am afraid, Lizzy, your behaviour of late is more than enough to persuade me that the gentleman has legitimate cause for disdain."

"Jane, I do not understand your meaning." Elizabeth sat and reached for her sister's hand. "What have you to accuse me of, that you might believe anything Mr. Collins might say against me?"

Jane pulled her hand away. "Lizzy, surely, you must see how this looks to all of us. Did you not run to Mr. Darcy the first chance you saw? Are you not living in his sister's home? Did you not arrive in a fine carriage befitting a gentleman of immense wealth?"

"I ask you, Jane, not to believe what your eyes and ears tell you, but rather that which you must know in your heart to be true."

Jane said nothing. Elizabeth continued to reason with her sister. "Mr. Collins is determined my life should be miserable, out of spite and contempt. He is only courting you as a means to get back at me!"

"Of course, Lizzy, why else would a gentleman, as handsome and as decent as Mr. Collins, wish to spend time with *me*?" Jane asked, her voice teeming with sarcasm Elizabeth theretofore had never heard fall from her lips.

"Jane, that is not what I meant, and you very well know it."

"I know nothing of the sort. There is a matter, however, upon which you need to be enlightened regarding Mr. Collins. He has assured me he sees the error in choosing you initially and had he to do it all again, his choice surely would have been different. He has asked for, and subsequently received, permission to court me."

"You cannot be serious, Jane!"

"Indeed, I am. I am six and twenty with no hope and no prospects. Moreover, Lizzy, I am afraid." Jane looked about her uncle and aunt's drawing room with a look of longing, a measure of regret. "This is not the life I wish for, to be the governess and nurse to my cousins. I want a life of my own, my own home and children. If Mr. Collins asks—nay, *when* Mr. Collins asks, I will accept him, Lizzy. You have said nothing of his behaviour as a gentleman which gives me cause to believe he would not be a good husband. As you have said yourself, he is an honourable and respectable man. There is no reason at all I should not be as happy with him as with any other gentleman."

What Elizabeth wished for most upon her return to Mayfair that afternoon, was a relaxing evening. It was not to be. Fairly bubbling with excitement, Georgiana raced to her side as soon as she entered the bright, airy drawing room, eager to share her news.

"Elizabeth, you will never guess what took place during your absence!" Georgiana exclaimed.

Elizabeth could not help being heartened by her warm reception, so different from the frosty parting with her own sister. "I can hardly imagine, but judging by your enthusiasm, I suppose it was of considerable delight."

"Oh yes! My aunt, Lady Ellen, called," Georgiana said. "She was eager to make your acquaintance. She has invited us to dine in her home this evening."

Somehow, the prospect of meeting Darcy's aristocratic relatives was not met with quite the same degree of enthusiasm in Elizabeth as shown by Georgiana. However, she saw how much it meant to her hostess, and Elizabeth did not want to dampen her anticipation. "What sort of affair do you envision? Will it be small and intimate or an elaborate dinner party?"

"My aunt's dinner parties are never small and intimate, especially during the height of the Season. Even on such short notice, it is bound to be a grand occasion. Because I am not yet out, I am not often invited. When presented with an opportunity to attend, I always look forward to it with such delight. My brother even encourages my attendance tonight, as long as there is no occasion to dance or the like."

"You are not allowed to dance, even at your aunt and uncle's home?" Elizabeth asked, thinking of her sisters, the youngest out at the age of fifteen.

"No, my brother says I must wait until my coming out."

Elizabeth could hardly be surprised by that particular declaration. During the past weeks, she often had chided Mr. Darcy on his tendency to arrange things for his own convenience. "You are nearly eighteen. When is your coming out?"

"Next Season!" Georgiana eagerly exclaimed. "I can hardly bear to wait. It is my greatest wish that you will be here to share it with me."

"It is difficult to predict with any certitude where Ben and I might be this time next year, Georgiana," Elizabeth spoke wistfully.

"Are you quite certain of that Elizabeth? I am sure my brother might have something entirely different to say on that topic. Ben, too, for that matter," Georgiana expressed with some confidence.

"It is complicated, Georgiana." Endeavouring to steer the conversation towards innocuous grounds, Elizabeth said, "Speaking of Ben, where is he? Is he with Mrs. Annesley?"

"No, he is out with my brother. He also called whilst you were out. He had hoped to accompany us to an exhibition this afternoon."

Elizabeth thought of all Darcy had done to see to their entertainment of late. Not a day went by that he did not call on them to accompany them to the park, a museum, or even outings to one of Georgiana's many favourite shops. Elizabeth marvelled at how his attention towards Ben and her, equalled that towards his sister. It seemed there was nothing he did not do himself to see to their pleasure. He was always on hand to share a bedtime story with Ben before tucking him in, and he often stayed to enjoy a late dinner with Georgiana and her.

"Will your brother dine at your aunt and uncle's home this evening, as well?" Elizabeth asked. She hoped.

Georgiana imparted a knowing smile. "I do not imagine he would miss it for the world, especially given you will be there."

Darcy and Ben had just finished their third game of chess. Ben was disheartened. He made no attempt to hide his dismay. He had yet to best his older friend, after so many attempts.

Darcy brushed the unruly curls atop his young friend's head. "Do not look so discouraged, Ben. Surely, you cannot expect to excel at the game when you have only been introduced over the past week."

"I am terribly frustrated when, try as I might, you always gain the upper hand."

"You would not want to win because I simply allowed you to, now would you? What would be the fun in that?"

"I believe it would be good fun regardless, as long as I should win," Ben expressed truthfully.

"Then, I encourage you to practise. You will never be truly accomplished, unless you practise," Darcy uttered the words reminiscent of his aunt, Lady Catherine, before he realised what he was saying. "Practise every chance you find. A brave knight such as yourself is sure to master this game in due time.

Ben, who had been slumping in the chair opposite his friend, sat up straight upon taking in those words. "I will do as you say. I will practise each and every day, and very soon it will be me who yells 'Checkmate'! Will that not be fun for a change?"

"I eagerly await the day, young sir," Darcy assured him.

Ben looked at Darcy intently for a long moment. "Will we always be together?"

"I believe we shall," Darcy said, "in one way or another. I promise I will do everything within my power to make it so."

Darcy stood from his chair and stretched his long legs. Ben mirrored Darcy. "Now let us return to Miss Georgiana's home. Your mother will have returned by now, and is probably wondering where you are. We must not give her any cause to worry about you."

From time to time, Darcy was obliged to be seen amongst society. It was expected, after all, of young men of his station. Growing more confident with each passing day that it was merely a matter of time before he would persuade Elizabeth to put her own interests before all else and accept his hand, he generally was amenable to an occasional appearance at private dinner parties, the theatre, and a private ball or two. Besides, it would give rise to the perception he was still on the market, and thus temper any speculations he enjoyed a secret engagement, or worse, a scandalous affair with the beautiful young widow who resided in his sister's home.

A heightened measure of anticipation he normally did not suffer with the prospect of an evening amongst society, engrossed him that night. It was not that he was to dine at the Matlocks, but rather, Elizabeth would be there. For the first time in their acquaintance, he would be able to engage her amongst those he considered his equal in consequence.

Darcy arrived at Lord and Lady Matlocks' home in time enough to espy his uncle escorting Elizabeth from the room, arm in arm. Knowing his uncle as he did, he fretted that they had not returned after a quarter-hour had passed. He set off to locate them and rescue Elizabeth from what he by now suspected to be a verbal skirmishing.

Darcy was too late in seeing the path he had chosen would lead him directly past Caroline. *What on earth am I to do now?* He had no one to blame but himself. He wanted to kick himself, for it was at his insistence some years ago that the Bingleys were even received by the Matlocks. His cousin excluded, the Fitzwilliams were a proud lot, not known to associate easily with those who had ties to trade. Ever since his ultimatum to his aunt and uncle to receive the Bingleys or risk alienating him, it seemed he could not go anywhere that Caroline did not also go. It was as though his aunt was punishing him, for she seemed to delight in Caroline's antics to ensnare him and his desperate attempts to avoid being snared by anyone, especially Caroline.

Caroline's eyes were trained directly upon him from the moment he entered the room. Timing his imminent approach, she placed herself directly in his path. "Is it true what I hear, Mr. Darcy? Is Eliza Carlton living with your dearest sister? Moreover, is it true she has a son?" She was standing much too close to him, for his taste. All attempts on Darcy's part to put a respectable distance between the two of them were in vain.

"Mrs. Carlton is a guest in my sister's home, and yes, she has a young son."

"How very interesting!" Caroline raised her fan to her face. "Rumour has it she is something more than a friend of your dear sister," she purred.

"Of what concern is any of this to you, Miss Bingley?" He spoke in a cool tone meant to discourage her from any attempt to disparage Elizabeth.

"Seeing how you practically threw me out of your home the evening she arrived, I would say this is a matter of great concern to me. You treated me abominably. Have I not always been welcome in your home, Mr. Darcy?"

"Given your propensity to come and go at your leisure, with nary an invitation, you seem to think so."

"Unless I am mistaken, Eliza Carlton arrived at your doorstep without an invitation, as well," Caroline opined. She had not forgiven him for his ill-treatment.

"It is quite different with Mrs. Carlton, as you very well know."

"I certainly know how it seems," Caroline spoke in a hushed tone, for his ears alone. "Come now, Mr. Darcy, you are fooling no one with this subterfuge. Why did you choose Eliza Carlton, of all people? Was I not here first? What has she that I have not?"

Darcy leaned down and spoke to her in a hushed tone, so close the warmth of his breath sent tremors along her spine. "My heart...." Having instigated the response that caused no one any harm but her, she stood foolishly by and watched as he walked away.

Being the determined old rogue he was, Lord Matlock was as eager for the combining of the estates of Rosings and Pemberley as was any of the Fitzwilliam family. To his way of thinking, it would only enhance his own overly inflated opinion of himself as the powerful patriarch of the Fitzwilliam dynasty. It did not sit well with him at all that his sister, Lady Catherine, seemed resigned to Darcy's declaration that a marriage to his cousin Anne would never be.

Two things had bothered him most upon first hearing of the beautiful young newcomer. Who was the young woman who had taken up residence in his nephew's home? His nephew could pretend all he wished that he had not taken on the role as the young woman's protector. In the end, he and he alone authorised the goings-on in his sister's establishment. Moreover, what of the young boy his nephew had been seen with on numerous occasions? Might these two possibly be his mistress and his illegitimate child?

Those two mysteries were solved immediately upon Georgiana's arrival. The truth behind his niece's guest was not nearly as nefarious as he had envisioned. The young lady who accompanied his niece could not possibly have been the mother of his nephew's *supposed* child. She was the young widow his sister Catherine had spoken of in her missive. Still, he was determined to carry his point. On the pretence of escorting Elizabeth to another room where there were other guests to whom he wished to introduce her, he informed Georgiana he wanted to steal her lovely friend for a moment.

Alone in his study, he offered Elizabeth a glass of wine, which she politely declined. He poured himself a stiff drink and took a seat behind his desk. Elizabeth sat down in a large, hard leather chair.

"So you are Mrs. Elizabeth Carlton. My sister, Lady Catherine de Bourgh, spoke of you in one of her letters. She made your acquaintance during your recent stay in Kent, if I am not mistaken."

"Indeed, you are correct."

"Capital! When I first learnt that my young niece had welcomed a beautiful young widow and her son into her home, I feared you might be someone else entirely. I am glad my initial suspicions are unfounded," Lord Matlock confessed. He spoke of his concern that Darcy might have fathered an illegitimate child, but Elizabeth could not have suspected that. "Lady Catherine mentioned in her letter that your son is the sole heir of her late friend, Mrs. Sara Carlton."

Elizabeth offered no confirmation. The more he spoke, the more he reminded her of the grand lady. She suspected he needed no encouragement when it came to letting his sentiments be known.

He continued, "Lady Catherine also mentioned you had an arrangement with her vicar's older brother to be united in marriage, one that ended abruptly. However, she did not inform me of the details regarding your broken engagement."

"Why would anyone have informed you, my lord? What concern is any of that of yours?"

Not one to be put off so easily, the earl insisted, "I should say it is of great concern, especially if it has anything to do with my nephew and the fact that you are now living in one of his homes."

"If Mr. Darcy does not object to my being a guest in his sister's home, why should you?"

"If you were merely a guest of my niece's, I would not be troubled, I assure you. You and I both know better than that, do we not?"

"I have no idea what you mean, I am sure."

Lord Matlock slammed his glass to the table, forcefully. "I will not play games with you, young lady. You are residing in my niece's—no, my nephew's home because it suits him to have you there!"

Her courage increased with his attempts to intimidate her. Elizabeth declared, "Think what you like, Lord Matlock. I am a guest in *your* home because your wife invited me here tonight. I doubt she invited me here to be subjected to such an unwarranted attack." Elizabeth spoke in haughty disdain, intended to match her host's.

"I am used to making my opinions known, young woman. Heaven only knows what my nephew must be thinking in allowing you to share his sister's home. Perhaps it is a part of his body, other than his head, with which he is thinking, madam. You are as beautiful as any other woman with whom I have ever known him to associate. The one thing you lack and all the women before you possessed, is a fortune.

"Even so, should you possess all the wealth in the world, I would not condone a marriage between my nephew and you. He is intended for my niece!"

"I am afraid you are greatly misinformed if you believe that to be true. Perhaps it is your nephew with whom you should be speaking."

At that moment, the subject of their discussion walked into the room. Completely ignoring his uncle, Darcy strolled directly to Elizabeth. "Mrs. Carlton, how delighted I am to see you this evening."

Elizabeth stood to return his greeting. "Indeed, the pleasure is all mine, Mr. Darcy." In a bold show of defiance towards Lord Matlock, Elizabeth offered Darcy her hand. He bowed before her and bestowed a warm kiss.

"I see you have met my illustrious uncle. I apologise I was not here, as I might have had the honour of introducing you, myself. I trust he has been a *gracious* host," Darcy said in a mocking tone, intended to vex his dear uncle.

Lord Matlock raised himself from his chair and baulked at his nephew's impudence. "Now, now, Darcy!" he exclaimed. "How would you expect me to comport myself towards a guest in my home?"

Darcy ignored his uncle's rebuke. With all his attentions focused on Elizabeth, he said, "If you will grant me the privilege, I look forward to escorting you to dinner."

"You are very kind, sir," she responded. "If the two of you will pardon me, I find myself in need of refreshment. Shall I see you in the drawing room, Mr. Darcy?"

"Yes, madam, I shall be there shortly."

Upon Elizabeth's quitting the room, Darcy and Lord Matlock wasted no time at all in speaking their minds.

"Your behaviour was uncalled for, Darcy," the earl raged bitterly.

"The look on Mrs. Carlton's face upon my entering the room told me otherwise, my lord."

"I am the head of this family, young man! I have every right to know more of the young woman who has taken up residence with my niece!"

"As long as you regard Mrs. Carlton with respect, I shall have no cause for concern that you might wish to know her better. However, I will not allow you to demean her in any way, as you are so wont to do."

"Respect, you say!" He spat the words. "Does the fact that you appear to have your mistress residing under the same roof as your sister not constitute blatant disrespect towards Georgiana and the rest of the Fitzwilliam family?"

"I will not be accountable for any misapprehensions you needlessly suffer regarding the nature of my affiliation with Mrs. Carlton. My intentions are honourable. I would marry her today, if she would but say yes."

"I am not the only one who suffers this *'misapprehension,'* and you would do well to know that, regardless of whether or not your intentions are honourable! You very well may intend to marry the woman; however, you are not yet married—nor will you ever be if I have any say in the matter.

"How fortunate it is then, for all concerned, you do not have a say!"

Darcy and Elizabeth were not seated close enough to each other at dinner as to make it possible for them to converse, nor were they close enough that he might catch any of her conversations with those around her. The ease with which she engaged her dinner companions and the spark that shone brightly in her fine eyes, gave him to know she was enjoying the evening. He was pleased. If only Caroline had not been seated directly across from him, he might have enjoyed the evening too. Would his aunt ever cease in punishing him?

Mindful of his wish that Georgiana not remain in society any longer than was warranted, Darcy saw to it she returned home almost immediately after the meal, along with Elizabeth and Mrs. Annesley. He had remained long enough to enjoy port with the gentlemen, departing his uncle's home shortly thereafter.

Soon after his arrival at Georgiana's residence, she excused herself for the evening, thereby affording Darcy and Elizabeth time alone. Darcy and Elizabeth sat opposite each other on facing couches. More space was between them than either of the two would have wished, but warranted if they were to keep up their tacit agreement of a chaste relationship.

Elizabeth spoke to him of her pleasure at having been received favourably by so many, including his aunt, Lady Matlock, on the one hand, and her general displeasure with the scrutiny she had received from his uncle, on the other.

"Elizabeth, I apologise for my uncle's deplorable treatment. I assure you that I will make certain he is on his best behaviour when next you two meet."

"It is not solely your uncle, I am afraid. Others uttered thinly veiled, snide remarks regarding my association with you and your sister; Miss Bingley amongst them."

"What is your greatest concern? People will think what they want, will they not? You know the truth. What concerns have you of what others so wholly unconnected with you might think?"

"If only it were so. My dearest sister Jane has been keeping company with Mr. Collins. Can you imagine that? It seems he is courting her. He may very well ask for her hand in marriage. From all indications, she is quite prepared to accept."

"I can think of worse things than that," he mumbled, nonchalantly.

"Can you Mr. Darcy? What do you suppose might be worse than my sister marrying Mr. Collins?" Elizabeth challenged.

"He might have married YOU!"

Elizabeth was not amused. She rested her head in her hands. "Would that I could get away from it all," she uttered wearily. Not wishing to minimise all he had done on her behalf, she raised her eyes to meet his. "Not that I do not enjoy it here, mind you. I am very grateful Georgiana has extended such hospitality. It is just that I feel so much a prisoner here—having to be ever cognizant of society's rigid expectations. I can scarcely step out of doors for a solitary breath of fresh air without giving rise to a scandal."

Darcy wanted desperately to offer Elizabeth solace. Giving up all pretence of not wishing to be near her, he abandoned his seat and moved to her side. Faint traces of lavender flooded his senses. He took her soft hand in his and placed his free hand lovingly on her cheek. "There is a matter I have been putting off discussing with you. In fact, I have been putting it off, not wanting to leave you and Ben so soon after you settled in with my sister. Now seems an apt time. I have been summoned back to Pemberley by my steward, to resolve an escalating dispute amongst my tenants."

He gently caressed her tiny hand. "What say you we all travel to Pemberley? I am sure Georgiana will be agreeable since we had planned to spend the summer there. We will simply arrive a little ahead of schedule. This way, you can take your time in deciding your next step, away from prying eyes, wagging tongues, and interfering uncles. You and Ben will have a chance to enjoy the freedom of Pemberley, and Ben will have leeway to roam a bit farther than I am comfortable with here in town."

Elizabeth looked deeply into his eyes. Her eyes then fell to his lips and remained there for as long as it took to remember herself. She then gazed at his beautiful face. Say what she would for the benefit of everyone else, she was in his power, completely. Elizabeth would deny him nothing.

Darcy traced his fingers along her cheek. Speaking in a deeper, more seductive tone, he continued, "Please, say you will accompany me. You are sure to enjoy yourself—I promise."

Between Darcy and Bingley, there had always been a very steady friendship. On the strength of Darcy's regard, Bingley had the firmest reliance, and of his judgement the highest opinion. Therefore, when Bingley became aware of the talk circulating amongst the *ton* that Darcy was often seen around town in the company of an unknown country beauty, he sought to know what his old friend was about.

Try as he might to call on Darcy at his town-house, he had yet been unable to accomplish that feat with any success. Bingley, being a single man, was not apt to call upon Miss Darcy, a young woman not yet out amongst society.

His sister Caroline's account that Mrs. Elizabeth Carlton of Hertfordshire was the mystery woman rumoured to be his friend's mistress, he regarded as complete nonsense—as clear a sign as any his sister continued to delude herself where Darcy was concerned. Elizabeth's presence at the Matlock's dinner party had solved the mystery of the woman's identity for Bingley, even if it had not lent credence to his sister's theory. The last he had heard, Mrs. Elizabeth Carlton was engaged to be married to her cousin.

His late arrival to the Matlock home along with Elizabeth's early departure provided little by means of satisfying his curiosity. With his friend's eagerness to leave early as well, the best he could secure from his friend had been a promise to meet him at White's for drinks the next day.

Bingley greeted his friend with warmth and enthusiasm, but uncharacteristically wasted little time with pleasantries, preferring instead to get straight to the point.

The drink orders had not been placed when he asked, "How in the world did Mrs. Elizabeth Carlton become a guest in your sister's home? If my memory serves me correctly, you two were not the best of friends whilst in Hertfordshire. How is she now rumoured to be regularly in your company about town?"

Darcy responded, "The answer is simple—I am in love with her. I believe I have been in love with her since the day I first laid eyes upon her. She is indeed a guest in Georgiana's home. In but a few days, we shall all travel to Pemberley. There, I hope to persuade her to accept my hand in marriage."

"What of your objections to her family, or does your intolerance of the Bennets and their lack of connections only apply to my situation?"

"Bingley, if this indeed has anything to do with your regard for Miss Bennet, I shall not accept the blame for your decision to leave Netherfield Park in such a precipitous manner. Certainly, I am not responsible for your decision not to act upon your regard for the lady."

"Yet, you hardly encouraged me to stay. You even suggested Miss Bennet was indifferent towards me—you said her smiles were as likely to be bestowed upon me as any other man."

"You asked for my opinion and I offered it in good conscience. I neither encouraged nor discouraged your decision to pursue Miss Bennet."

"I will grant you that, Darcy. With such being the case, is there anything you might tell me of Miss Bennet? Seeing as how her sister is residing in your own sister's home, surely you must have knowledge of the particulars of her situation."

Darcy had always enjoyed an easy manner of directing his friend. This time would prove no different. *Perhaps if Bingley should arrive in Cheapside in time to interrupt Collins's pursuit, then so much the better. Indeed, Elizabeth would be pleased,* Darcy considered.

"She resides in Cheapside with her Uncle and Aunt Gardiner. However, I must forewarn you, my friend; I have it on good authority she is admired by another man."

"In Cheapside—and admired by another," Bingley pondered aloud. "I appreciate this information, my friend. Indeed, I shall seek out Miss Bennet and determine what I must as regards this other man."

"May the better man win," Darcy said.

"Indeed, may the better man win," Bingley reiterated with confidence.

Chapter 22

Elizabeth sat alone, her elbows resting on her uplifted knees, in harmony with her surroundings as she looked around her and admired various remarkable spots and points of view. Once in a while, she glanced towards Darcy and her son. *Inseparable,* thought she with a smile lighting her face, *is the word that perfectly describes the two.* She would never forget the grin on the face of her young son when Darcy had invited him to ride along atop his prized stallion once they approached Pemberley Woods.

Elizabeth enjoyed a tranquillity she theretofore had never known, not even during her earlier years at Camberworth. The heartbreak she had suffered in being denied welcome by her father into Longbourn, her childhood home, was erased by the sense of well-being she now enjoyed. Elizabeth thought to be mistress of Pemberley might be something after all!

Just off a short distance, Darcy and Ben were at the top of a rise of considerable eminence where the wood ceased. Pemberley House, situated on the opposite side of a valley, caught Ben's eye right away. The prospect of one exciting adventure after another stoked his fertile imagination. He pointed to the large, handsome, stone building standing well on rising ground and backed by a ridge of high, woody hills

"Is that your home?" the lad asked reverently.

"Yes, I live here," Darcy announced. "Welcome to Pemberley."

"Your home is just as you described it. I think I shall be happy here."

"I am counting on that, Ben."

The lad caught sight of the stream in front of the great manor. "Look, Mr. Darcy! A river runs in front of your home. May we spend the day fishing?"

"What you see is not a river, Ben. It is a stream. Although you and I might fish there, should you insist, I believe we shall have far greater success if we take advantage of my well-stocked lakes.

"Have you had many opportunities to enjoy fishing in the past, Ben?"

"Not as I recall, but I imagine I must have when I was younger," the young lad replied with confidence.

"Why do you say so?"

"My mama said my grandfather Carlton and my papa enjoyed fishing. Do you imagine they would not have included me?"

Darcy's heart broke whenever Ben spoke in such terms. He understood Ben's loss well, having lost both of his parents, albeit his beloved mother as a boy and his beloved father as a young man. He had his memories to cherish. Ben had none.

"I cannot imagine such a thing, Ben. They surely would have demanded your company. I am certain they would be exceedingly proud of you now, as is your mother."

"What about you? Are you proud of me?"

Darcy placed his hand atop Ben's head and tousled his curly hair, "Yes, indeed, most ardently. You mean the world to me, both you and your mother. I am delighted you are come to Pemberley."

"As am I," Ben affirmed. "Let us make haste. I cannot wait to go fishing!"

A week into their stay at Pemberley, whilst returning from a visit amongst his tenants with his steward, Darcy came across Elizabeth, sitting alone in a little alcove. Deciding to join her, he dismounted and told his steward to attend his stallion. He indicated he would meet with him later in the afternoon.

The welcoming smile Elizabeth bestowed on Darcy as he made his approach gave him to know he was not intruding on her solitude.

"You have been quiet of late," Darcy expressed.

"Yes, you are correct. I suppose you think me an abysmal guest."

"Not at all. I invited you here to afford you the opportunity to escape from your worries in town. Yet, it seems you have brought them along with you."

"I am afraid you are once again correct."

"I wish you would talk to me about whatever this is that troubles you and steals your happiness. I have been told by others I am a good listener." Darcy reached for Elizabeth's hand. "Shall we take a walk?" With Darcy's aid, Elizabeth stood and brushed her skirt of tiny traces of clinging debris.

She was agreeable to his scheme. In fact, she welcomed the chance to share her burden. The manner in which she had parted with her relatives in Cheapside bothered her still. The last thing Elizabeth had wanted was to hazard seeing Mr. Collins again. Instead of returning to Gracechurch Street, she had invited her Aunt Gardiner and Jane to join her for tea in Mayfair. Any tension that remained had sprung from the fact that Jane had elected not to come. Mrs. Gardiner could not help but feel drawn into the middle of the two sisters' misunderstanding. Her aunt understood Jane's position, even if she did not agree with her assertion of not wishing to show disloyalty to Mr. Collins, who indeed had requested and gained acceptance of Jane's hand in marriage. Mrs.

Gardiner's advice to Elizabeth was to know what she was about and not to be dissuaded by the opinions of others.

Still, Elizabeth had been determined to be disturbed by Jane's attitude. She wondered what she might have done to heal the rift between them.

Darcy had other thoughts on the matter. "You must not take all the blame on yourself," he urged.

"I recognise an equal share of blame between us. Nevertheless, I am pained my dearest sister would believe I did not have a legitimate reason for acting as I did."

"Perhaps she will, in time. Your sister is practical in choosing not to live her life as a lonely spinster when she is just as likely to find happiness with Collins as anyone else."

"I am surprised you would express such sentiments when you swore I might find misery with the gentleman!"

"What did I suspect that was not true? Your lively spirits, as well as those of your son, placed you in grave danger of an un-happy life with such a man. Your eldest sister, on the other hand, has a temperament more suited to his officious manner."

"So, you think me a lively sort, Mr. Darcy?"

"I do."

"On what basis is your opinion formed, if I might be so bold as to ask?"

"I see it in your eyes when you look at Ben, even when you look at me, when you suspect I am unaware. I sense it in our touch whenever I have ventured to hold you, and I feel it in your presence whenever we are near," Darcy spoke softly, touching Elizabeth on her face. He wanted nothing more than to kiss her lips. The sound of his sister's voice urged him to surrender his hands to his sides.

Georgiana and her young companion approached Elizabeth and Darcy in the lane. Georgiana sensed something in the air. Instead of an awkward apology, she said cheerfully, "Ben and I are out for a walk."

"I say we all enjoy a leisurely stroll," Darcy responded as he offered Elizabeth his arm, and they set off happily on the path.

Although Darcy may not have been thrown by the interruption, Elizabeth was all aflutter. If ever there had been a moment she did not wish to be interrupted, it was then. Memories of the first time he had kissed her lips were fading. How she longed for a reminder. Elizabeth's silent musing recalled her to a time from the not very distant past when she imagined she might satisfy her aching, longing for his touch. Her learning he had placed her in the mistress's suite at his town-house was met with a mixture of anxiety, anticipation, and tension laced with excitement. On the one hand, she wondered what on earth he might be thinking. On the other hand, she wondered whether he was thinking the same thing she was thinking. Not only was she no stranger to desires of the flesh; he was the one person on earth who stirred those desires like no other had or could.

Elizabeth suppressed a smile in remembrance of the last night in his London home, as she stood at the door adjoining the mistress's suite to the master's suite, with her hands placed on the centre pane. Her dilemma, *If it is honourable for him not to venture through this door would it prove dishonourable should I venture forth, instead?*

Of course, she would never know. Elizabeth determined she would follow his lead. *Mr. Darcy is in love with me after all,* she reminded herself time and again. *He offered his hand once. Surely, he will offer again; his actions suggest it is only a matter of time, Might pride prevent a man such as Mr. Darcy from offering twice to the same woman?*

Georgiana and Ben raced ahead, whilst Darcy walked along the narrow path, arm in arm with Elizabeth, his thoughts of a similar vein. The gift of time had allowed him to think with greater discernment back to the nights Elizabeth and he had slept just a doorway apart in his London town-house. His excuse of wanting her to be close to her son had been part of his reasoning, of course. Indeed, he had been most considerate in settling her within feet from her son's apartment. Without a doubt, Darcy had wanted her close to himself, as well. Darcy's dilemma had been overwhelming, knowing as he did how Elizabeth's desire for him was as potent as was his desire for her. To have ventured through the door connecting their adjacent suites, amidst the quiet stillness of the night, might well have led to the fulfilment of their shared utmost yearnings, but would it have been any less dishonourable? Darcy would never know. Furthermore, he would not chance it again. For the time being, the mistress's suite at Pemberley remained unoccupied. Darcy determined he would follow Elizabeth's lead.

The following days and nights at Pemberley were filled with harmonious accord. Elizabeth had ample opportunity to enjoy Pemberley at her leisure. Darcy and Georgiana made sure of that. Both devoted as much time and attention to Elizabeth's young son, as did she. They were becoming a family. The prospect of their newly formed relationship ending—of Elizabeth yielding to the threat of censure from both their families and even society and denying herself, denying them all the happiness they richly deserved—was too much to fathom.

One morning whilst Darcy was in the stable yard with Ben, teaching him the finer points of horsemanship, Georgiana accompanied Elizabeth on her walk. Not usually an early riser, Georgiana was on a mission.

"Though I am not yet out in society and thereby not expected to discern such things, it is clear to me that my brother cares deeply for you and your son. Have you any affectionate regard for him?"

Elizabeth often wondered what the young lady suspected of the nature of Elizabeth's association with her older brother, although she would never broach the subject. "Georgiana, there are certain things one does not discuss with a prospective suitor's younger sibling by ten years."

Not to be discouraged, Georgiana persisted. "Ah, so you DO consider my brother a suitor. I cannot imagine he has asked for your hand in marriage, for what woman would reject him? On the other hand, realising the way he feels, I cannot envision what is keeping him from offering for you."

As Elizabeth had supposed, Darcy had not discussed the circumstances of their past with his sister. "Georgiana, I shall not discuss such matters with you."

"Why will you not, Elizabeth? Is your reluctance merely a result of the difference in our ages?"

"Our age difference is a consideration, of course. The other matter has to do with the history between your brother and me, matters which neither of us would care to talk about with others, I am sure."

"If you insist, then I shall not pry. However, I ask one thing. WHEN my brother offers his hand in marriage, will you please say yes?"

"At times, you are as incorrigible as Ben!" Elizabeth exclaimed to the younger woman.

"Indeed, I shall consider that a compliment, for Ben is wise beyond his years." Georgiana and Elizabeth paused and embraced in an unspoken truce before resuming their stroll.

రావ

After dinner, neither of the Darcys had seemed much in the mood for company. Darcy parted with the ladies following a single exhibition by his sister on the pianoforte. Soon afterwards, Georgiana pardoned herself from Elizabeth's company as well, with the excuse of wanting to retire early.

Elizabeth, however, had no wish for an early end to the evening. Furthermore, she had no wish to spend the evening by herself. She wanted to spend time alone with Darcy, for they had rarely done so since their arrival at Pemberley. She found him on one of Pemberley's many balconies, one overlooking a small, glistening pond.

She approached him from behind. "Are you wishing on a star, Mr. Darcy?" Elizabeth asked.

Darcy was not expecting company, as the surprised look on his face attested. A further testament was the casual state of his attire. Having discarded his dinner jacket and vest, he was dressed solely in a shirt hanging loosely from his breeches. The bright moon and the brilliant stars above conspired to cast a perfect glow on Darcy's profile. He was such a pleasure to behold—broad chest, long legs, taut muscular thighs, and tight leather boots hugging his calves as if painted in place.

Turning to face her, he said, "Indeed. It seems my wish has been granted, for here you are." Darcy extended a welcoming hand, which Elizabeth graciously accepted. He then raised her hand and brushed his lips unhurriedly against it in a lingering kiss.

"Pray tell, is this a favourite pastime of yours?" Elizabeth asked in reference to his stargazing.

"If you are referring to this," Darcy turned her hand upward and kissed her palm gently, "I should say so."

"Mr. Darcy, you are a shameless flirt," Elizabeth teased as she withdrew her hand.

"I remind you, it is only with you that I behave this way. You, woman, have bewitched me."

Elizabeth eased towards the edge of the balcony and placed her hands thereupon. She looked to the stars. Darcy joined her. Standing but a few feet apart, he too took up watch.

"Is gazing at the stars a favourite pastime of yours?"

"Not since I was a child, I am afraid. Even then, I could identify but a few constellations."

"Allow me to guess, Ursa Major and Ursa Minor."

"How ever did you surmise that, Mr. Darcy?" Elizabeth asked, allowing his teasing without taking offence.

"I suppose it to be part of one's childhood teachings. What of the others: Orion, Canis Major, Canis Minor, Perseus, and Taurus, just to name a few?"

"I am afraid my teachings were lacking in that regard," she confessed as she resumed her study of the heavens.

"Allow me to make up for any deficits," he whispered. By then, any response other than yes on Elizabeth's part would have proved disadvantageous. She stood captured in his embrace. With one hand resting on her waist, Darcy's other hand slowly guided her hand across the night's sky. In no hurry, he traced the path of the stars forming the various constellations, one after the other, whispering the names of each softly in her ear.

Lost in the moment, Elizabeth remained silent throughout as she nestled in his arms. She could not imagine a better moment; the sheer delight of his arm freely resting along her waist, the warmth of his breath tracing softly along her neck, and his hands gently touching hers. As much as it was a pleasure for Elizabeth to be ensconced in Darcy's embrace, and as much as she relished the intoxicating effects of the excitement engendered by his tender, arousing voice, their intimacy was a torment to Darcy's sensibilities; painfully aching, sweet, torture. Darcy unhurriedly relinquished his impassioned hold, though he could not bring himself to let go of her hand.

"Elizabeth, I have but one wish to voice before we part for the evening…surely, you must know what it is. My greatest wish is that you will marry me, that I shall soon be a husband to you and a father to Ben. Please do me the honour of accepting my hand."

After what seemed an eternity in his mind but was merely a few seconds, Elizabeth raised Darcy's hand and brushed a light kiss across his knuckles. "Wish granted," she whispered.

"Yes?" Darcy asked. He had waited long. He needed to hear her speak the word.

"A thousand times, yes!" Elizabeth exclaimed. Her eyes sparkled with unshed tears of joy. A bright smile graced her lovely face. "It seems you were not the only one who used the night's stars to their greatest advantage this evening."

"Truly, Elizabeth?"

"Indeed, it has been my greatest wish, as well, that you would ask me again. I was beginning to think you might not, you know. However, I can by no means fault you in taking so long. I needed time to put my recent past in its proper perspective, and you allowed just that. How shall I ever thank you enough for your patience?"

"My wish did include we should be married soon," Darcy reminded.

"Although not too soon, for we must observe all the requisite decorum." Elizabeth's last sentiment was met with a furrowed brow, hinting at a measure of dismay. Elizabeth placed her hand lovingly on his cheek. "Please, do not look so forlorn. I am asking you to bear with me but a short while longer. After all, we are a family already, are we not? You are as much a father to Ben as anyone might expect or even dare to wish."

"Yes, but I am hardly a husband to you," Darcy spoke in a soft, tender voice.

"Are you not? Have you not cared for and provided for me for the past months as a husband would care and provide for his wife?" she teased. "Might I expect something more upon taking the actual wedding vows?" Elizabeth asked. She called on her best imitation of a fair maiden in so doing.

Darcy took her delicate wrists in hand. "Teasing woman, were I your husband, without fail, you would know the difference." He trailed kisses along her wrists. "Every night would find you drifting asleep in my arms, wonderfully satiated from the feast of our lovemaking." He resumed his pleasing kisses. "Every morning would find you rousing in my arms, ravenous for more."

Elizabeth had no doubt of the veracity of his words. Did she not fall asleep so many nights with pleasant dreams to that effect? She blushed and turned slightly away from him. "You make the prospect of our life as husband and wife sound delightful, Mr. Darcy."

"Indeed. When shall we be married?" Darcy drew Elizabeth into the cradle of his arms, her back meshed snugly against his chest. "What amount of time constitutes proper decorum?"

"Two months seem a respectable period." Elizabeth reclaimed the warm, comfortable spot she had treasured some moments earlier as she snuggled in closer.

Darcy removed the pins from Elizabeth hair, freeing it to cascade down her back. He wove his hand in her long, dark tresses and took in the delightful scent of lavender, before gently brushing her locks aside to find a most enticing spot behind her ear. "A se'ennight," he whispered. The soft music of his voice sent tremors through her body.

"At least six weeks," Elizabeth whispered in kind.

Darcy trailed his fingers along Elizabeth's slender neckline and traced a subtle pattern on her bare shoulders before guiding her to face him. He chose a spot at the tip of her brow on which to lavish his attentions, effectively commencing the next round of debate. "A se'ennight," he insisted before breaking off talks.

Once Elizabeth sensibilities recovered enough to allow her to speak, she said, "Clearly you are not in tune with the finer points of negotiation, Mr. Darcy."

"Am I not?" His eyes etched a tempting path from her eyes to the enticing décolletage of her evening gown. The rise and fall of her chest told him all he needed to know of the efficacy of his approach. With a slight sweep of his lips against her bare shoulder, he murmured, "You have yet to counter propose, my love."

The burning shiver of desire coursing through her body threatened to melt every bit of her resolve. "A month—" she managed to utter.

Darcy teasingly brushed his lips against hers. "A se'ennight," he repeated as he drew Elizabeth ever so slightly nearer to his body, close enough that she might realise the strength of his desire.

"A fortnight..." Elizabeth whispered. Her heart raced. Her thoughts shouted, *Should he keep at this, we might very well be planning a trip to Gretna Green in the morn!* She placed both hands on Darcy's broad chest, initially hoping for a moment to catch her breath but instantly losing herself in the pleasure of the touch of his skin underneath her palms. He had discarded his cravat, as well as his dinner jacket and vest before she came across him. The sight of the soft hairs of his chest threatened to strip away all her sense of purpose. She closed her eyes and relaxed.

Darcy rested his head atop hers as he gently caressed her curves. "Half a fortnight, Elizabeth," Darcy murmured.

"How would we manage that, Mr. Darcy?"

"We shall be married by special license[1], of course."

"Does a special license not take time to procure?"

"What if I confess I took care of the matter before leaving town?"

Elizabeth raised her head and looked into his eyes. "I would say you are rather presumptuous."

"I would rather you say I am determined. Which I am, you know. I am determined to make you my wife as soon as can be." Darcy kissed Elizabeth on the tip of her nose. "The ball is in your court, Elizabeth, my love. What say you?"

"Even with this new disclosure, I am resolved. I say a fortnight, Mr. Darcy."

Darcy smiled. "A fortnight it is."

---

1 For entertainment purposes only. Historical accuracy is not intended.

Chapter 23

It seemed to young Ben as if everywhere he ventured in the grand halls of Pemberley, he had been met with the commotion of people as they ran back and forth in preparation for the wedding. The auspicious occasion was days away. What joy he felt when first told of the pending nuptials! What excitement! His mama and his best friend were to be married! Mr. Darcy would no longer just be Mr. Darcy, King Arthur, his best friend in the world. He would be his father.

After a day or two, all such talk of the exciting prospect the future held had made little difference to the young fellow who had grown accustomed to being the centre of attention.

His sense of feeling left out of things had hardly gone undetected. Thus, Darcy, Elizabeth, and Ben set out for a day of adventure amidst the Derbyshire countryside. It was meant to be a simple outing comprised of only the three of them, not counting the carriage driver, a footman, and Elizabeth's maid. Although the news of the master's engagement had spread throughout the land, it would not do for Elizabeth to be seen by the locals, unescorted in the company of two handsome young gentlemen, even if they were her betrothed and her son. People talked.

Elizabeth rode along in the open carriage with her parasol cast aside, enjoying the warmth of the sun on her face. Darcy took advantage of the open stretch and raced ahead in the field with Ben nestled closely in his saddle. Ben spread his arms and glided in flight with his eyes closed tightly as the wind blew through his hair.

As much as Ben enjoyed their countryside excursion, concern over Miss Georgiana's absence persisted. Once again, as they sat on a blanket spread over the lush green under a towering tree, he sought reassurance there was nothing amiss.

"This outing is for the three of us, alone. Miss Georgiana understands. Your mother and I wish for us to spend time together, before she and I are married," Darcy explained. "We will depart soon afterwards for our wedding journey."

"May Miss Georgiana and I come with you?"

"I am afraid not, son," Elizabeth responded as she drew Ben close.

"Why not, Mama?" Ben implored.

Darcy offered an explanation. "Ben, it is not as though either of us would wish to be parted from you. Your mother and I would do anything in the world for you, except in this case. When a man and his bride are married, they take a honeymoon journey where they might spend some time alone, solely the two of them."

"But my mama and I have never been separated for so long, except the night she spent apart from me to care for my Aunt Jane. I was asleep most of that time."

"I understand your anxiety of being separated from your mother for the first time, which is why I shortened our travel plans by half. We will return before you know it, and Miss Georgiana will care for you in our absence."

Ben drew himself even closer to his mother's side and clung to her. "Mama, it is not fair. You and I have never been apart for so long. I am young, and I am small. You would hardly even know I am around. May I come along, please? Moreover, Miss Georgiana might come along, as well. We shall have a grand time."

Elizabeth's eyes drifted towards her intended. His countenance spoke volumes. She gazed down at her son, into the sweetest eyes. His face spoke volumes, as well. "Please, do not leave me, Mama."

Sensing his intended might give in to her son's irresistible heartfelt plea, Darcy stood and extended his hand to the lad. "Come, Ben. Walk with me so the two of us might talk, man to man."

Ben accepted Darcy's proffered hand without reservation. The two walked towards a small, shallow pond. Darcy bent and picked up a few pebbles from the pond's edge. Ben did likewise. The two skipped the tiny pebbles across the water. After a spell, Darcy sat on the ground and recommended a spot for Ben.

"Tell me, Ben. What is this about? You and I have spoken of my marriage to your mother often of late. I thought we agreed this match was a good thing for all of us. We will be a true family, at last."

"Indeed, sir. But now it seems clear to me that not only am I losing my best friend, I am losing my mama, as well," Ben expressed sadly.

"You are mistaken. You are not losing your mother. That would never happen. She loves you more than anything in the world."

"It will not be the same. Already things have changed. You and my mama spend far more time together now than ever before, and now you are talking of taking her far away from me."

"Ben, I understand your sentiments, truly I do. You have had your mother all to yourself for as long as you can remember, and now for the first time, you are expected to share her time and attention, even her love with someone else.

"You must trust me. It is true—our lives will not be quite the same as before. Our lives will be better. Your mother and I will be husband and wife. You and I will be father and son. Just think, in time, you will have brothers and sisters, as well. Will that not be wonderful?"

Ben pondered the matter. "I suppose so. I have always wanted a baby brother. Can I have all brothers? I am certain I do not wish to have sisters."

Darcy chuckled. "No sisters? Why not?"

"Sisters are girls!"

"Indeed. What would the world be without little girls?"

"Girls are nothing but trouble," Ben spoke from his limited experience with the fairer sex.

"Oh! What about Miss Georgiana? She IS a girl, you know."

"That is not the same thing. Although she is a girl, she is not JUST a girl!" Ben explained. He thought but did not say, *She is a fairy princess, an angel.*

"Indeed. She is not JUST a girl. She is my sister. I love her dearly. I cannot imagine life without her. One day, you shall feel the same way I do towards my sister, towards your own little sister. Trust me."

"I trust you, sir. Moreover, I love YOU dearly." Ben embraced Darcy. "I can hardly wait to call you papa." Ben reflected for a moment on his chosen appellation. "Shall I call you father, or shall I call you papa, or perhaps even Pa?"

"I addressed my parents as father and mother. That said, it is entirely up to you. I shall find whatever suits you agreeable."

"Then, I think father is pretty formal. I think I shall call you father when I am particularly vexed. What say you to that?"

"I say it is good to be forewarned," Darcy jested. "What shall you call me when you are exceedingly happy?"

"Oh! You shall find out."

"I can hardly wait."

"Nor I, to be sure," Ben said. "Look after my mama and take good care of her on your wedding journey. I shall look after Pemberley, as well as Miss Georgiana, in your absence."

The history between Lord Matlock's only nieces could never have been described as anything akin to cordiality. Far from it. The unfortunate fact was borne out by Georgiana's reaction to the footman's ushering in a dark cloud, with his entrance into her favourite room in all of Pemberley.

"Miss Anne de Bourgh," he announced.

Georgiana could not have been more displeased, as the unmasked look of dismay on her countenance surely attested. In keeping with her station as hostess in her brother's home, Georgiana arose from the pianoforte and walked over to greet her cousin.

"What are you doing here, Anne? Why have you come all this way, uninvited? Should you not be at Rosings Park on your deathbed feigning illness of some sort in a desperate attempt to lure my brother back to Kent?"

"I have come all this way to confront MY intended—to put an end to this nonsense once and for all," Anne bitterly retorted. "I suppose the better question might be what are you doing here, or is your presence required to lend an air of legitimacy to the presence of his mistress living under his roof?"

"Poor deluded Cousin Anne. If only you knew," Georgiana smirked.

"From what my uncle conveyed in his missive to me, you have been a party to this sordid affair from the start," Anne accused as she brushed her cousin aside and walked about the room. "Have you no shame? Accepting your brother's mistress, first in your home, and now here! For crying out loud, that the shades of Pemberley are thus polluted."

"You ARE your mother's daughter, are you not? You sound exactly like her. How did you manage to come all this way without her?"

"You never mind that. The whereabouts of my mother is none of your concern. You need not pretend with me, young lady. You have never looked on me with favour since it was made clear to you that despite your objections, your brother and I were to be married."

"I confess there is no love lost between us, but that has nothing to do with your misapprehensions that you and my brother are intended for each other. Had my brother expressed any desire in the slightest to go along with that foolish notion, I would have made every attempt to welcome you with open arms."

Anne looked at the large mantle clock she had admired for so many years. "Where is Fitzwilliam? Surely, you do not suppose I came all this way to waste time pontificating with you."

"My brother is out. I do not expect his return for hours. Are you staying at the inn in Lambton? Shall I inform him upon his return that he might find you there?"

"Do not be ridiculous, foolish child! I shall stay here, as I have always done when in Derbyshire. I believe Pemberley is as much my home as it is yours. I daresay it is certainly destined to be."

"I would not hold my breath whilst waiting for that to come about, if I were you. On second thought, DO hold your breath, dear cousin," the younger woman suggested derisively.

"Pardon me, *dear* cousin. I should like to go to my room. I am certain Mrs. Reynolds will have arranged for me to be comfortably settled in the blue bedroom, where I normally stay." Anne headed towards the door. She paused. "Do make yourself useful and ring for tea to be served in my room. I am rather parched, and I much prefer my own company than to suffer your impertinence a minute longer than is necessary."

"Oh Anne! Why do you not go away and let us be? My brother does not intend to marry you; on the contrary, he is promised to another."

"We shall see about that!"

Several hours later, Anne stood at the window of her apartment, the same room she had occupied whenever she had visited Pemberley for as long as she could recall. *I shall not be consigned to this room much longer,* she considered. *I shall reside in the mistress's suite soon enough.* Such grandiose scheming was halted when she espied her cousin. She could recognise his fine gait from anywhere. The pleasure she enjoyed from the sight of him was soured by the sight of the two companions who joined him. They united hands and ambled along together, the smallest of the three in the middle. *One big happy family,* she considered mockingly. Anne then recalled Darcy's attachment to the child whilst in Kent. At first, she had thought it all a ruse, a not so subtle attempt to garner the favours of the mother.

She was no fool. Surely, her intended was no stranger to the arts and allurements of beautiful women. If he deigned to have a mistress, who was she to object, as long as he did not flaunt it in her face? However, THIS was too much. *Did he just lift the child in his arms, then lean forward, and place a kiss on the mother's forehead?* Anne had seen enough.

This ends TODAY!

Anne stalked out of her room and stationed herself in the hallway where she would be sure to intercept Darcy on his way to his apartment.

Darcy was not surprised to see his cousin. Georgiana had mentioned she was there. He had thought to speak with her later—much later, after she had rested from her long journey from Kent. He had not expected to find her standing in the hallway with her arms crossed in front of her, awaiting his approach.

Darcy cast any semblance of formality aside. "Anne, you should not have come. Where is Lady Catherine? Did you travel without her?"

"I believe it is your mistress who should not be here," she accused at the top of her voice.

Neither Darcy nor Elizabeth wanted Ben to bear witness to Anne's unseemly behaviour. Taking her son by the hand, Elizabeth excused herself and ushered Ben to his room. Georgiana, who by then had joined them, took the opportunity to accompany Elizabeth and Ben.

"Disparage my intended again, and I shall demand you leave my home," Darcy spoke harshly.

"Nonsense! How can you speak such foolishness? Have I released you from our engagement?"

"I was never yours to release, Anne."

"It is well established that our engagement has been of a peculiar nature. We are bound by honour, by blood. We are family. It was our mothers' greatest wish we should be married."

"It has never been my intention to honour our mothers' wishes. In truth, I have always hoped to marry the woman I loved. Finally, I have found what I have been searching for all these years. Can you not understand, Anne? I love her! She and her son mean everything to me. They are my family. I would never settle for you when I might have the woman I love."

"What about me?" Anne begged. "I love you, too. I have loved you the longest!"

Darcy looked at his cousin in exasperation. "Do not be absurd, Anne. You do not love me."

"In our world, what is love when there is mutual consideration and respect? Furthermore, I need you."

"I need HER!"

"What about the promises you made? Have you no feelings at all for me? No honour?"

"What has honour to do with this? I made you no promise!" Darcy ran his fingers through his hair whilst he contemplated his next words. He glared at her. "I do indeed have intense feelings for you, Anne. However, not the feelings you would wish. For I no longer care for you, even as a cousin. You have taught me to loathe you. I detest you! Moreover, I pity you for coming as far as you did only to make a fool of yourself!"

It pained him to utter such words to his own flesh and blood. It seemed the only way to get through to her—to wound her so critically she might then despise him. At least he would be free of her. Darcy turned to walk away, a clear signal the conversation had ended.

Anne had other ideas. Deranged, infuriated, and confused, she did not intend to broker disappointment. He was hers! He would regret speaking to her as barbarously as he had, in such denigrating terms of disparagement.

As if floating along on a dense cloud of rage, all sense of reason escaped her as she followed him down the corridor. He had dared to utter those words to her—that he loved another woman, needed another woman. She would be damned if she allowed him to walk away from her.

The pain and disappointment of the past years overtook her. It had not been all for naught. Had she even been capable of admitting the truth to herself, she would have confessed she never truly wanted him at all, until at some point in time, ALL she wanted was him. Suddenly, there was no turning back from the path she had set upon.

Possessing a strength she did not even know she had, she caught up with him at the top of the stairs. Trying desperately to halt his descent, to force him to hear what she had to say that she might persuade him to see things her way, she grasped at him just as he halted of his own volition. A split second too late and taken quite by surprise, Darcy tried but could not grab hold of her.

Anne grappled at anything that would break her fall, but alas, there was nothing. She tumbled. Mindless of nothing other than the pain she endured, soon enough her contorted body rested at the foot of the stairs on the hard, cold ebony and ivory marbled landing. Then darkness.

Chapter 24

Elizabeth cuddled close to Ben to read his bedtime story. Darcy's continued absence was conspicuous. The more that time passed, the more difficult it became to explain away his lack of attendance. After what seemed in Ben's young mind to be a mighty long time since he had last seen his friend, Ben began to fear something was amiss. The last time he had glimpsed him, he had been in the hallway when the unpleasant lady arrived. Ben had not missed noticing that the newcomer amongst them was a presence unwelcome by all, most notably by Mr. Darcy, judging by the sternness of his countenance, as well as the hushed whispers after Miss Georgiana and his mama had scurried him off to his room.

"Mama, where is Mr. Darcy? Let us wait until Mr. Darcy joins us this evening. I like it when both of you read to me," Ben expressed.

Visions of the terrifying scene that had taken place just down the hallway, days earlier, flooded her mind. She had seen it all, heard it all, and watched in fear as Anne fell down the stairs. She observed Darcy's frantic race down the steps after his cousin. She stood frozen at the top of the stairway and watched as Darcy lifted his cousin's limp body in his arms and called out in alarm to summon a doctor.

Elizabeth had done all she could to protect Ben and to reassure him nothing was wrong. However, he was far too astute not to discern their idyllic life at Pemberley had taken an unexpected turn. Even more, he was too curious not to start asking questions.

Elizabeth sat Ben's favourite storybook aside and embraced her son. She kissed him lightly on his forehead. "Mr. Darcy is tending to a relative who is gravely ill," she said, hoping her explanation would be enough to pacify her child.

"Is it the lady I saw in the hallway when we came back from our family outing? I have not seen her since."

"Yes, Ben, she is Mr. Darcy's cousin. She suffered a serious mishap."

"Is Mr. Darcy terribly upset? Is that the reason he does not spend time with me any longer?"

"Mr. Darcy does not mean to neglect you, Ben. I am sure he misses you as much as you miss him. He believes his cousin has a greater need of him during this time." Elizabeth did her best to make the situation clear, for even she was beginning to be concerned about Darcy's attentiveness towards Anne. Georgiana explained to her what Darcy had failed to mention; how he had maintained a vigil over Anne the last time she had fallen victim to a strange deathbed malady, and how he had uttered those poorly chosen words which led Anne to believe she held some claim over him—that he would do anything to see her recover, that he might even go as far as to marry her.

The anguish Elizabeth suffered in merely recollecting Georgiana's words must have been etched on her face. Ben placed his tiny hand lovingly on his mother's chin and peered into her eyes. "Will Mr. Darcy's cousin die?"

Ben's question, innocent though it was, brought to Elizabeth's mind a paradoxical scenario she had never even considered. *What if Anne recovered? What if Anne recovered, but not fully? What if Anne never recovered? What would become of their lives?*

Elizabeth answered her son, solemnly. "I pray she gets well, my child." She kissed him atop his head, softly. "We all do."

It seemed all Darcy wanted to do when he did not choose to be alone to berate himself for Anne's accident, was to remain by his cousin's side, to pull her back from the brink as he had done before, thinking his presence as truly what was needed to accomplish such an end.

He had been assured by the physician the scrapes and sprains she suffered would indeed heal, and the bruises would disappear. What the doctor could not account for was her deep state of unconsciousness. Whether she would ever open her eyes again, he could not say with conviction. Only time would tell. Such was the matter weighing heaviest on Darcy's mind.

Anne was suffering as a result of his actions, his words. He might as well have pushed her, he managed to persuade himself. He could not have suffered more guilt.

Colonel Richard Fitzwilliam, who had come to Pemberley expecting to stand as groomsman for his cousin, arrived at what might easily have been described as a house of mourning. A brief conversation with Georgiana spurred him into action.

Darcy was surprised to see Richard after he entered the master's suite. Apparently, Richard had been waiting there for some time. Darcy had hoped for a chance to refresh himself and perhaps have a nap before returning to his post by Anne's bedside. He did not expect, nor did he care for, another lecture from well-intentioned relatives.

Richard wasted no time in his chastisement of the younger man's behaviour. He pointed out Darcy's inattention to his own health and his neglect of the people who meant most to him. The two men wrangled back and forth. Darcy thought surely everyone must understand. Richard expressed doubts. Even knowing Anne as he did, he could not say for certain whether Darcy's vigil made a difference. Nonetheless, he spoke with certitude of the undesirable consequences of Anne's latest crisis on Georgiana and young Ben. Georgiana, for one, was sceptical and afraid it was another of Anne's ploys—one she would play out until Darcy capitulated. Young Ben was lonely and confused. He missed his friend, and Richard could do little to make up for Darcy's absence.

Talk soon turned to the wedding. Richard asked, "Have your intentions changed?"

"How can I possibly wed Elizabeth whilst Anne is wasting away up the corridor, clinging to life?"

"What are you saying, Darcy?" Richard asked. "Do you mean to say after all the two of you have overcome to reach this point, you do not intend to marry Elizabeth?"

"No, that is not what I am saying. This is not the time to be planning a marriage, especially in light of the circumstances. It is MY fault Anne lies in bed, fighting for her life!"

"How on this earth do you suppose any of this is your fault?"

"I drove her to this! I mocked her! Do you fail to recall my parting words to her in Kent? How I would sooner see her dead than to marry her. And now…" Darcy threw himself in his chair, slumped forward in resignation, and buried his face in his hands.

"Darcy, you are taking too much blame upon yourself. How could you have known she would go to such lengths?"

Darcy stared at his cousin in dismay. "How might I expect you to understand my torment? You have never looked upon our cousin sympathetically."

"On the contrary, I have long seen her for the person she is. You have always looked naively at her manipulative antics."

"Well, here we are!"

"Indeed, you have allowed yourself to be drawn in by Anne's problems once more. What if, Heaven forbid, she should not recover from the fall? What IF it is no pretence? What IF she dies? Do you then intend to ask Elizabeth to wait until you have observed a proper period of grief for our cousin? Think about what you are doing, man! Is that how you intend to start your newly-wedded life, on the heels of mourning?"

"What is the alternative, oh wise one?"

"Proceed with your plans. Marry Elizabeth, NOW! Delay your wedding journey for a week at the most, but for heaven's sake do not put your life on hold waiting for Anne to decide to recover."

"I do not believe Anne is pretending. I was there! I will not abandon Anne when she needs me most. Nor will I marry Elizabeth when I am consumed with worry over Anne's well-being. Elizabeth deserves more than that. She deserves better than I am able to offer just now."

Darcy was on his way to look in on Anne, when he came across Elizabeth, who placed herself directly in his path.

"Hello, stranger," Elizabeth's visage offered far more than her words conveyed.

"Elizabeth, I know we have much to discuss," he offered apologetically.

"Indeed, we do. Thus, I am standing here in the hallway. I mean to spend the rest of the day with you, Mr. Darcy."

"Elizabeth," he began, "not today. Anne—" Darcy started to say before Elizabeth intervened.

"You have hired an army of nurses to care for Anne. Meanwhile, no one is looking after you; least not yourself. I mean to do just that, starting now," Elizabeth insisted.

Darcy opened his mouth to form an objection, but Elizabeth placed a silencing finger on his lips. "I refuse to accept no as an answer. Come with me."

A quarter of an hour later, Darcy and Elizabeth strolled together along a winding path bordering a quietly flowing stream. Occasionally, Elizabeth cast a glance towards him and wondered what had become of her passionate lover. His hands were tightly clasped behind his back. His countenance was crumpled. His mind seemed miles and miles away. He barely noticed when she laced her hands through his arm and rested her head thereupon as they walked.

It was destined to be a far greater challenge than she had envisioned. Elizabeth broke the inexcusable silence. "Mr. Darcy, I do not mean to make light of the pain you surely must be suffering; however, I was there, you know. You have nothing to feel guilty about."

Darcy wondered to himself, *Why must others insist on telling me how I should feel during this time? I know their intentions are good. No one understands.* It was his burden and his burden alone. He did not mean to share it with anyone, not even Elizabeth; especially not Elizabeth.

"Elizabeth, I do not wish to speak of any of this."

Elizabeth did not argue. They continued to walk in silence and soon came across the spot of a cosy picnic she had arranged through his staff. It was a delightful prospect, exactly as she had in mind. Elizabeth pulled him along by the hand and urged him to sit on the large blanket arranged on the ground.

Darcy was forced to shed his mask of remorse and despair in response to Elizabeth's warm gesture. After studying the contents of the baskets and retrieving a bottle of wine and two glasses, he endeavoured to make amends for his aloofness.

"Thank you, my love," he began, "I apologise for my sour mood of late. I am especially sorry for the havoc the situation with Anne has wreaked on our wedding plans."

"I accept your apology, Mr. Darcy, and I have tried to understand, believe me, though it has been rather difficult at times."

"I know," said he, "which brings to mind a matter which I have given some thought."

"What is it?" Elizabeth asked as she set the preparations of fresh fruit aside, and beheld him intently.

How he adored her. He missed her. His gaze rested on her tempting lips, but alas, he turned away. *How can I even think to kiss her, when poor Anne clings to life pursuant to my cruelty?*

"I received a letter from my uncle, Lord Matlock. Lady Catherine continues to recover from her recent bout with ill-health.

However, she is not yet fit enough to travel. Lord and Lady Matlock will come to Pemberley in her stead." Darcy took Elizabeth's hand in his and caressed it gently. "You should not have to suffer the indignities that are sure to come with my uncle's arrival. I think it will be best if Georgiana, Ben, and you return to town."

Elizabeth attempted to withdraw her hand. Darcy would not allow it.

"Is that what you want, Mr. Darcy?"

"I wish to protect you from what might be a long drawn out wait, as Anne's situation remains unchanged."

"Do you wish for me to leave Pemberley?"

"I never wish to be parted from you."

"Good, for I shall never leave you. You might as well accustom yourself to that fact."

"I would much rather you stay. However, my guilt is compounded when I think of how my attendance to Anne comes at the expense of Ben and you."

"You must allow me to worry about such matters. Ben misses you to be sure, and only you can fill that void." Elizabeth covered their joined hands with her free hand. "Allow me to share this burden with you. What this situation calls for is far more objectivity and fewer guilt-ridden obligations.

"I shall be mistress of Pemberley soon enough. I shall act accordingly. From this point, I shall assume primary responsibility for Anne's care."

"No, you do not understand. I cannot expect that of you. After all, she should see my face if, NO, when she first opens her eyes."

"On the contrary, sir, yours is the LAST face she should see when she first opens her eyes. This clinging spiral will never end otherwise."

Darcy's countenance was riddled with doubt. Elizabeth traced her fingers along his cheek. "Anne does not need you to tend to her, not as much as you have done thus far. You, on the other hand, are very much in need of some tender loving care, and I mean to be the one to provide just that."

Elizabeth leaned forward to kiss him on his cheek then sat back. The two lovers gazed into one another's eyes once again. Darcy studied her lips intently then leaned forward and kissed Elizabeth softly, tenderly, and ever so sweetly. His kiss was filled with all the love he had for her.

The two young lovers were in accord. They would try it Elizabeth's way.

Elizabeth took over the care of Anne. Her army of nurses notwithstanding, it was Elizabeth, who sat with her, read to her, and saw to it the nurses treated her in a manner befitting the master's first cousin.

As Elizabeth's stamina waned, Georgiana, and even Richard, aided her in her care of Anne. Darcy too maintained a vigil of sorts, even if not allowed by those who cared for him most to remain in Anne's room for anything longer than to look in on her and then promptly take his leave.

What is occurring with Miss Anne? Ben's curiosity would no longer be satisfied with vague responses, having asked the question of his mama, his friend Mr. Darcy, Colonel Fitzwilliam, and even Miss Georgiana on many an occasion. One day, whilst the grown-ups were having dinner, he took it upon himself to learn what was afoot.

Ben slowly pushed the door of Anne's apartment open and peeked inside. No one was about, save an elderly woman. The sounds emanating from her corner of the room confirmed Ben's suspicion she was asleep.

Ben looked up and down the corridor, and seeing no one around, slipped inside. He tiptoed across the fine thick carpet to have a better view of the woman in the bed. It was the first he had managed a glimpse of her since her arrival some time ago. He had imagined her to be a wicked witch—clothed in black, a long crooked nose, warts and all—given the storm that had descended upon Pemberley with her arrival. He stared at her for a full minute. *She does not look like a witch. In fact, I have seen her before. We met at Camelot!* Ben eased a bit closer to the bed. *She does not stir. Is she dead? Is she merely asleep?* "Miss Anne," Ben spoke softly, taking care not to disturb the loud woman in the corner. He was about to reach over to tap Anne's shoulder, when the grip of someone's hand upon his own caused in him quite a scare! Wide-eyed, his heart racing, Ben lifted his head to see Darcy towering over him.

"Mr. Darcy! You startled me!"

"I should think so. What are you doing in here, Ben?"

"I-I wanted to see for myself what is taking place. I want to know if what everyone is saying is true."

"Everyone, Ben?"

"Yes, everyone! Everyone says Miss Anne may never recover. Everyone says should she recover, she will be the next mistress of Pemberley!" Ben wrapped his arms around Darcy's legs. "I pray with all my heart Miss Anne recovers, truly I do." He looked up to meet Darcy's eyes. "Should Miss Anne recover, what does that mean for my mama and me? Shall we be forced to leave Pemberley?"

Darcy lifted his young friend in his arms and settled in the chair beside Anne's bed. "Ben, why would you ask such a question? You know your mother and I are to be married."

"The wedding was to have taken place by now. I cannot help thinking you might be obliged to reconsider once Miss Anne recovers. She is family. My mama and I are not—not really."

"Ben, you are mistaken. There is no one else on earth who means more to me than your mother and you." Darcy held Ben closely. "You are my family. Nothing will ever change that." Just then, Darcy noticed what Ben had been clutching in his hands.

"What is this you have here?"

Ben offered up the book he had brought into the room. "I thought I might read to Miss Anne for a spell," he confessed.

"Why don't I read to both of you?" Darcy suggested while reaching for the book and adjusting Ben in his lap so he might follow along. Darcy observed the inside pages and noted, "Ah, another tale of the Knights of the Round Table. Do you imagine Miss Anne will enjoy hearing of fierce battles, evil enemies, treachery, and the like?"

"Why, of course," Ben asserted, feeling much more assured than he did a few moments earlier. "What is there not to like?"

"Indeed," uttered Darcy. "Now where do I begin?"

With Ben's assistance, the two flipped through the well-worn pages of the book. "I suggest we start here! This is one of my mama's favourite passages. I am sure Miss Anne would approve."

"We shall see," Darcy uttered wistfully, "we shall see."

Later on, Elizabeth entered Anne's room planning to spend time with her and was surprised to find her two favourite people. Both of Anne's guests had fallen asleep, Ben in Darcy's lap. The hired nurse was fast asleep, as well. *What is it about this room that encourages such lethargy,* she wondered as she attempted to remove the book, already threatening to fall from Darcy's hand on its own. Darcy stirred and opened his eyes.

Elizabeth placed the book aside. "I never thought to find the two of you here. What are you doing?"

Darcy slowly recalled himself to his surroundings and was slightly embarrassed to have dozed off. "I followed this young lad," he began. "It seems he was interested in reading to Anne."

"That is surprising."

"Indeed, it turns out the little fellow has been spending time in the kitchen or elsewhere amongst the servants, who no doubt have been speculating about my cousin's fate and her opinion she has some claim over me."

"Oh dear! Were you able to put his mind at ease?"

"I hope so. I reminded him the two of you mean more to me than anything in the world. It is absolutely true, you know. I love you with all my heart. Nothing will ever come between us—ever again."

In a bold display of "public" affection, Darcy graced Elizabeth's lip with a passionate kiss. "I love you, Elizabeth."

❧

Richard happened upon a startling discovery when he entered Anne's room the next morning. She sat in the window seat overlooking an expansive maze garden, her eyes flooded with tears. Richard's approach from behind caught her unawares.

"Anne?"

"Oh, Richard, I have been such a fool!" she confessed, not bothering to turn and face him.

"Anne, how long have you been awake?"

"They are a family," she spoke poignantly.

It was enough said. "Yes, Anne, they are a family—never to be parted."

"Whilst I stand here on the outside, looking in."

"You know, it does not have to be that way." Richard sat beside his cousin and lifted her chin to meet his gaze. "You can always make amends."

"After all the havoc I have wreaked upon Fitzwilliam's life, I hardly know where to begin."

Not long afterwards, Richard joined Darcy, Georgiana, and Elizabeth in the drawing room. He stood in the middle of the room and announced, "Anne is awake."

Abruptly tossing his paper aside, Darcy jumped to his feet. "How long has she been conscious?"

"Anne has been awake for some time. I had a good long talk with her this morning," he uttered.

"I must see her, at once," Darcy proclaimed.

Richard raised his hand to halt his cousin's progress. "And you will, in time. For now, she asks to speak privately with Mrs. Carlton."

Darcy and Elizabeth glanced towards each other. Elizabeth smiled at him in reassurance, and then walked up the stairs to Anne's apartment.

The mid-morning sun beamed through the crack in the shades, prompting Elizabeth to walk over to open the curtains as had been her habit each morning. Elizabeth did not know what she might expect and thus was surprised to see Anne sitting up in her bed. She was even more startled by Anne's extended hand, silently beckoning Elizabeth to sit with her.

"I feel I owe you an apology, Mrs. Carlton," Anne explained. "Cousin Richard tells me that you would be enjoying your wedding journey, if not for me."

Elizabeth was not quite certain how to respond to what surely must have been the greatest change in sentiments she had ever witnessed. Perplexed, she responded tentatively, "You are correct. Mr. Darcy insisted on postponing our wedding until you recuperated. Are you saying you are reconciled to this fact?"

"Indeed. Some would say it is about time."

"What has occurred to bring about this change of heart?"

"I had a long conversation with Cousin Richard. He spoke at length of the mayhem my stubborn persistence has hurled on our family. However, that alone was not the deciding factor."

"Then what was, if I might ask?"

"It was you, Mrs. Carlton. You see, I have come to realise it was you who sat by my side for so many hours, read to me, cared for me. You demonstrated such selflessness when you could just as easily have exhibited scorn or derision towards me, as I surely meant to do towards you, or would have done if the situations were reversed."

"How did you ascertain my part?" Elizabeth asked in a half-whisper.

"Does it matter?" Anne asked. "Suffice it to say, I have it on good authority." Elizabeth then wondered whether Anne had feigned unconsciousness. Had she recovered sooner than was known by her nurse? The question would remain unasked. Anne espied a glass of water on her bedside table. She attempted to prop herself up, so she might have a drink. Elizabeth reached for the glass and handed it to her, even held the glass in her grasp as she aided Anne in taking a sip.

Anne smiled in gratitude. "You see I do not begrudge my cousin his happiness one bit," she continued. "I deluded myself far too long in believing he and I shared a future, despite his words to the contrary. I mistook his kindness for something more. He is a good man. He deserves more than the utter disregard for his feelings I have shown him these past years."

Anne reached for Elizabeth's hand. "He deserves happiness. I believe he has found that with you. Though I would never presume to think you two need my blessing, I wish to tell you that you have it."

Chapter 25

D arcy had just returned from a visit with Anne. He was engaged in pleasant repartee with Richard and Georgiana
when the butler entered the drawing room.

"Lord and Lady Matlock," he announced before stepping
aside in deference to the noble party.

"This is a surprise," Darcy said, as the face of all those in the
room with him attested. "I had not expected to receive you until
tomorrow."

Lord Matlock responded, "Not an unpleasant surprise, I hope?"
The elderly man scrutinised the room as if expecting to find something amiss. He returned his suspicious regard to his nephew and
asked, "What difference does it make when we arrived, unless you
are attempting to hide something?"

So, this is how it is, Darcy considered. Seeing no cause for
subjecting the rest of the family to the imminent verbal sparring
with his uncle, Darcy went to his aunt and welcomed her properly.
He returned his attention to his uncle.

"My lord, please join me in my study." Lord Matlock was not
impressed, far from it. Had Darcy lingered long enough for a

reply, he might have witnessed his aristocratic uncle's dismay, having been ordered about by the younger man.

Moments later, Darcy and his uncle sat across from each other in Darcy's study.

"I had hoped to receive you in my home with some expectation you would be more reasonable. If such is not the case, I suggest you depart my home post-haste."

"Though, I am a guest in your home, young man," his lordship began, "I AM head of this family! I demand you treat me with the respect inherent in my standing! That being said, I came to look after my niece! I shall not take my leave of Pemberley until I am assured she is being cared for, and ALL her needs are met to my satisfaction."

Darcy regarded the older gentleman with a knowing smile. "Then, you shall be pleasantly surprised to hear she is well on her way to recovery. She awakened this morning. She spoke with Richard and then asked to see my future bride."

"Your future bride, indeed," Lord Matlock spoke derisively. The good news about Anne was seemingly disregarded. "Do you mean to suggest you intend to go forward with your selfish plans? Do you intend to marry that woman after all that has occurred?"

"I fail to discern anything that has transpired that would have persuaded me to change my mind about marrying the woman I love. I only regret Anne's accident was a cause to delay the wedding. Elizabeth and I shall be married tomorrow."

"What of Anne's sentiments? Do you not have the dignity to allow her time to recover before you bestow the title of mistress of Pemberley on another woman, when it has long been considered amongst the Fitzwilliam family as Anne's birth right?"

Darcy cupped his forehead with his fingers and massaged his temples in annoyance. "Must I be subjected to this foolishness, yet again, and on the eve of my wedding, no less?"

"Foolishness? Why it was the fondest wish of both of my dear sisters!"

Darcy interrupted. "Yes, yes, at our cradles—I have heard it all before." Darcy sat back in his chair as he mocked.

"That is enough of your disrespect towards your elders," Lord Matlock warned. "What has Anne to say of your plans to allow another to usurp her rightful position?"

Darcy looked at his uncle in disbelief. "Although it is not as if either of us sought it, Anne offered her blessing. Furthermore, she has asked for and received my forgiveness."

"I hope you do not expect me to stand by as a silent witness to this vulgar spectacle. I have not been in the habit of brokering disappointment, young man."

Darcy had heard enough. He stood and faced his uncle. "No disrespect intended, my lord. However, I suggest you get used to it."

꙳

Lord Matlock remained in Darcy's study long enough to enjoy a stiff drink and settle on his next move. Soon enough, he found himself sitting in a chair in Anne's room, next to her bed, uncharacteristically contrite.

With her hand in his, he affirmed, "This is not how I had intended things to turn out when I arranged for you to come here against my sister's knowledge. I believed Darcy would be persuaded to do right by you if you were here. It pains me to see how much you have suffered. I am sorry. Can you forgive me, my dear child?"

Anne smiled at her dearest, in truth, her only uncle and gently squeezed his hand. "I can hardly blame you for my literally throwing myself at my cousin, now can I?"

"I blame myself. Darcy waited all these years to commit to marriage. When he did at last, it was to a widow with a child from a previous marriage. I never supposed his intentions towards the woman were honourable. I considered the entire affair as a mere dalliance. When he did not choose a young lady from our own circle, I surely thought he would honour our family's wishes by marrying you." He glanced towards the window, as if in search of an answer. "How could I have been so wrong about him?" Lord Matlock pondered aloud.

"As I said, I do not bear you any ill will, my lord. You were only looking out for my best interests. You thought you were doing what was best for our family.

"However, I must confess this is an agreeable alternative. At the end of the day, this is what I have wanted all along—to be part of a family. Cousin Fitzwilliam and his intended have forgiven me. I hope Georgiana will, as well, in time.

"So you see my lord, I can have a family with Fitzwilliam, Elizabeth, Georgiana, and little Ben. Even though I might continue down a path of vindictiveness, bitterness, and isolation, why would I, when I can be a part of something wonderful?"

Darcy went to Ben's room bright and early the next day. Ben, who had not been impressed with the outfit he had been forced to don, smiled with glee when he noticed his finery was much the same as his friend's handsome, rich attire.

"Good morning, Ben."

"Good morning! We are dressed nearly the same," the eager lad exclaimed excitedly.

"Indeed," Darcy replied and then walked over to Ben and knelt to his eye level. He dismissed Ben's attendant with a nod, signalling his intention to take over from there. Darcy began arranging Ben's cravat. "I am informed you are not too keen on the idea of dressing this way, young man."

"No, not at all, I do not know why I must wear such finery, and why on earth must someone help me to dress?"

"It is expected for young masters to be attended in this manner. One day, you shall have your own valet."

"My own valet," Ben uttered in wonderment. "What is a valet?"

"A valet is a man who is hired to perform personal services for a gentleman, such as assisting with one's morning and evening dressing and what not. You know my man, Waters. He is a good man, is he not? When you are older, you shall require your own man."

"I can hardly imagine needing someone else to help me dress every morning, much less help me undress each night. That is what my mama does!"

Darcy could not help chuckling at Ben's pronouncement. "Surely, you will reconsider that notion in time." As Darcy continued to fuss with Ben's cravat, he said, "In time, you shall appreciate having someone to tend to such matters as this."

"Indeed," Ben said teasingly in response to Darcy's second attempt to get it just right. "Your hands are unsteady, my King. Why is that?"

Darcy thought about it. Had his man, Waters, not expressed words of a similar vein earlier as he attempted to complete his morning toilette? Darcy considered it was not so much anxiety over the day's impending events, as it was anticipation of how his night would unfold. He had not bothered to mention it to his valet, who had been with him most of his life. He surely would not confess it now.

With the task at hand completed, at last, Darcy helped Ben don his jacket. "It is an important day for me, Ben. It is the most important day of my life, in fact. I am allowed to be just a bit anxious, am I not?"

Ben placed his hand reassuringly on Darcy's broad shoulder and looked at him straight in the eye. "Then you should stay close to me, for I am not anxious at all."

Darcy smiled. "I knew you would not be nervous, which is precisely why I am here. That and the fact that I wanted to spend time with you before the ceremony, solely the two of us."

Darcy sat on the bed and entreated Ben to sit beside him. He continued, "Things will be quite overwhelming today, from the moment your mother and I take our wedding vows. I do not want you to feel left out or to consider you are less important to either of us.

"I realise how you felt neglected over the past weeks, what with my cousin Anne taking away so much of my time and attention. I never want you to feel that way again."

"My mama always says family comes first," Ben declared professorially.

"You ARE my family, you and your mother," Darcy spoke proudly. "What say you we head on over to the chapel straight away and make it official?"

The pristine chapel settled amongst its lush green surrounds and the clear blue of the sky above, decorated with fluffy white clouds, allied to supply the perfect setting for the long-awaited matrimony of the master of Pemberley.

On reflection, all those in attendance would admit to an impeccable execution of the ceremony with nary a tense moment save when the vicar spoke those fateful words of The Book of Common Prayer: "If any man can show just cause why they may not lawfully be joined together—"

Georgiana glanced about as if expecting the doors to fling open, in hobbling her cousin Anne, whilst both Richard and his mother cast a wary eye towards Lord Matlock.

The vicar continued in a measured yet reverent drawl, "Speak now or forever hold your peace."

Nary a sound was heard. The ceremony proceeded to its crowning moment, to young Ben's way of thinking.

The vicar asked, "Who giveth this Woman to be married to this Man?"

Young Ben offered over his mother's hand to his best friend —the only father he would ever know—as he loudly proclaimed, "I do."

Minutes later, Mr. and Mrs. Fitzwilliam Darcy emerged from the chapel to a throng of well-wishers and a sense of merriment, joy, and celebration that lasted for hours, long after the Darcys took their leave of Pemberley.

Once they were well beyond the sight of Pemberley, Darcy attempted to distract Elizabeth, whose countenance bore a mixture of delightful anticipation with subtle traces of forlornness.

"I know you will miss Ben terribly, my love. I shall miss him, as well," Darcy said as he gently laid his hand atop hers and caressed it. "Even if it is not with the same depth of your emotions, I have some sense of what you are suffering."

Elizabeth smiled faintly, almost apologetically.

Darcy continued, "We need this time together. Should Richard or Georgiana report the slightest bit of malaise on Ben's part, I shall invite them to join us at the Lakes, if that is your desire."

"No, I would not expect such a change in plans," Elizabeth responded. "I shall be fine, and so will Ben. You are correct, Mr. Darcy. We need this time."

Darcy leaned forward and kissed her lips. "There will be no more of that, least not when you and I are alone."

"No more of what?" Elizabeth responded in earnest.

"Never call me Mr. Darcy when we are alone; otherwise, I shall consider you are displeased with me."

Elizabeth raised a quizzical brow. "Then what shall I call you —King Arthur, perhaps?"

"King Arthur and his queen Guinevere, together at last. I like that very much," he murmured. A sudden jolt landed Elizabeth into Darcy's arm. Not one to let such an opportunity as this go wasted, Darcy adjusted his position to afford his wife a more comfortable seating arrangement.

Conspiring to keep her there, he traced a soft, gentle pattern along her bare shoulders and the length of her arms. An occasional remark on seemingly insignificant matters, which could only be meaningful to two young people violently in love, was soon interspersed with teasing, enticing kisses over her décolletage—slowly and deliberately, at first, along her slender neckline, up and down her throat and back again.

His deft fingers worked magic of their own—caressing, stroking, and bestowing similar pleasures to other parts of her body crying out for his touch. The mounting evidence of his desire encouraged Elizabeth to draw the shades, move purposely to his lap, and do what she might to elicit deep moans of pleasure from her husband.

At length, Darcy gently eased his satiated bride onto the carriage seat. "I can hardly wait to make you mine," he murmured bestowing a light kiss on her temple. He opened the shades so they might enjoy the passing Derbyshire countryside, and she leaned back in the circle of his arms, rested her head on his broad chest, and enjoyed the view.

Darcy and Elizabeth arrived to find everything in the honeymoon cottage to their liking. Members of Pemberley's household staff had arrived before the newlyweds and arranged things according to their master's taste.

After a perfunctory tour of their lodgings, Darcy was impatient to release the staff for their other responsibilities. Once they were on their own, Darcy looked at Elizabeth, as if anticipating what her greatest wish might be. She looked at him, likewise. It was as though their thoughts sang out in unison—there would be time enough for talking later on. They had matters of far greater consequence on their minds.

Darcy swept her up in his arms and carried her up the stairs. With her aid, they managed to open the door. He crossed the room swiftly and placed her gently on the bed.

"I am told it is customary for the groom to allow his bride some time alone to prepare for the wedding bed," he uttered between kisses.

"Indeed."

"May I persuade you to forego such formalities, just this once? I need you now."

"Patience, my King," Elizabeth voiced, although in opposition to her body's urgent yearning. "I insist on it."

"How much time must I wait?" Darcy beseeched after he tore himself away from her lips.

Thirty minutes, Darcy thought, as he closed the door separating his suite from his lovely wife's bed. *Thirty minutes! What am I to do for thirty minutes?* Darcy asked himself.

Darcy then noticed his man had ordered his bath. *I might as well take advantage of it. Where is Waters?* In the next breath, he recalled Ben's words on the futility of a valet. Did he really need Waters to help him prepare for his bath? He nearly laughed aloud.

Moments later, Darcy relaxed in the steamy, hot water. He shifted about from side to side and considered the tub's size. *Next time, I shall invite my lovely bride to join me.*

One such thought led to another of all the exciting prospects that awaited him in that very room over the days to come. Time passed so quickly that before he knew it, thirty minutes had come and gone. Darcy jumped out of the tub in a flash and walked across the room, dripping wet, to retrieve a towel. He had not bothered to secure one earlier. Now, there was none to be found. Soaking wet, he pulled the light bed-cover from his bed, draped it around his waist, and made his way back to his wife's room.

The sight of her husband's torso, glistening wet, delighted Elizabeth. "Had I known you were enjoying a long, warm bath, I might have joined you," she teased.

"I shall make a note of your declaration," Darcy responded as he held fast to his cloth, wrapped securely around his waist, as if in protection of his modesty. It was no use. Elizabeth's eyes were drawn to the ever-increasing tell-tale sign of his desire. She boldly approached him and tore away his cover.

Before the bed-cover landed on the floor, Elizabeth found herself nestled against his firm body. His longing, hard and sharp, was immensely evident as he held her captive in his loving embrace.

Having surrendered herself to his passionate kisses, Elizabeth was enthralled as Darcy lifted her and carried her to bed, where he suspended his adoring onslaught long enough to reveal all of her. He took his time whilst his fingers traced a path to their long-awaited destiny. He was pleased to learn his beautiful bride was ready. Darcy's own excitement increased more than he had imagined as even possible. He relished the moment as long as he could bear, and wishing the night would never end, he made her his wife.

Pleased, joyful, and utterly satisfied, Darcy and Elizabeth slept.

Hours later, betwixt quiet whispers of love, Darcy made slow, reverent love to his wife once again, this time until the wee hours of the morning.

In the early dawn, Elizabeth lay spooned in her husband's loving embrace, both in quiet reflection. Each supposed the other was asleep.

Elizabeth thought back to a moment in time she was sure she would never forget—the first glimpse of him walking through the crowded Meryton assembly. She recalled feeling as though she had peered into the eyes of her soul mate. With tears she sought not to hold back, silently streaming from her eyes, she knew at long last she had found a place in her life she had always been searching for. She thought she had known love before. It hardly compared with this. She wondered whether she would ever get enough of this beautiful man.

At the same time, Darcy thought with certainty, *this is what I have waited for my entire life. I love Elizabeth above all else. I shall never get enough of her—my wife, my lover, my goddess divine.*

Chapter 26

The full moon suspended high above Derbyshire on that gentle autumn night, bathed the grand corridors of the stately manor with soft light.

Inside one of the many ostentatious apartments, her ladyship, who had retired for the evening, sat perched in bed, her head resting on beautifully adorned satin pillows. Closing her book, she placed her spectacles aside and glanced towards her husband of five and thirty years.

"I shall not rest until you confess your new-found adoration of the youngest member of our family."

The cantankerous aristocrat merely harrumphed. "The precocious lad sees to it that he is impossible to ignore."

"Indeed, I suspect you were not the least put off."

Lord Matlock smiled as he recalled Ben's antics during their stay at Pemberley in Darcy and Elizabeth's absence. "Indeed. He is witty, even if a bit impertinent. His high-spirited manner provided a refreshing change."

"I say our nephew has made an excellent match."

"The young lady brought nothing to the alliance, save herself and her son."

"I am certain our nephew would not sacrifice what he has found in his wife and her son for all the wealth in the world. His happiness seems beyond measure."

"Only time will tell," Lord Matlock offered, still reluctant to embrace the union wholeheartedly.

Lady Matlock leaned forward and placed a loving kiss on her husband's cheek. "Is your stubbornness to admit our nephew has made an excellent match the reason you insisted Anne remain at Pemberley? What of your earnest desire to bring her to Matlock, so she might continue to recuperate under our care?"

"Did you not recognise the bloom in her countenance when in the company of our son? Even Georgiana is beginning to warm to Anne's presence."

"I agree. Georgiana is making a good effort where Anne is concerned. But what does Anne's apparent admiration for our son have to do with anything?"

"A second son might do far worse than marry an ailing heiress, do you not agree?"

Under the brilliance of the same moon, many miles far south of Derbyshire, Mr. Bennet rested his head atop a firm pillow next to his wife. As she did most often of late, Mrs. Bennet extolled her blessings to anyone who would pay attention. Not for the first time, her husband listened with amusement.

"Thank the lord, our prayers have been answered. Two fine sons-in-law, my Jane rescued from the threshold of spinsterhood, thanks to the benevolence of Mr. Collins. He is such a handsome man! I was sure she could not be so beautiful for nothing!

"And Lizzy, OUR Lizzy—the mistress of Pemberley! Mr. Darcy has more than ten thousand a year! What fine carriages she shall have! What pin money she shall enjoy." As if experiencing an epiphany, she sat up and exclaimed, "Our Lizzy will be able to put her younger sisters in the path of many rich gentlemen!"

Mr. Bennet could not help scoffing at his wife's assertion. "I would not count on it, my dear. Have you forgotten your daughter's propensity to be selfish and put her own interests before those of the family?"

Mrs. Bennet regarded her husband with some degree of vexation. "Do you not think it is time to give up this foolish vendetta against Lizzy, Mr. Bennet?"

"I am not the one who turned my back against the family time and again. I have no reason to suspect she has changed in that regard."

"I, for one, have no intention to allow your grudge against Lizzy to interfere in my other daughters' prospects," she proclaimed.

My dear Mrs. Bennet, what became of your hopes of seeing the amiable Mr. Bingley as a future son? Have you abandoned those plans completely?"

Again, she looked at her husband, as if he had taken leave of his senses. Did he not know how much she suffered? She blurted, "After his wretched treatment of Jane, I care not the least for Mr. Bingley! I am sure I quite detest the gentleman!"

Mr. Bennet smoothed his pearly grey beard. His eyes twinkled with merriment. "Then you will not be interested to know the master of Netherfield Park is coming down in a day or two to shoot there for several weeks. If our wayward neighbour remains a single man in possession of a good fortune, surely he remains in want of a wife. So you see, my dear, we have no need to rely on Lizzy and the proud Mr. Darcy's generosity at all."

This gives me cause to reconsider, thought Mrs. Bennet. She wondered which of her daughters would suit. *With Jane out of the question, Mr. Bingley is sure to favour my Lydia.*

"My dear Mr. Bennet," she began, "our daughters being the sisters of *the* Mr. Fitzwilliam Darcy of Pemberley and Derbyshire must increase their odds of making advantageous matches considerably."

Mr. Bennet continued to rub his hand along his beard. *I knew my Lizzy could not be so clever for nothing.*

From the heights of Grosvenor Square to the narrow streets of Cheapside, the moon shone just as luminously.

Caroline had not seen Mr. Darcy since he so rudely had expressed his preference for Eliza Carlton over herself. The news of his nuptials with the chit dealt the crushing blow. Her exasperation with her brother, that he had not done more to encourage an alliance between the Darcys and the Bingleys, was increased by the knowledge of his pending travels. "For Heaven's sake, Charles, why on earth do you insist on spending time in Hertfordshire?"

"Because, my dear sister, it is my country home, and it has remained unoccupied for far too long. Why are you complaining now? I recall the last time we travelled to Hertfordshire; you were beside yourself with joy!"

"The last time we travelled to Hertfordshire, we had the pleasure of Mr. Darcy's company. I shall never consider it the same without him there."

"You speak as though he is not a newly-wedded husband. Even if he were in attendance, he would have little to do with either of us."

"Still, it would be a magnanimous gesture on your part to extend an invitation to him and his new family to join us, especially given the proximity to his new in-laws." She barely contained her smile at the prospect.

"Indeed. For once, I find myself in complete agreement with you. I shall write to him at once."

Bingley set about his task with thoughts of the last time he had seen his friend. True to his word, Bingley had indeed gone to Cheapside in search of Miss Bennet. What he discovered, he had not discussed with anyone. His friend had spoken the truth. Miss Bennet had an admirer. Bingley had observed them from afar and saw in Jane's eyes the same warmth he had believed reserved solely for him, bestowed upon someone else. He was too late. She had given her heart to another. Bingley could blame no one but himself for his loss.

Caroline's motives in inviting the Darcys for a visit at Netherfield were simple. Of course, it would be wonderfully entertaining to observe Mr. Darcy amongst his lowly Meryton relatives. The added prospect of future invitations to Pemberley was further inducement. Caroline, too, commenced writing a letter addressed to Mrs. Elizabeth Darcy with the purpose of paying off all arrears of civility.

As for Mr. and Mrs. Gardiner, all the way across town, both suffered elation over the marriage of their niece to Mr. Fitzwilliam Darcy. Mr. Gardiner was in receipt of a heartfelt letter from Elizabeth, forgiving him, not just for the ill-considered investment scheme, but for any financial considerations, as well. More than anything, she wanted to see the Gardiners as financially whole once more. It was so much the better, if the complete discharge of any further liability to her might help.

Mrs. Gardiner was delighted, having received an invitation to Pemberley for the following summer, not only because she spent the better part of her youth in the neighbouring town of Lambton, but also because she had long marvelled at the sight and splendour of Pemberley. To her way of thinking, to be welcomed to the grand estate by her favourite niece, the new mistress, would indeed be something!

Geoffrey Collins sprang from his bed, strode over to the window, and drew the curtains open in welcome of the luminous, full moon's ardent light. Its magnificence cast a romantic glow throughout the room. Having donned her silken gown, Jane sat up, and resting her head on her hand, watched in appreciation of her husband's handsome physique as he returned to their bed.

He reached for her proffered hand and raised it to his lips. "How are you this evening, my beautiful, passionate, and wonderfully amenable, acquiescent bride?"

"Not so acquiescent," Jane spoke as she assumed the dominant position and playfully tossed her flowing hair aside, bringing to his mind their amorous endeavours thus far that evening.

He reached up and fingered an errant lock. He inhaled its sweet scent deeply. "Indeed. You are perfect. You, my dear, are everything I would ever wish for in a wife." He placed his hand behind her neck and pulled her gently towards him to brush her lips with his own. "You must remind me to write to the proud Mr. Fitzwilliam Darcy of Pemberley to thank him for his interference in my life."

Comfortably astride her husband, Jane sat up and regarded her husband intently.

Trailing his hands along the curves of her body, he continued. "His Highness shall have his hands filled with your impertinent sister and her unruly child."

Jane placed a loving finger against his lips. "Whatever you may think of him," she gently admonished, "that is my brother to whom you refer with such acrimony."

"Indeed, and it is my sister to whom he is married," he bemoaned.

Jane sacrificed her position and moved into her husband's welcoming embrace. "Oh! How shall we meet again?" Jane inquired. "Seeing as how the circumstances turned out so advantageously for us all, I can hardly imagine the occasion as anything but a cause for joy. However, knowing my sister as I do, I can hardly imagine her as being very accepting of our marriage and my decision to find happiness with you."

"Perhaps, then it is left to the two of us to extend an olive branch." He kissed her on her temple. "After all, my misunderstanding of the *truth* of their acquaintance coloured your feelings towards your sister."

"I do not blame you at all. Even I was convinced of the unseemliness of my sister's association with Mr. Darcy."

"Perhaps we were all mistaken. Nonetheless, the fact that they are married does not minimise the lack of propriety shown by either of them. However, we are all family now. For the sake of our family, it is incumbent upon us all to let bygones be bygones."

ॐ

Ben pushed the heavy door of Darcy's study ajar and peeped inside. His mother had reminded him more than once that Mr. Darcy was not to be disturbed when in there with his steward, for they were attending to estate business. He was delighted to find him there, alone.

Darcy sat at his chair with his head buried in the paperwork before him. Ben raced to the desk and cajoled his way into Darcy's lap.

"Good morning, Da!" Ben eagerly expressed.

"Good morning, son!" Darcy responded in kind, before regulating his tone. "Where have you been this morning? I looked for you in your room. You were not there. The servants were unable to account for your whereabouts."

"I waited for you for as long as I could bear, Da. Any way, you do not rise nearly as early as when we first arrived at Pemberley."

Darcy thought of his increasing reluctance to leave his bride's side each morning. "Indeed."

Ben regarded Darcy's far-away gaze curiously. "May we commence our riding lessons now? I am eager to see my new pony."

"I have no doubt of that. Unfortunately, I expect my steward to arrive any minute. We have much to discuss before I am free to accompany you to the stables."

Ben looked about Darcy's desk. "What are you working on? Perhaps, I might be of service."

Darcy chuckled. "In due time, son, for I intend to teach you all there is to know about the management of the estate. However, for now, you are to enjoy your carefree youth a bit longer."

Ben would not be dissuaded. He continued to look about for a means to be of use. "What is that?"

Darcy retrieved the object of Ben's curiosity. "This is a rendition of Pemberley." Darcy stretched out the parchment, placed it on the desk, and began to point out various spots of interest, some of which Ben had seen already, many he had not.

In the midst of their perusal, Ben danced around the question that lingered in the back of his young mind. "Da, do you suppose I shall ever own an estate as fine as Pemberley?"

Darcy spoke gently. "As a gentleman of means, which you shall one day be, I have no reason to suspect otherwise, Ben."

"Is my family's estate of Camberworth forever lost to me?" Ben asked tentatively, recalling how his mother had spoken of the entail, the details of which were too complex for even his inquisitive mind.

"For now, you are not to concern yourself with such matters. I shall endeavour to explain the nature of entailed estates to you when you are older. Does that sound agreeable?"

Ben did not answer, but rather draped his arms around Darcy's neck. "I love you, Da."

"As I love you," Darcy responded.

Darcy and Elizabeth lay in bed together basking in the warmth of their shared passion. He held her in his arms and rested his head atop hers. "Are you happy, my love?"

Elizabeth stroked her hand across his broad chest. "Exceedingly so," she whispered.

A light scratch at the door prompted the two lovers to look at each other in silent acknowledgement. Elizabeth smiled apologetically. Darcy placed his finger gently on her cheek and then followed through with a light kiss. Ben had suffered unpleasant dreams for the past two nights. Darcy could only imagine the young lad had met with fierce two-headed dragons, ferocious beasts, and what not, yet again.

Darcy got out of bed and donned his breeches and robe quickly. Tying it at the waist whilst walking over to unlock the door, he glanced back at his wife to assure that she too had recovered her silken nightgown and robe.

Darcy opened the door. Ben only had eyes for his mother. He walked right by Darcy and climbed into bed. He was fast asleep in his mother's arms before Darcy had managed to close the door and return to bed.

Elizabeth whispered. "I am sorry. It is just that it has been solely the two of us for so long."

Darcy silenced her with a soft, reassuring kiss. "I understand, my love. We shall allow him to remain a short while longer before carrying him off to his own bed," Darcy affirmed.

Nearly a half-hour later, Elizabeth awakened from a quiet slumber. She had dozed off. Now, neither her son nor her husband was in the bed beside her. Darcy had carried Ben to his room some time ago. Ben had stirred as Darcy tucked him into his bed.

He rubbed his eyes. "Da, where is my mama?"

Darcy placed his finger to his lips, beckoning the young child to hush. "Your mother is asleep, as you should be," he whispered.

"But I am not tired," Ben yawned. "I am wide awake."

"On the contrary, young man, you are quite sleepy. Now, get some rest." Darcy leaned forward and bestowed a light kiss atop Ben's head. He picked up the candle the servant had placed on Ben's bedside table and turned to leave.

"But I am not tired," Ben repeated, this time trying his best to stifle a yawn.

Darcy had had enough experience tucking Ben in bed to know how that would go. He set the candle down and retrieved the book from the table. "Very well—I shall read to you for a spell. That always helps." Darcy relaxed in the chair and started reading.

Awhile later, Elizabeth entered the room in time to espy her son drifting off to sleep. She crossed the room quietly and sat in her husband's lap. "What are you reading?"

"An account of The Knights of the Round Table," he whispered, as he pointed out the title of the book.

Elizabeth smiled. She spoke softly, "Indeed, is there *anything* else?"

Epilogue

During the Darcys' first year of marriage, Elizabeth gave birth to two healthy boys, an heir and a spare, as it were. Darcy was ecstatic. All of Pemberley was overjoyed, especially young Ben. He was delighted, so much so he reckoned a little sister would suit nicely.

While Darcy did not give Ben his name, teaching the child instead to honour his birth right and bear the Carlton family name with pride and dignity, he gave him an incredibly wonderful story of his own to tell. Not of kings and brave knights from distant, enchanted lands, but one firmly steeped in reality.

Through Darcy's marriage of profound love and deep affection for Elizabeth, he proved a strong and caring father figure who loved Ben as surely as if they were of the same blood, as much as the two younger brothers and a sister who grew up in adoration of him. In short, he gave him a loving family such as Ben truly had never known, secure in a place that held magical allure all its own.

Pemberley.

Acknowledgements

The highest praise goes to Miss Jane Austen's timeless works, as well as the JAFF community and its curiosity to ask, "What if?"

Other *Pride and Prejudice* Variations

by

P O Dixon

To Have His Cake (and Eat It Too)
Mr. Darcy's Tale

What He Would Not Do
Mr. Darcy's Tale Continues

Available online and where books are sold.

Discover much more at PODixon.com

Made in the USA
Lexington, KY
13 November 2011